THE MAJOR MEETS HIS MATCH

She was dressed in the most ridiculous gown he had ever seen. Great masses of floppy pink lace billowed around the high neckline, all but swallowing the lower half of her face in their effusion. A great, gray turban, sporting a bobbing pink ostrich feather, drooped so low on her head that the only clearly discernible features were the bridge of her nose and her incredible green eyes.

"I'm very frightened, you see."

"You?" he teased. "You are bamming me, my lady. Surely a woman who could cross a ballroom in the middle of a country dance and accost a strange man could never be afraid of anything."

Lady Mirthton had the good grace to blush furiously. "It is my kneecaps. Why, even now, if you but lifted the hem of my gown you would see that they are bouncing up and down across my knees like a pair of boiled eggs in aspic."

Marc swallowed his sudden burst of laughter so quickly he choked on it.

"Oh dear, my lord!" cried Lady Mirthton as she began to pound with all her might upon his back. Her turban slid precariously close to the end of her nose. "Oh dear," she repeated more urgently, and spun about wildly in the shadows in her sudden disorientation. Marc had just enough time to grab her arm and drag her tightly against his body before, kneecaps, turban and all, she would have tipped over the balustrade into the garden below.

She fit him perfectly. From the top of her forehead, which bumped his chin, to the flare of her slender hips, which meshed so nicely with his, she was his perfect match. Marc smiled, captivated.

D1603301

ZEBRA'S REGENCY ROMANCES
DAZZLE AND DELIGHT

A BEGUILING INTRIGUE   (4441, $3.99)
by Olivia Sumner

Pretty as a picture Justine Riggs cared nothing for propriety. She dressed as a boy, sat on her horse like a jockey, and pondered the stars like a scientist. But when she tried to best the handsome Quenton Fletcher, Marquess of Devon, by proving that she was the better equestrian, he would try to prove Justine's antics were pure folly. The game he had in mind was seduction — never imagining that he might lose his heart in the process!

AN INCONVENIENT ENGAGEMENT   (4442, $3.99)
by Joy Reed

Rebecca Wentworth was furious when she saw her betrothed waltzing with another. So she decides to make him jealous by flirting with the handsomest man at the ball, John Collinwood, Earl of Stanford. The "wicked" nobleman knew exactly what the enticing miss was up to — and he was only too happy to play along. But as Rebecca gazed into his magnificent eyes, her errant fiancé was soon utterly forgotten!

SCANDAL'S LADY   (4472, $3.99)
by Mary Kingsley

Cassandra was shocked to learn that the new Earl of Lynton was her childhood friend, Nicholas St. John. After years at sea and mixed feelings Nicholas had come home to take the family title. And although Cassandra knew her place as a governess, she could not help the thrill that went through her each time he was near. Nicholas was pleased to find that his old friend Cassandra was his new next door neighbor, but after being near her, he wondered if mere friendship would be enough . . .

HIS LORDSHIP'S REWARD   (4473, $3.99)
by Carola Dunn

As the daughter of a seasoned soldier, Fanny Ingram was accustomed to the vagaries of military life and cared not a whit about matters of rank and social standing. So she certainly never foresaw her *tendre* for handsome Viscount Roworth of Kent with whom she was forced to share lodgings, while he carried out his clandestine activities on behalf of the British Army. And though good sense told Roworth to keep his distance, he couldn't stop from taking Fanny in his arms for a kiss that made all hearts equal!

Available wherever paperbacks are sold, or order direct from the Publisher. Send cover price plus 50¢ per copy for mailing and handling to Penguin USA, P.O. Box 999, c/o Dept. 17109, Bergenfield, NJ 07621. Residents of New York and Tennessee must include sales tax. DO NOT SEND CASH.

A Merry Escapade

Jenna Jones

ZEBRA BOOKS
KENSINGTON PUBLISHING CORP.

ZEBRA BOOKS are published by

Kensington Publishing Corp.
850 Third Avenue
New York, NY 10022

First Printing: September, 1995

Printed in the United States of America

To Tonya Peterson, a dear friend and former neighbor who never once laughed when I said I was writing a book.

Chapter 1

London—1813

I cannot do it, thought Lady Mirthton as she gazed across the crowded ballroom of Heatherton House at a small group of elegantly clad aristocrats engaged in animated conversation. *I simply cannot do it.* Yet in spite of her trepidation, her attention remained riveted on one particular gentleman in the group; so much so, in fact, that she was as oblivious to the lilting strains of the orchestra, the brilliant sparkle of the crystal chandeliers, and the vibrant hum of flirtatious conversation as the others of the *haute monde* were of her. She scooted forward in her chair, one of a battalion of delicate damask-covered ones that lined the ballroom, and twisted the pale gray brocade of her ball gown around her trembling fingers.

What could I have been thinking of to come up with such a plan? she wondered as an intrusive blade of a parlor palm frond attached itself to the moistness of her pale pink lips. She made a soft "pffft" sound and wiggled her mouth to detach it, but it did not annoy her. She was much too grateful for the palm's concealing foliage. She would have been quite happy, in fact, to stay hidden behind the protective palm forever, for, as much as she may have wished to avoid it, this was to be the night of her social ruin.

Oh, cease this silliness! she scolded herself. *He is here tonight. If you do not seize the opportunity now, when it practically thumps you on your noggin, you are the veriest twiddle-poop!* Still, in spite of her self-chastisement, the tiny oval of her fingernail drifted nervously up to her mouth and wedged itself in the slight overlap of her two front teeth. She sucked on the tip of her finger absentmindedly. Finally she sighed, and once again leaned back against the soft damask.

I simply have no choice, she concluded as she tugged at the voluminous pink flounce that threatened to engulf her chin. *I must do it. And as for the consequences, I will just have to learn to live with them. I am quite persuaded that after tonight, I shall probably not be able to show my face in society again. And if that happens, I will never be able to go home again, for I shall be tossed out on my ear!* She shivered slightly as she straightened the tangled folds of her gown and vainly attempted to brush away the wrinkles she had created. *But I must do it,* she silently vowed.

She glanced once more at the man standing so gloriously tall and erect in his black evening garb across the room, and watched as he took a glass of champagne from a passing footman and put it to his lips. She knew it was now or never. The chance would not come again. *I will do it,* she affirmed, and, braced with renewed resolve, she took a deep breath and rose to her feet. It took only this action for her natural liveliness of spirit to reassert itself: She smiled, and as she shrugged her shoulders at the inevitability of her course, found to her amusement that her face was all but buried in a cascade of pink lace. *When all is said and done,* she thought as she battled the pink fabric, *it is far better to be socially ruined, an old maid, and homeless, than to be dead.* Strangely bolstered by the bizarre turn of her thoughts, she pushed aside the invading palm fronds and stepped out onto the ballroom floor.

* * *

Marcus Forester, tenth Earl of Clairmont, accepted the sting of Lady Samantha Peters's fan with a polite smile and good grace, but the gray emptiness that had taken root inside him since his return to London seemed to grow a little larger. He was thoroughly, overwhelmingly, bored. And not just temporarily in the clutches of a spate of *ennui,* either, he realized, as Samantha trilled another of her melodious, delicate laughs that marched down his spine like an elephant in hobnail boots. No, this was serious boredom. The kind that made a man of action do foolish things, like volunteering to face the latest bare-knuckle champion with one hand tied behind his back, or going to war, or swimming the Channel with a weight around his neck, just to alleviate the unending sameness.

He had not realized a few months ago how much he would miss his former occupation. He had always led a physically demanding life, full of action and adventure. He had spent five years as a major in the Royal Horse Artillery; five years fighting the French on the Peninsula under Wellington. But that was closed to him now, and he was pierced with regret. It was not that he gloried in war. He was not sorry to be free from the death and destruction. It was just that his life now offered him no suitable alternatives. He found the endless round of parties, routs, and balls as insipid as the conversational attempts of the scores of childish debutantes who were continually foisted upon him by their match-making mamas as day followed tedious day.

The direction of his life had been abruptly taken out of his hands. He had been seriously wounded during Wellington's victorious battle at Vittoria in June, and had been obliged to sell his commission. And then his older brother had died of typhus and he had become, at age eight and twenty, Earl of Clairmont, and had been forced to assume, along with his title, a mass of ensnaring obligations, the huge Clairmont fortune, and the dubious renown as Catch of the Season. It chafed. Almost as badly as the healing scar that rippled across his abdomen.

''La, Marc, darling, I am persuaded that you do not find my

company at all to your liking," pouted Lady Peters prettily. She unfurled her fan, and suddenly the pastel pattern of yellow roses and bluebirds flashed briskly before his eyes.

Startled out of his reverie, Marc took another sip of champagne from the delicate crystal of his fluted glass and tried once again to focus his attention on his companions. "My apologies, my dear," he replied with a half-smile. "I have merely been stunned into silence by your beauty."

He captured her hand while she blushed becomingly and touched his lips to her fingers, thinking as he studied her *décolleté* that he might not have said such a plumper after all. She was very much the simpering deb, of course, and he found her mannerisms tedious, but she was undoubtedly the most beautiful woman he had ever seen. Her skin was all milk and roses, and her hair floated above piercingly blue eyes in a cloud of golden curls. She was wearing a gown of diaphanous yellow tissue over a white silk underskirt. The sleeves were tiny puffs at her shoulders, and the bodice, fitted to her generous breasts by a wide blue ribbon, was cut daringly low. He found himself swallowing as his body reacted, and quickly forced himself to look away.

"Have a care, Samantha," teased Marc's good friend, Peter Babbington, Viscount Eversley, with a grin. "We are fortunate to have Clairmont's company tonight. He is still in mourning, you know. It would not serve to lay more guilt upon that which he already has for allowing me to draw him into attending this frivolous function."

"Oh, pooh!" she responded with a playful tap of her fan upon Eversley's arm. "It is enough that he will not dance with me. I refuse to feel badly if I make him suffer for it."

Marc felt a pang of irritation at her self-centeredness. His response was out before he could stop it. "And I, my dear Samantha, refuse to suffer for it," he answered quietly. At the lady's indrawn gasp, he turned his attention toward his friend. "How goes the war, Peter?"

"Better than we ever could have expected. Wellington has pushed all the way to the Pyrenees and is moving into southern

France. Lord Castlereagh told us in a meeting yesterday that he doesn't think Napoleon can last much longer. Even now the Allied forces are massing for an assault on Leipzig. I think it is the beginning of the end for the little Corsican."

"Damme, that's good news!" responded Marc enthusiastically. "I only wish . . ."

"*I* only wish for another glass of champagne," interrupted Lady Peters, once more demanding the gentlemen's attention. "Would you get it for me, Peter darling?" she asked as she smiled prettily and rested her fan on his forearm.

"It would be my pleasure, of course," he returned, bowing over her hand. He turned and waggled his eyebrows knowingly toward Marc, and then melted into the crowd.

Marc forced himself to unclench the jaw that had tightened at her obvious manipulation. He suddenly wished to be anywhere else but at Heatherton House, struggling to keep his head above social waters that were filled with giggling, fan-snapping, husband-hunting sharks. He smiled at the beauty who had maneuvered herself into his solitary company, and a proximity far closer to him than propriety would allow, then pointedly stepped back from her nearness. She immediately filled the gap.

"Marc, darling, are you sure you do not wish to dance?" she asked as she inched closer and her blue eyes blazed into his. "I've managed to keep this dance and the supper dance open just for you. The orchestra is going to play a waltz next and I would so love to partner you. I can, you know," she continued, again tapping him with her fan. "Countess Lieven gave me permission last week."

"How very nice for you," Marc mumbled, as he fidgeted with the stiff collar of his snowy white shirt. He stepped away again.

"Yes, isn't it?" she replied, again moving closer. "To dance the waltz is to be *aux anges,* is it not? When I am waltzing, I feel as if I am floating on a cl—"

Marc's eyes flew to hers, startled by the abrupt ending of her conversation. He watched in fascination as her lovely face wrinkled into a look of sheer disgust, then quickly observed that her eyes were now fixed on a point beyond his broad shoulders.

"Oh, this is the outside of enough!" she uttered vehemently. "That . . . that *creature* is coming right toward us! Never say that she actually intends to approach us!"

Marc lost no time in turning to follow the line of her vision. What he saw caused him to struggle to keep his jaw from dropping like a round of uncharged grapeshot. A young woman was indeed making her way toward them, plowing her way across the ballroom floor like a ship under full sail, parting the astonished participants of a lively country dance like the waters under a sharp keel.

She was dressed in the most ridiculous gown he had ever seen. It looked to be at least a half-century out of date, although some attempt had been made to modernize it. Of heavy gray brocade, the gown was as out of place in this room filled with frothy pastel silks and muslins as the low, snug-fitting waist that hugged the woman's willowy figure. Great masses of floppy pink lace billowed around the ends of the half-sleeves, the hem, and the high neckline, all but swallowing the lower half of her face in their effusion. A great, gray turban, sporting a bobbing pink ostrich feather, drooped so low on her head that the only clearly discernible features on her face were the bridge of her nose and her incredible bright green eyes. She kept those eyes trained steadily upon Marc as she closed the distance between them, and when at last she came to a halt before him, she took a firm grip on her heavy skirts and sank into a deep curtsey.

"My lord," she began, quickly reaching up to snare her toppling turban, "I am . . ."

"How dare you!" gasped Lady Peters as her hand clenched the scanty muslin covering her bosom. "How dare you accost his lordship and try to insinuate yourself into our group! It is the outside of enough! Unless you leave this instant I'll see that you are *de trop* at every gathering of the *ton* for the rest of the Little Season, just see if I won't!"

"Restrain yourself, Samantha," Marc ordered with a hard glare. He had no liking for the scene she was undoubtedly enjoying creating. He was well aware that his group was fast becoming the focus of an amused crowd of curious onlookers, and he had no wish to become the object of their night's entertainment. Yet he was equally appalled by the attention the strange young woman had drawn to their party by her unheard of intrusion into their midst. He wanted nothing more than to be rid of her. Indignantly, he assumed a haughty air, and watched as she rose to her feet and stood straight and tall before him.

What he saw was unsettling. The woman's gaze was respectful, unwavering, and very green. Marc was disconcerted by that. She should have been hanging her head in shame. Yet her behavior did arouse his curiosity. Who the deuce was she? She was probably just another pushy debutante, of course, and from the looks of her, one that had a disastrous Season ahead of her. He again decided to brush her off quickly. He even had the words of his setdown framed in his mind, but just as he was about to utter them, she blinked her bright green eyes and instantly the words were forgotten. It was inexplicable, but he was sure that something needful shone brightly in their verdant depths. He sensed Viscount Eversley's return with Samantha's champagne, but still continued to stare at the intriguing woman for long moments. Then, finally, he spoke.

"I do not believe we have met, ma'am," he began.

"Clairmont, certainly you do not mean to speak to this person?" interjected Lady Peters. "Why, I should give her the cut direct! She is nothing but a wallflower!"

Marc studied the strange woman's reaction to this blatant slur, and became even more intrigued when he saw that Samantha's words sparked a flash of amusement in her emerald eyes.

"You are quite correct, my lady," the woman replied brightly. "I am but one of a vast legion of women who take great pride in the important service we perform."

"Important service?" interjected Viscount Eversley, becoming fascinated by the strange woman who stood before them in spite of her appalling behavior.

"Oh, yes, my lord," she replied, swinging her gaze to him. Marc watched as she batted down a layer of errant lace at her throat and squelched a sudden urge to smile. "Why, if it were not for us, how would the ladies of the *ton* be able to judge how beautiful they are? You must agree that without plain women with which to compare themselves, they would never really know. And just think of how much better a woman like Lady Peters, for instance, feels, knowing that she has such as I to look down upon. Why, it does positive wonders for the ego! But these piddling services are nothing compared to the most important thing we do," she said with an emphatic nod of her head. The movement dislodged her turban once again and set her lace adrift. She quickly clamped her hands on the sides of her head and ruffled her lips to unstick a section of the pink fluff that had wandered into her mouth.

"And what is this most important service, ma'am?" inquired the viscount with a warm smile of amusement. Marc remained silent but his fingers were pressed suspiciously to his lips.

The woman lowered her voice to a conspiratorial level. "It is little known outside our ranks, my lord," she began, "but we are the ones who make all these balls and parties possible."

"Indeed," replied the viscount as Lady Peters gazed at the woman with her mouth formed in a horrified "O."

The woman cast an uneasy glance at the earl, but could read nothing in his bland visage. Taking a deep breath, she continued. "Oh, yes," she said with a grin. "Why, with the way the *ton* packs itself into its routs and balls like passengers into a public conveyance, who do you think holds up the walls?"

Marc suddenly found it necessary to turn away as he struggled to mask his broad smile. Viscount Eversley had no such compunction. He immediately burst into laughter.

"Really, Eversley," chided Samantha with a scowl.

"My dear," said the viscount to the strange woman when at last he had composed himself enough to speak to her through the remnants of his chuckles, "I will forever more regard you who buttress our walls with a new respect." He took the young woman's hand and kissed it heartily.

"Thank you, my lord," replied the woman as her eyes gleamed with mischief. "However," she continued, and her countenance sobered somewhat, "I did not interrupt your conversation so that I might entertain you with my somewhat unusual sense of humor." She turned, then, to bravely face the earl. "I am well aware that it is not at all the thing, my lord, but please allow me to introduce myself. I am Lady Mirthton, and I have sought you out because I wish to speak with you."

"Mirthton?" interrupted Lady Peters. "Mirthton. Ah, yes. You would be Viscount Collingwood's daughter, then."

"I was. My lord, if I might . . ."

"That explains a good deal, does it not?" insisted Lady Peters triumphantly.

The young woman flushed with embarrassment but held the earl's gaze. "If I might see you alone for just a few moments, my lord," she said as her spine straightened.

Instantly, all the earl's defenses against predatory females came alive. "Alone?" he questioned. The chit was set on trapping him after all!

"He gambles quite heavily, does he not?" Lady Peters inserted.

Lady Mirthton determinedly ignored the inner pain that flared at her words. She kept her focus on the earl. If she failed now, the consequences could be severe. "For a few moments only, my lord, and in plain sight if you wish." And then, as if she had read his mind, she added, "I assure you, I have no design to compromise you."

Marc knew he should just turn from her and walk away. The strange woman had, after all, done the unheard of. She had boldly insinuated herself into their presence without an introduction, struck up a conversation with them, and made a spectacle of herself as she did it. It was all very bad *ton.* Yet still he hesitated. There was something about her that drew him, a genuineness and sincerity that shown in her eager eyes. Try as he might, he could see none of the guile that seemed so evident in her peers.

"He is a drunkard, I believe," stated Lady Peters sweetly.

Marc's eyes flew to Samantha's. The behavior that he himself was set on displaying only a few moments before now seemed appallingly callous when he observed it in her.

"My lord?" Lady Mirthton again entreated as her eyes sought his. She clasped her hands together to still their trembling. Her heart knocked against her ribs and she knew she was scarlet with embarrassment, but she could not back down now.

Marc felt an uncomfortable squeeze of annoyance. He knew very well what a gentleman of the *ton* should say to this impertinent baggage, and he was fully prepared to do so, but when his answer was finally uttered, no one in the vicinity was more shocked than he at the words he heard coming from his mouth.

"Perhaps if we stand on the terrace in plain sight of everyone . . .," he offered, totally astounded with himself.

The gust of air that Lady Mirthton released waffled the lace at her throat and sent it flying. She grabbed at it with one hand, steadied her turban with the other, and grinned radiantly.

"Thank you, my lord," she breathed.

Marc tilted his head and gave her a wry grin. He had discovered yet another flaw in this most odd woman. One of her front teeth overlapped the other. But somehow, hidden as the flaw was behind the brilliance of her smile, it did not seem in the least significant.

Chapter 2

With his hand in a socially correct position beneath her elbow, the earl escorted Lady Mirthton under the glassed arch above a set of open French doors and out onto the flagstone terrace behind Heatherton House. Anxious not to compromise the earl in any way, the lady came to a halt while still within the wedge of wan light that spilled out onto the terrace from the ballroom. It pleased her that the light seemed to warm the cold stone beneath her slippers as it illuminated the crisp autumn night. She rested her gloved hands upon the balustrade and looked up into the depths of the evening.

"It is a lovely night, is it not, my lord?" she softly asked.

Marc was somewhat taken aback by her comment. As far as he could see, which wasn't very far at all, the sky bore a distinct resemblance to India ink. "Do you think so, Lady Mirthton?" he politely inquired as he clasped his hands behind his back.

"Oh, yes," she responded readily. "We cannot see it, of course, but it is. Just imagine, my lord," she continued as she swung her slender arm in a wide arc, "a million people are living all around us. And each one of them is keeping warm tonight beside a fire that is spewing tons of foul-smelling soot into this beautiful night sky. I must confess, sir, that the air is so dirty I would dearly love to take a clean cloth and rub away a patch for the stars to shine through."

Marc smiled at the image her words provoked. His gaze alighted on her face and he found himself studying her. Her slim nose ended in a tiny ball. He thought that most unusual. But then, so was she. He wondered about the color of her hair, hidden as it was underneath that atrocious turban. Her skin was creamy and reminded him of peaches. He thought she might taste quite good, too. And then she shivered.

"You are cold," he stated immediately.

"No, I am not," she shot back quickly. Her green gaze caught his for only a moment before she again looked away.

"I saw you shiver," he challenged firmly.

"Yes, but it wasn't a cold shiver," she confessed as she turned toward him. Her turban again sagged dangerously toward her left eyebrow and she quickly dragged it back into place. "I am quite frightened, you see."

Marc was once again caught off balance by her honesty. He immediately thought to set her more at ease. "Frightened? You?" he teased. "You are bamming me, my lady. Surely a woman who could cross a ballroom in the middle of a country dance and accost a strange man at his pleasure could never be afraid of anything!"

Lady Mirthton had the good grace to blush furiously, but her bright grin negated the effect completely. "It is quite true, though, Lord Clairmont, I assure you," she said in a prim voice. "It is my kneecaps, you see."

"Kneecaps?" queried the earl as laughter threatened.

"Yes, indeed," she sighed. "They are my greatest trial. I give thanks to God for every long skirt I have. I do not wish to boast, my lord, but I possess the very fine gift of always appearing on the surface to be quite calm and completely poised. However, at times like this, if you could but see my kneecaps, you would soon discover how thoroughly I am betrayed. Why, even now, if I but lifted the hem of my gown, my lord, you would see that they are bouncing up and down across my knees like a pair of boiled eggs in aspic."

Marc swallowed his sudden burst of laughter so quickly he choked on it. He grabbed the balustrade and hung over it while a spasm of coughing wracked his chest.

"Oh, dear, my lord!" cried Lady Mirthton as she immediately stepped to his side and began to pound with all her might upon his back. Her turban, as might be expected, slid precariously close to the tiny ball on the end of her nose, just as a gust of sooty air wafted a billow of pink lace in front of her eyes. "Oh, dear!" she repeated more urgently, and spun about blindly into the shadows in her sudden disorientation. Marc had just enough time to grab her arm and drag her tightly against his body before, kneecaps, turban, and all, she would have tipped over the balustrade into the garden below.

She fit him perfectly. From the top of her forehead, which bumped his chin, to the flare of her slender hips, which meshed so nicely with his, she was, incredibly, his perfect match. The thought stunned him. For a fleeting moment he was certain that a few guards from Bedlam were going to appear to carry him away, but then Lady Mirthton lifted her head and he looked deeply into her viridescent eyes, and every thought that was boiling around in his brain simply melted away.

"I've lost my feather," she whispered, as enthralled with his nearness as he was with hers.

"Your feather?" he responded stupidly. He was enmeshed in a feeling he couldn't begin to describe if it took him a thousand years.

"Yes," she breathed. "My ostrich feather. It went over the side." She gestured with the only finger that was yet free from his ensnaring arms. Her turban slipped a fraction lower and covered one green eye.

Marc smiled, captivated, and moved his hands up her back until he held the turban between his two tapered hands. Slowly, carefully, he set it back in its proper place, then let his fingers trail softly across her downy cheeks as he reluctantly distanced himself from her.

Lady Mirthton marveled at how bereft she felt at the absence of the earl's powerful body pressed so tightly to hers. *How odd,* she thought as she lowered her eyes and clasped her hands together in embarrassment. She had never experienced a man's touch before. Not even her father's.

"Shall I get it for you?" the earl inquired softly.

"What? Oh, no . . .," she replied, dismissing the bothersome thing from her mind with a wave of her hand. "I only wish I'd thought to throw it over the side when we first came out here." Her eyes widened then, at her abrupt confession, and she broke into a wide grin.

Marc found himself drawn to her as he had never been drawn to a woman before. He couldn't understand it. He smiled, joining in with her amusement, and wondered at how this complete Original could have affected him so quickly and so deeply. She was not at all like the woman of his dreams, the fantasy woman with whom he had always pictured himself when the time came to choose a bride; yet somehow her very uniqueness had him thinking thoughts about her that, until tonight, he never would have imagined entering his mind. His smile deepened as he remembered how adamant she was about not compromising him. And then he sobered. He was in danger of doing the same thing to her. They had been out together on the terrace far longer than was proper and had been embracing in the deepest of the shadows. He needed to get her back inside, and he needed to do it quickly.

"Perhaps you could tell me why you wished to speak with me?" he asked gently.

Lady Mirthton's eyes flew to his. "Oh! Forgive me, Lord Clairmont. I am persuaded that my brain must have flown away with my feather. I have kept you here far too long, have I not? I shall be brief, then." She straightened her spine and looked at him squarely. "I wish to speak with you, my lord."

There followed several seconds of silence. "You *are* speaking with me, Lady Mirthton," he pointed out.

She grinned at him again, and he felt himself responding in kind. "You misunderstand, my lord," she said with a burble of laughter. "I wish to speak with you at sometime in the near future. Tomorrow perhaps. I wish for you to call on me so that I might speak with you privately and for a short time only."

"Let me see if I have this straight, Lady Mirthton," he said with a finger alongside his chiseled chin. "You wished to speak to me about wishing to speak to me?" His eyes sparkled with a very unlordly mischief.

"Yes, well . . . it does sound rather peculiar when you put it that way, my lord, but, essentially, you are correct." She touched her cheeks as a sudden blush warmed them and Marc found the movement captivating.

"Would it not have been easier, my dear, and certainly far less taxing on your reputation, to have sent a note around to my residence asking for an interview?"

"That was my assumption also, my lord," she responded, "but as I received no response from you when I attempted it, though I had the note delivered three days ago, I came to the conclusion that another method of contacting you was called for. Time, I fear, is a somewhat important factor." Her eyes shone into his with sweet sincerity.

Marc's brow wrinkled into a frown. "Are you saying that you sent me a note?" The earl thought furiously. Had he seen such a thing? More than likely he had, and probably had tossed the unsolicited summons into the waste can as being beneath his notice.

"Please, my lord," Lady Mirthton said as she placed a warm hand on his forearm, "give it no further thought. In your position, receiving such a note from some unknown female, I would have reacted just as I am sure you did." She frowned slightly, but he barely saw it beneath the layers of her overwhelming turban. "You would have concluded, would you not, that I was some scheming woman intent on having you for my husband. You would have surely thought that I had plotted some thoroughly scurrilous situation in which to entrap you, and that my machinating mama was no doubt waiting in the wings with a parson ready to do the dirty deed as soon as you so foolishly appeared."

Lord Clairmont released a rather guilty chuckle. "I suppose the thought might have crossed my mind."

Lady Mirthton's eyes began to sparkle with the warmth of her smile. "I thought as much. But you have no need for concern, my lord." Her unusual face suddenly became serious. "This I vow on my life. I have no wish to put a period to your bachelorhood. I promise you that if you will but call on me, I will be well and properly chaperoned. I will give you no cause to regret your decision to pay me a visit. Will you come, my lord?"

Marc leaned against the cold stone of the balustrade and studied the engaging woman who stood patiently before him, awaiting his decision. He knew without even having to think about it that he would go to her house tomorrow whether she was setting a trap for him or not. She fascinated him. She intrigued him. She was so honest in the revelation of her thoughts that she took his breath away. She was not at all a beauty, but there was something so compelling about her that he knew he had to have more. He would see her tomorrow, all right, and he would hear what she had to say. And then he would begin the pleasant task of making this thoroughly refreshing woman his.

"Shall I time my visit to avoid your other callers, my lady?" he asked, pleased to see a look of relief wash over what he could see of her face.

She surprised him yet again. A low gurgle of laughter spilled from her throat and the pink lace somehow managed to snag itself on one of her eye teeth. As she unhooked it, she confessed, "There will be no other visitors, my lord."

Marc cocked an eyebrow. He allowed that this was a rather happy turn of events. "Indeed. Then you do plan to ensnare me in a matrimonial scheme." His eyes were gleaming into hers.

Again she laughed. "I have promised you that I would not. I have had only three visitors since I came to London for the Little Season, and those were all former friends of my mother. No, my lord, you will only find myself, my companion, Miss Plumley, and my butler, Beedle, to receive your call." Lady Mirthton suddenly found the toes of her slippers most interesting. "Does that put you off coming?" she asked quietly.

Marc lifted her chin with his finger. "Not in the least. But

I do have several calls I am obliged to make tomorrow, so if I may, I'll make it early."

"Of course, my lord," the lady responded happily. "Whenever you can come, we shall be at home."

"Then may I escort you back inside, Lady Mirthton?" he asked as he extended the curve of his elbow.

"Thank you, my lord," she replied graciously.

Once inside the glittering ballroom, Lady Mirthton quickly gave Marc her direction and took her leave of him. He watched her make her way through the crush, pulling the heavy brocade of her gown close to her legs while she twisted her slender form to avoid contact with those around her. He was careful to observe the reaction of the members of the *ton* as she passed them by. Almost to a person they looked at her as if she had just crawled out from under a rock. He conceded that she was now an object of ridicule. One had only to look at her to be appalled by what one saw. That turban alone would be enough to put a period to any social ambitions Lady Mirthton might have had. But none of them, of course, had been with her on the terrace. None of them had probably ever even spoken to her. But he had, and had come away captivated. And that was another thing the *ton* didn't yet know. They didn't know that he was about to change her circumstances. They didn't know that she now belonged to him.

"Marc, darling, I thought that woman would never take her leave," breathed Samantha as she breezed up to his side with Peter and Lady Heatherton in tow.

"There was no reason for your concern, my dear," the earl responded with an effort to control his irritation.

"Is all well, Marc?" asked the viscount as he noticed the dusky flush that washed over the earl's face at Samantha's words. His first thought was that Marc's wound might be bothering him. He and Marc had fought side by side on the Peninsula, getting each other out of more scrapes than either cared to remember, and it was he who had dragged Marc, bleeding and near death, to safety. They had even sold out together. Their lives had taken different paths since then, though; Peter's into service under the Foreign Secretary, Lord Castlereagh, and Marc's into the demands of his earldom, but they were still the best of friends.

"Quite," Marc replied, turning toward his friend. "I fancy finishing up the evening at White's, Peter. Do you join me?"

"Never say you're leaving, Marc," pouted Samantha. "Why, I've even brought Lady Heatherton to apologize to you and to assure you that she has no idea how that odious woman came to be at her ball tonight. Surely you have not taken such a disgust of her forcing herself upon you that you will take yourself away before dancing even one dance with me?"

"I do wish to extend my most profound apologies, Lord Clairmont," interjected Lady Heatherton from the depths of her most profound bosom. "I assure you the chit was not invited. Nor shall she ever be again by any of the *ton.* I shall personally see to it." She raised herself up to her full dignity and pressed a silver lorgnette to the bridge of her nose.

"How unfortunate," the earl replied glacially. "Since I intend to pay a call on the odious chit tomorrow, perhaps you should also withdraw any further invitations to me." Glancing with considerably more warmth toward his friend, he concluded, "Coming, Peter?"

Amid the ladies' gasps of surprise, Peter grinned and answered, "Absolutely. But you had better take the lead. It seems you are not yet finished with needing me to watch your back."

It was well before the fashionable hours for morning visitations when Marc sawed on the ribbons of his four matched bays and brought his midnight blue curricle to a stop before Number Eight, Half Moon Street. His tiger jumped down immediately and ran around to take the horses' heads. Marc stepped down onto the cobbled street and looked up at the narrow townhouse that stood before him.

It was an unpretentious dwelling as London townhouses went, having a brick facade, a curved portico, and sets of dark green shutters putting parentheses around each window. But there was ample evidence of neglect. Marc noted that the bricks were covered with gray smut. It had obviously been a long time since they had been cleaned. And the paint on the shutters was chalky and peeling as well. Yet somehow the condition of the house did not surprise him. His lips curved into a smile. He pictured Lady Mirthton's appalling ball gown. Why should he expect her home to be any different than she was? He shook his head and, with a few energetic steps, stood before the door, rapping on the dull, white paint with the head of his walking stick while he awaited entry.

Lady Mirthton answered his summons. Marc was completely caught off guard. He stared at her, blinking in surprise.

Merciful heavens! she thought as her green gaze absorbed the earl's splendor. He was wearing a cutaway of burgundy superfine that showed not even the suggestion of a wrinkle. His waistcoat of embroidered fawn silk rode over buff pantaloons that might have been painted on his muscular legs. A starched muslin neck cloth of pristine white softened the hard lines of his masculine garb and set off the deep tan of his handsome face with dramatic effect. Lady Mirthton's hand, of its own accord, rose slowly to her throat and pressed ineffectively at the hammering heartbeat that pulsed against her fingers.

Oh, my, she almost said aloud as she remembered the state of her own attire. She quickly stuffed her dusting cloth under the apron bow that was tied behind her back and rubbed at a smudge of dirt she had noticed adoring her cheek earlier when she had passed the cheval glass. She had known he was coming, but never expected him to arrive so early! And here she was, dressed in her grubbiest gown and, of all things, cleaning! *Ah, well, there is no help for it,* she thought resignedly. *I am what I am.* Taking a deep breath, she opened the door wider to let the earl in.

"Lord Clairmont," she said with a blindingly bright smile, "I am so pleased that you have come. Won't you come inside?"

The earl stepped across the threshold with decidedly different thoughts assailing him. He was not quite able to believe what he was seeing. Lady Mirthton's slender form was encased in a long-sleeved gown of aged gray muslin. The gown was devoid of any ornamentation but the bib and heavy folds of a large, white apron! And if that wasn't shocking enough, the whole of her head was covered by an enormous mobcap whose gathered flounce drooped sadly across her forehead. Slowly he let his eyes travel over the length of her, thinking she looked scandalously adorable. When at last his gaze rested questioningly upon hers, he found himself noticing a very odd thing. Lady Mirthton certainly must know that a proper lady would never receive callers dressed as a maid, yet she did not seem the least bit embarrassed to be seen by him.

He was suddenly suspicious. And then he smiled.

"Good morning, Lady Mirthton. And how are your kneecaps today?"

Lady Mirthton blushed to the tips of her ears, but she smiled broadly. "They are quite busy at the moment, my lord. How kind of you to ask." Her green eyes glittered with humor.

"Madam, you have got the door again," scolded a wavery masculine voice from somewhere down the dim hallway. The earl turned in surprise toward the sudden sound and the scraping of slow, shuffling feet that followed directly thereafter.

"Yes I did, Beedle," called the lady. "I have told you that when you are taking your rest period you needn't heed a summons at the door." There was a loud clearing of an aged throat from somewhere down the long passageway, and the shuffling sound inched closer.

"And I have told you, miss," came the wheezing rasp of a reply, "'t'aint proper!" The shuffling came closer still until, at long last, the oldest man Marc had ever seen emerged from the dark recesses of the hallway and began his slow creep toward them.

Lady Mirthton wore a look of resignation. Lord Clairmont's emotion could only be called astonished amusement. But the two of them waited patiently for the excruciatingly slow progress of the ancient elder across the floor.

"Beedle, dear," said Lady Mirthton when the wizened man finally drew close enough to embrace, "you are supposed to be resting. You were up far too late last night waiting for me to return from the ball."

The old gentleman straightened his curved spine into less of a curved spine and threw off his mistress's protective arms. "Am I, or am I not, the butler, madam?" he asked in his loftiest tones.

"You are, of course, Beedle. You are well aware of that," responded his mistress as she stepped back to the earl's side.

Beedle's nose lifted perceptibly. "Then kindly allow me to buttle." The old retainer slowly swung toward Marc and relieved him of his hat, gloves, and cane, then began his shuffling journey to the coat closet.

Lady Mirthton burst into laughter. Marc's grin covered most of the bottom half of his face. "That, as you have no doubt discerned by now, my lord," said Lady Mirthton between her chuckles, "is Beedle." She turned, then, and began to escort the earl toward the parlor.

"How old is the fellow?" asked Marc, *sotto voce.*

"Do you know, I am really not at all sure," she responded. "I do know that he was with both me and my mother from our day of birth, and I am certain with her mother for at least a part of her life, also. I think it quite possible that he was here before William the Conqueror." Marc's smile became a deep laugh, and Lady Mirthton opened the door leading into a sunny, but shabby, room.

The parlor in Lady Mirthton's townhouse was decorated tastefully, but it had certainly seen better days. Faded pale blue silk wallpaper dressed the walls above dark mahogany wainscotting. Ancient gold draperies, tattered where they touched the floor, adorned the windows, and a threadbare blue and gold carpet drew the furniture, perched in pleasant conversational areas, together.

Marc let his gaze drift over the room and then settle on Lady Mirthton. He was still somewhat disconcerted by her attire. He could not understand how her family would allow her to live in such obvious penury. He decided to get to the bottom of it before things went any further between the two of them. "I wish to ask you a question," he said, as his eyes again perused her form.

"Then we have common purposes for this meeting, do we

not?" she responded with a smile. "But I have promised to be well and properly chaperoned, so I must ask you to hold your question until I have summoned my companion. You may ask whatever you wish when she is present." Lady Mirthton then gestured toward a threadbare sofa. "Do be seated, my lord. I shan't be but a moment." And before Marc could raise an objection, she had breezed through the parlor door.

Marc settled himself as best he could amongst the horsehair cushions. He took a closer look at his surroundings, noting with interest that the room was not at all unclean, merely worn. Someone was at least taking pains to see that the furniture was dusted and polished. A delightful fragrance of lemon and beeswax formed a pleasant counterpoint to the ancient mustiness of the furnishings. He relaxed against the faded brocade and thought about Lady Mirthton. The minutes ticked steadily by.

He smiled. He had known from the moment he set eyes on her earlier that he had not been mistaken about her. He had been somewhat concerned that when he saw her again by the light of a new day, her appeal would have somehow dissipated. But it had not. If anything, it was far stronger. Just seeing how she cared for her ancient butler had taken care of that. She was truly one of a kind, and Marc could not wait to possess her.

She was poor, of course, and almost surely without a dowry, but that fact did not bother him unduly. He had no need for a woman of means. He would have to do something about the way she dressed, though. She obviously lacked any sense of taste. Perhaps he could bring his mother in from Stonebridge to advise her. He wondered if Lady Mirthton would take it amiss. And, damme! He still didn't know the color of her hair!

The door opened suddenly and the object of his ruminations backed inside, her arms laden with a heavy silver tea tray. She was followed by a small, dumpling of a woman dressed completely in black. Marc rose to his feet immediately, then hurried over to take the tray from her hands.

"Thank you, my lord," Lady Mirthton said brightly. "I fear I might not have made it to the table without your assistance. Please set the tray in front of the sofa and I will pour." When

Marc had done as she asked and straightened, Lady Mirthton pulled the small gray-haired woman to stand before him. "May I present Miss Plumley to you, my lord? Plum, the Earl of Clairmont."

"Oh, your lordship!" tittered the round little woman. "Such an honor. Such an honor."

Miss Plumley folded herself into a surprisingly good curtsey, then blushed furiously when the earl raised her and brought her pudgy fingers to his lips. "Oh, my lord, please, do sit down. Do sit down," she blustered, flapping her hands at the earl and creating quite a breeze.

"Thank you, Miss Plumley," Marc replied as his eyes gleamed with amusement.

"Oh, quite, quite," giggled the woman as she cupped her cheeks with pleasure. "Now my dear," she said as she turned toward Lady Mirthton, "I shall just take a cup of tea and two of your delicious scones over to the window, and there I shall continue my sewing." Suddenly she tittered again and pressed her fingers to her lips. "Such an honor, my lord. Such an honor. But you'll not even know I am there. Not even know I am there." With another radiant blush, she took up her embroidery and scurried over to the window.

Lady Mirthton helped the older woman settle into a comfortable chair that was bathed in bright sunlight, then served her a dish of tea and scones. When that was gracefully accomplished, she returned to the earl's side. She seated herself next to him on the sofa and poured him a cup of tea. "You wished to ask me a question, my lord?" she began as she lifted the jug of milk to his cup and noted his refusal.

"Yes," he responded, nodding his head to her offer of lemon, "though it is a difficult question to ask without bringing offense, my lady . . ."

"I shall not be offended, my lord. Do go on," she urged, handing him his cup and offering him the plate of raisin scones.

"Lady Mirthton . . .," he hesitantly replied, taking a scone onto his plate, "You are wearing a mobcap and apron."

"Oh, that," she laughed as she poured herself a cup of the fragrant tea. "Would it be better, do you think, to do housework in my ball gown?" Her eyes were alight with sparkles of mischief.

The earl sighed. "I was afraid you might say something like that. So you were doing housework?"

"Dusting, as a matter of fact."

Suddenly the earl remembered something she had told him on the terrace the night before. "So it is true, then? Your household consists only of yourself, Miss Plumley, and Beedle? No maids?"

"No, no maids. Do have another scone, my lord. I made them myself," she said, offering him the plate again. "And yes, before you ask it of me, I do all the cooking, as well." She took a bite of her own scone and removed a tiny crumb from the corner of her mouth with a slender finger.

"But why, Lady Mirthton?" he asked, wondering again about her family.

"Because both Beedle and Plum are getting too old for any but the lightest of tasks," she replied easily.

Marc gave her a wry smile. "You know very well that is not what I meant."

"Yes. But I am avoiding the answer, you see. It really has no bearing on why I asked to see you today. And I must try to not keep you any longer than is necessary. Shall we get down to the reason for my asking you to call?"

Marc's head was spinning with hundreds of questions, but he held them at bay. There would be time enough for explanations later. Instead, he smiled into her emerald eyes and nodded.

"Very well," Lady Mirthton said briskly. "I am sure you are wondering why I chose you out of all the *ton* to come calling. The answer is that I needed a man of your singular accomplishments to give me some advice."

"Advice?" questioned Marc, his curiosity now pricked. He had thought surely she intended to ask him for money.

"Yes. It will take a man with certain attributes to tell me what I wish to know, and I have decided, my lord, that you are that man. You are a former soldier, skilled in weapons and fighting techniques, are you not? I have read many times in the *Gazette* of your heroics on the battlefield and the decorations

you received because of them. And as for the life you now lead
as a gentleman, sir, why, the whole of the *ton* knows that you
are the veriest Corinthian! Oh, yes, indeed, my lord, you are
exactly the one to give me the advice I need." She nodded her
head briskly and smiled at him with confidence.

Marc set his cup and saucer on the table before him and
leaned back into the cushions once again. Then he fixed Lady
Mirthton with a steady gaze. "A female usually seeks out her
male relatives for advice, my dear. Why do you not go to
them?"

"I cannot," she said simply, and her gaze dropped to her
lap.

"And why is that?"

She slowly raised her lovely eyes to his. He noticed that
their emerald color had darkened to moss with sadness. She
drew in a deep breath and let it out slowly, and then she spoke.
"Because, with the exception of my two younger cousins, my
lord, they have all been murdered," she calmly replied.

Chapter 3

"Do take a deep breath, Lord Clairmont," urged Lady Mirthton after her stunning revelation had caused him to choke on an inhaled raisin. "All the coughing you seem to do cannot be good for your wound, you know." She lowered her eyes and took another sip of tea while the earl cleared the rest of the scone out of his airways and wiped his streaming eyes with a fine linen handkerchief.

_ He turned to her then and shook his head. "If I failed to take you seriously before, my lady, I have now amended my opinion. You will start at the beginning, my dear, and you will tell me everything," he ordered in his best battalion commander's voice. Lady Mirthton thought it quite likely that when the earl still had his commission he never experienced problems with discipline. "You may begin now."

Lady Mirthton smiled gently. The sweetness of it did strange things to Marc's pulse. "I perceive that you are a very kind man, my lord, but you must not take my situation so to heart. We are strangers, you and I. And I would not involve you in my life any more than is necessary. All I ask is to be given the benefit of your knowledge, and just for this one time only."

The earl almost laughed out loud. If his adorable lady thought that she'd be free of him after today, she was very much mistaken. She did, after all, belong to him. She just did not know it yet. He did not want to frighten her, however, so he sought the information he needed by approaching her from a different direction.

"Very well, my dear, let us get to the heart of the matter. Suppose you tell me what advice you are seeking."

Lady Mirthton set aside her tea cup and looked at him earnestly. The flounce of her mobcap settled over her finely arched brows and she unthinkingly pushed it aside. The earl smiled. "I wish to know how to defend myself, my lord. I thought perhaps you could show me how to fend off an attack by . . . well, by someone who might wish to do me harm. Perhaps you could show me how to load and fire a pistol as well."

The earl merely stared at her; a hard, piercing stare that caused her conversation to falter awkwardly. She was quite put out of countenance, and felt a somewhat panicky need to fill in the heavy silence coming from her glaring guest. "I . . . well, I suppose you have concluded by now that I have a problem of sorts . . ."

The silence continued. Lady Mirthton could not know that Marc was struggling with a powerful rage. Someone was threatening his lady. He knew it as assuredly as he knew his own name. But he knew he must contain his emotions. He could not risk frightening her. It would not be impossible, but he would not be able to protect her nearly as easily if she sent him away.

"Please, my lady, do continue," said the earl finally, and very quietly.

"But I truly do not wish to involve you, my lord. If you could just tell me what to do . . ."

"You are trying my patience, my dear," interrupted the earl, not unkindly. He gave her a reassuring smile.

Lady Mirthton's eyes turned mossy green again. Marc knew it signalled her sadness. "Oh, very well," she responded with a sigh. "It is not a complicated problem, really. It is just that I do not quite know how to handle it. It is somewhat beyond my experience. That is why I came to you."

"Tell me the problem, my dear," ordered Marc softly.

Lady Mirthton struggled for a moment, wondering how to make her answer sufficiently vague. More than anything, she sought to spare her father's name. "The problem is this, my lord," she began. "There is a certain item that has been lost, and I have been directed to find it." *There,* she thought, *that doesn't tell him anything.*

The earl gave her a hard stare. "It won't fadge, my dear," he said bluntly. "Simply finding a lost item would hardly require lessons in self-defense. I would have the truth, Lady Mirthton."

Lady Mirthton's eyes glowed bright green with indignation. "That *was* the truth, my lord," she snapped.

"But not all of it," he countered with a gleam of appreciation for her lovely emerald fire.

Her irritation fled instantly. "Well . . . no. Oh, very well, my lord," she sighed, "the persons requiring me to find this item are the same ones who killed my family."

Marc was instantly alert. At last she was getting to the core of the matter. "And if you cannot find it, what will happen?" he questioned calmly.

Her words were barely whispered, but Marc heard them with bell-like clarity in spite of the blood pounding against his ears.

"Then I shall be the next to die."

Marc clenched his fists against the surge of possessiveness that washed over him. The need to protect his lady was so strong that he had to fight to remain seated.

"You see now, perhaps, why my need for your expertise is so timely," she continued, clasping her hands together in her lap. Then she smiled brightly. "What will you show me first?"

"Madam," said Marc penetratingly, "if you think I am going to allow you to pit yourself against cutthroats and murderers, you are to let in your attic! Get your bonnet. We are going to Bow Street."

"No!" cried Lady Mirthton as she quickly laid a restraining hand on the irate earl's arm. "I cannot do that!"

Marc settled onto the edge of the sofa once again. "Why not?"

"I have been instructed not to do so." She withdrew her

hand from his sleeve, but Marc would not have it. He put it back again and covered it with his own.

"Indeed. And how was this accomplished?"

"I received a note a short time ago. My instructions were contained in it."

The earl relaxed against the cushions once again. "May I see it?" he ventured calmly. Inside he was a seething storm.

Lady Mirthton hesitated. She had hoped with all her heart, since the day of his death, that she could protect her father's name even in the midst of the scandal she had just brought upon herself, but now she realized that to do so would be impossible. She sighed softly and let that hope die. This morning, even as early as it was, she knew that every tabby in the *ton* would be bruiting about her behavior at the ball last night. She accepted the fact that she was now ruined and thought that one more item of juicy scandal attached to her name simply would not signify.

"Yes, my lord, you may see it," she softly acquiesced. "Please excuse me for a moment while I get it for you."

Miss Plumley's head bobbed up from her embroidery as her young charge rose to her feet and crossed the room to a well-worn rosewood desk inlaid with beech burl. She watched as she took a small slip of paper from the single drawer and started back toward the earl.

"Such a pother," she muttered to no one in particular. "Such a pother." Then her head bent once again over her work.

Lady Mirthton seated herself once again at the earl's side and handed him the piece of paper. He opened it carefully and scanned the childish scrawl.

Lady Mirthton,

You have one month in which to locate and bring to London a list that was in your father's possession. You will be contacted about where to bring the list after you arrive. If you fail to follow these directions, you will die as he did. Under no circumstances are you to seek the aid of either Bow Street or the Government.

"Well, this is a deuced coil," said the earl with a gentle smile. "But I am very much afraid that this note raises more questions than ever, my dear. I can understand why the writer would demand that you not seek help from Bow Street, but why would he tell you not to contact the government?"

Lady Mirthton's eyes dropped to her lap.

"You know, do you not?" asked Marc softly.

"Yes," she sighed, avoiding his eyes.

There was no help for it, she knew. She would have to expose her father now. She knew she could weather the ostracism certain to come upon her from the *ton,* but it was going to be a devilish task to remain composed when she saw the look of disgust that would fill Lord Clairmont's eyes at her revelation. Yet it had to come, and she would have to live with it. And who could tell? He was a man of honor. Perhaps he would still teach her what she needed to know in spite of his aversion.

"Will you tell me?" he asked as his gaze captured hers.

Lady Mirthton took a deep breath and looked squarely into Marc's eyes. "My father spied for the French," she said flatly. And then she waited . . . waited for the fire of revilement to kindle in his eyes, waited for the hatred to twist his handsome features. It never came. Instead, Marc reached over and drew her cold hand into his.

"My dear lady," he began gently, "how very difficult for you."

His casual acceptance of her plight was almost her undoing. "You do not hate me?" she blurted out before she could think better of it.

"Were you a spy as well?" he countered quickly.

"No!" she cried, drawing back from him.

"Did you aid your father in any way?" He took her hand and pulled her back again.

"No, of course not!" she exclaimed. "I only found out the truth myself very recently." She reached out, then, and cupped her free hand over his. She had no idea she had done it, but Marc certainly did. His heart smiled.

"Tell me about it, my dear," he encouraged. "Tell me how you found out about your father's treason."

"You truly do not hate me?" she whispered wonderingly.

"No," he said with a smile.

Lady Mirthton was so relieved that unthinkingly she nestled against Marc's shoulder. With her hands encased in his, she felt warm and safe for the first time since her father's death. "It was when he died, about four months ago, that I found out," she began. "We were living at our family home, Mirthton Manor, at the time. There were only the five of us: Father, Beedle, Plum, and I, and one village girl who served as our maid."

"And your mother?" queried the earl.

"Mama died when I was thirteen." Lady Mirthton's face sobered suddenly. "You must know the truth of something, Lord Clairmont. Last evening, when Lady Peters accused my father of being a gambler and a drunkard, she was quite correct. For most of my life, in fact, he was a consummate wastrel. Mama and I hardly ever saw him, and when we did, he hadn't a feather to fly with. But he was my father and I cared for him, and somehow he managed to come up with funds enough to keep us going. Toward the end, I believe he had come to regret his mistakes and was trying to make up for his neglect of me. We had begun to rub along quite well together, you see. He had stopped his drinking and gambling and stayed at the Manor with me nearly all the time." She smiled then at what Marc thought might be a pleasant memory. "He was even insisting on giving me a Season and had begun to make plans for it. I knew we could not afford it, but seeing to the arrangements seemed to make him so very happy."

"What happened then?" asked Marc with a squeeze of her hand.

"It was all so frightfully sudden," she continued. "One morning, as I had returned from my ride, I came into the drawing room to tell him something and found him lying on the floor near death." Lady Mirthton's hands were clutching the earl's, seeking solace from their strength and warmth. "I rushed to his side and tried to take him into my arms. I could see that he had been brutally stabbed. He was too heavy, of course. I could not lift him. But he began trying to whisper to me. I was sobbing by then. I remember struggling to control my tears so that I could hear what he was saying."

The earl tightened his grip on Lady Mirthton's hands. "What did you understand him to say?" he asked.

"He said, 'Forgive me. I have spied against my country.' Then he began to cough, and when he had controlled it, said, 'There is a list.' And then he said something that sounded like, 'The sign of the *sabot*.' He said only a few more words, but he began coughing again in the middle of them and it became difficult to understand him. And then he was gone."

"The sign of the *sabot*," repeated Marc pensively.

"Yes. Does it mean anything to you?" Lady Mirthton asked hopefully.

"Only in one way, at this point," he answered. "A *sabot* is the French name for one of the wooden shoes that were worn by the *sans-culottes* during the French Revolution. The name certainly establishes a link between your father and the French, but I suspect that it is much more."

"How so?" asked Lady Mirthton, intrigued by the thought.

"It is quite possibly our most important clue as to the whereabouts of your father's list, and I should not be at all surprised to find that it is the key to uncovering your father's murderer. Have you no idea what the list might contain?"

"None. I was completely ignorant of my father's activities until he told me of them, and I have given you his words just as he told them to me. You now know as much as I do, my lord."

"I see. One other question, then, if you please," said Marc as he stroked her fingers with his thumb. "You gave me the impression earlier that more than one of your family had been murdered. Is this true?"

"Yes," she replied sadly. "Upon my father's death, his brother, my Uncle Boggs, came into the title. He, my Aunt Beatrice, and their two sons, Lucius and Willard, moved into the Manor just before my father's funeral, and I was soon sent here to find myself a husband. Not long after Plum and I had arrived and my cousins had returned to Oxford to complete their term, robbers supposedly broke into the Manor. Uncle

Boggs must have come upon the intruders and tried to fight them, for in the morning, Beedle found my aunt and my uncle at the foot of the stairs. They were both dead."

"I am very sorry, my dear," said the earl as he pulled her a bit closer. "To lose so many loved ones so quickly must have been painful beyond belief."

"Thank you, my lord," she responded, "but I can only be truthful. I did not care for my aunt and uncle, nor do I care for my cousins. Uncle Boggs was deeply ashamed of my father's dissipations and the taint that he brought to our family name. It angered him that my father held the title and the right to the family fortune. He was forced to watch my father squander it over the course of his life, and, I am afraid, grew quite bitter because of it."

"And so, when, because of your father's death, he could claim the title and estate for himself, he at last had the power to make his brother's only child pay for all those years of frustration," concluded Marc as he at last understood Lady Mirthton's situation.

"Yes," she replied, "though in truth I cannot blame him for it."

"Gammon!" the earl replied. "You had no part in what your father did. Your uncle had a responsibility to you, and he dealt with you shamefully. But what of your cousins? Why did you not go to them for help?"

"I would not, my lord. They are toads."

"Oh," said the earl with a bark of laughter, "I see."

"In fact, they have always seemed somewhat sinister to me. They were nasty little children, and have grown into nasty young men. They are cut from quite the same cloth as their father, I fear."

Marc filed that bit of information away in his mind. "Let us go back to something you said earlier, if we may," he said, breaking off a corner of a fresh scone and popping it into his mouth.

"What was that?" she asked with a grin at his lordship's comfortable manners.

"You said that robbers 'supposedly' broke into the Manor.

Why did you use that term? Do you have doubts about the intruders' purpose?"

"I fear that I do. Plum and I traveled back to the Manor after the murders to set things in order again and to attend the funerals, and found that the house had indeed been ransacked in the way robbers are wont to do. But as we worked to clean and replace all the items where they belonged, it became obvious to us that nothing was missing. Absolutely nothing."

"As if whoever broke in was merely looking for something and wanted to cover their activity by making it appear to be a robbery," continued Marc, deep in thought. "Looking for a list, perhaps?"

"My thought exactly, my lord," she affirmed. "I am convinced that Uncle Boggs and Aunt Beatrice's deaths are tied somehow to my father's."

"If we are right about the intruders looking for the list, then it is likely that your aunt and uncle simply got in the way and paid the ultimate price for it, my dear," Marc said gently, "and that convinces me more than ever that you are in serious danger."

Lady Mirthton's shoulders trembled with an involuntary shiver. "Do you think they found the list?" she asked hopefully.

"I am afraid not, my dear," he responded. "If they had, there would have been no need to force you into finding it."

"Yes, of course, how foolish of me," she said sadly. She was suddenly feeling quite blue-deviled. She was no farther ahead in her pursuit of the infamous list than she had been the day before, and even her great plan had gone awry. She should by now be feeling confident in her ability to protect herself, but she had instead seen herself shorn of ancestral home, reputation, and future in one fell swoop. And to put the cap on it all, the earl had refused to teach her. She decided that his attitude made her the tiniest bit angry. Who was he to refuse her simple request? She was sure there were others in Town who could teach her just as well.

Of course! she thought, suddenly elated. *Why did I not think of that before! If this idea had been a foot, it would have kicked me in the shin.*

"Is anyone living in the Manor at present?" asked the earl, totally unaware of the new direction of Lady Mirthton's thoughts. "It does not have to be sold for payment of debts right away, does it?"

"What? Oh, no, my lord," she replied as she quickly determined that she needed to get rid of the earl as soon as possible. The day was wasting, after all, and she had to hurry if she were to accomplish her new plan. "The estate is entailed. My cousin, Lucius, is the new Viscount Collingwood, of course, but as far as I know, he and Willard are still away at Oxford."

Marc eyed Lady Mirthton suspiciously. Her eyes had suddenly transformed from moss into vivid emerald. He was grateful for the warning. "Is something amiss, my dear?" he asked resignedly, knowing of a certainty that he was throwing himself like a moth into the flame.

"Not at all," she replied with a brilliant smile. Marc lifted a wary eyebrow. "But I am reminded that I promised to keep you only for a short while this morning, and our time together has been far longer than I had intended." She quickly withdrew her hands from his grasp and stood to her feet. Marc followed her lead reluctantly.

"I have not minded," he said, watching her carefully.

"But I cannot in good conscience keep you longer, my lord," she stated as she began to lead him toward the door.

"I have all the time in the world, my dear," he countered, then awaited her next attempt to usher him from her home.

"Appointments!" she cried, snapping her fingers. "I do remember your telling me that you had other appointments this morning," she reminded him gleefully, and she all but shoved him to the coat closet.

Marc had had enough. He dug in his heels. "Cease, my dear. What is this all about? You have ushered me out so quickly I did not even have time to pay my respects to Miss Plumley."

"She will not mind," she said as she pulled on his sleeve.

"You have not answered my question," reminded the earl.

"Oh. So I have not," she said somewhat guiltily. Her eyes dropped to the pattern on the parquet floor. "Oh, very well, my lord. I have just thought of something I wish to do."

"I see," he replied. "And my continued presence is preventing you?"

"Yes. That is it exactly, my lord," she said brightly.

"And what is it that you wish to do, Lady Mirthton?" he inquired politely.

"I do not wish to tell you, my lord," she said in a small voice.

"But I am afraid you are going to have to," responded Marc with more force. "Otherwise I shall not move from this spot."

Marc did not think it was possible, but Lady Mirthton's eyes got even greener. She was silent for long moments while she scowled at him. He thought she looked entrancing. She had a lot of bottom, his green-eyed lady, and a bright, fertile mind. He knew she had hatched another scheme even as she sat talking to him, and he could not wait to see what she had come up with this time.

He did not have to wait long.

"I asked you here to teach me how to protect myself," she began.

"I am aware of that," he responded with an amused grin.

"You refused," she stated bluntly.

"Yes, I did," he agreed, loving her tiny display of temper.

"So I am going to a place where I can learn everything I need to know," she said crisply.

"And where might that be?" Marc asked with a sudden surge of alarm.

"Exactly where you would go, my lord," she answered as her eyes sparkled with excitement, "to Gentleman Jackson's Boxing Saloon."

Chapter 4

"The deuce!" shouted the earl as he punched his balled fists against his narrow hips.

Suddenly, Beedle's sonorous tones rumbled from somewhere within the recesses of the house. "Madam, you are at the door again," he called, and the whisper of his slow shuffle began to rasp across the floor.

Lady Mirthton rolled her eyes.

"Women do not go to Gentleman Jackson's Boxing Saloon, madam," continued the earl as he bent at the waist and situated his face just inches from hers. "Why not tell me that you intend stopping on the way to have luncheon at White's? The notion is just as cork-brained!"

"Fustian," the lady returned, not in the least intimidated. "I have no need to go to White's. What can they teach me except how to swill brandy and smoke those foul-smelling cigars?"

"You are deliberately missing the point," barked the earl with increasing exasperation. "You know as well as I that there are certain places that are strictly a gentleman's domain, places where a woman of breeding would not think to intrude, and Gentleman Jackson's is right at the top of that list."

"Why?" asked Lady Mirthton as she retrieved the earl's hat, cane, and gloves from the musty closet.

"Because," shouted the earl, "it just is!"

"You must do better than that, my lord," she returned with a challenging gleam in her eye.

Marc took a deep, calming breath. He had fought the French. He could handle one stubborn nodcock of a woman. "My dear," he began in soft, reasonable tones, "Gentleman Jackson's is a very rough place. Men spend good money to go there solely for the purpose of pounding on one another. Quite often their noses get bent in some rather unusual directions. Chins are buffeted and abraded. There is sweat everywhere, and more than likely blood . . ."

"I do not succumb to the vapors over the sight of blood, my lord," interrupted the lady. "As a matter of fact, I do not succumb to the vapors over anything. You need not be concerned on that score." She thrust the earl's belongings into his supplicatory hands as the creak of Beedle's ancient joints grated closer.

"Then what about the men themselves, my dear?" Marc asked in frustration. "Have you considered them?" Lady Mirthton gave him a puzzled frown, and the earl at last felt that he had opened a crack in the lady's monumental stubbornness. "It is a gentleman's establishment, you know," he continued, forcing the crack a little wider. "Men can be found inside in various states of undress, you know. Some in no dress at all." He crossed his arms over his broad chest and nodded sincerely. He was rather pleased with himself.

"Oh, dear," responded Lady Mirthton. "That does put a different complexion on the matter, does it not?" She stared at the earl for a moment and then her face brightened. "I have it!" she cried. "I shall simply keep my eyes closed until all the gentlemen present have put their clothes back on, and then I shall proceed with my plan."

The earl's head dropped into his well-manicured hand.

"You *are* at the door, madam," accused Beedle as he ambled into view, "*and* you have retrieved his lordship's belongings. Stand still, if you please, my gel, until I have had a chance to thump you."

Lady Mirthton's laugh was light and lovely and not at all contrived. Marc couldn't help but smile. He enjoyed her honest merriment immensely. "You see, my lord, what comes of keeping on old family retainers. They take the most amazing liberties with one's ego." Then she turned to Beedle. "I am going out immediately, Beedle. I shall need Plum to accompany me. Will you ask her to join us?"

"Wait a moment, Beedle," countered the earl as he held out a staying hand. He turned quickly toward Lady Mirthton. "You truly mean to go through with this nonsense, don't you?" he asked with an incredulous look on his face. "In spite of all I have said to the contrary?"

"Yes, I do," she replied readily. "I have nothing to lose, after all. My reputation is already in shreds."

Marc ran his fingers through his blond hair, then let his hand fall limply to his side. He could not let her do it, of course. She was not aware of it, but Marc had spent a good deal of the evening after she had left the ball working the tabbies to her benefit. He had told them of her refreshing sense of humor and penchant for taking on the most entertaining dares, and, by the time his *on dits* had circled the floor, the *ton* was calling her the most delightful Original to make her debut in years. Having gone to such lengths to preserve her reputation, he could not let her ruin it all over again now.

And, of course, there was the very large consideration of her safety. She was in danger. Marc could sense it with all the instincts that had kept him alive during the war. He knew he could not be comfortable unless she remained within his sight. Understanding this, he made his decision. He himself would take her up in his curricle, but he would see to it that she never came near her destination.

"Very well, my dear," he acquiesced, "if you are set on this foolish course, the least I can do as a gentleman is to accompany you. Your Miss Plumley would hardly be a suitable escort for this ill-begotten escapade."

"Nor would you, Lord Clairmont," she shot back quickly,

"since I would be alone with you and without a chaperone."

Marc smiled at her ready mind. She would keep him on his toes, this impertinent bit of goods, but he did not mind. He was, in fact, looking forward to a lifetime of delicious combat with her. "I give you my word, my dear, that we shall at all times remain in the public view. Will that satisfy your maidenly sensibilities?"

Lady Mirthton laughed delightfully. "Indeed it will, my lord, and you have my gratitude. If you will excuse me, I shall just get my hat and pelisse, and we can be off in a trice." She turned toward the stairs, but the earl stopped her.

"Just one small thing," he said with a grin, "I do not believe that aprons and dust cloths have yet become the highest stare of fashion." Before she could stop him, he slipped an arm around her waist and retrieved the dust cloth she had hidden beneath her apron bow. As he tucked it neatly into her pocket, she attempted to hide her embarrassed blush by tugging the ruffle of her mobcap low on her brow. He would not let her off so easily. "Perhaps before we go you would care to change into something a bit more ordinary," he suggested as he touched two fingers to the ruffle and flipped the confounded thing out of the way.

Lady Mirthton started, thought a moment, and then beamed. "I have just the thing!" she said with a snap of her fingers.

Lord Clairmont sighed.

She scurried up the stairs.

Marc feathered an exacting right turn onto Curzon Street, his bloods prancing in their eager desire to be free of his controlling hand on the ribbons. He kept them at a sedate pace, though, as they trotted past corner shops and townhouses, while he shook his head in bemusement. Lady Mirthton sat close beside him, glancing at him somewhat hesitantly.

She was wearing a gown of violet cambric with a fitted bodice that ended in a point over her lower abdomen. The bodice was held snugly over a white chemisette and was laced in front by a yellow ribbon from whose tapered ends dangled bright balls of *faux fleurs* in every color of the rainbow. Wrapped around her shoulders was a blue lace-edged fichu which crossed over her small bosom and tied at the back of her waist. A straw beehive bonnet, adorned with a large blue flower, completely covered her head. Her outfit was the most abominable combination of out-dated clothing Marc had ever seen.

She had brought along a plain brown pelisse of heavy wool, but the day had proved to be too warm for her to wear it, so she held it on her lap beneath her clasped hands while her pink reticule bounced against her knees. Marc wondered if she would take offense if he seized her pelisse and threw it over her head. He supposed she would. Women seemed to be sensitive about things like that. He cast her another glance and sighed. Not a wisp of her hair could be seen. The horrible thought came to him as he observed her that she might not have any. His wary eyes slid toward her again. At least she had eyebrows, he noticed, of a pleasant light brown color. She turned suddenly and gave him a bright smile. He immediately found the most interesting flaw on one of his horses' flanks.

"You are going the wrong way, my lord," said Lady Mirthton as Marc made a left turn onto Berkeley Street. He slowed while a white-aproned nanny pushed a perambulator across the street in front of him, and then headed for the plane trees that delineated Berkeley Square.

"I am going exactly the right way, my dear," he corrected.

"I beg to differ with you, sir," she argued, "but Gentleman Jackson's is in Bond Street. You are heading for Berkeley Square."

"Yes," he replied casually. "I am hungry. Before we go to Jackson's, we shall take tea at Gunter's and have an ice."

"That is very kind in you, my lord," she stammered with surprise, "but I wish to get on with my lessons."

"Come now, my dear," he cajoled, "certainly you would not force me to go hungry?"

"I hardly see how that can happen," she muttered in disgruntlement. "You have just finished eating six of my raisin scones!"

"And delicious scones they were, too, my dear," he said with an amused smile. "Yet my man's body requires something of more substance, and I very much fear that you will just have to accompany me."

Lady Mirthton eyed the earl suspiciously, but she could not fault his reasoning. Just then, adding weight to his argument, her own stomach rumbled noisily. The earl chuckled with amusement, and Lady Mirthton suspected with dismay that even her feet were blushing. "Very well, my lord," she agreed as the curricle pulled into the square, "we shall delay long enough to eat, but then we shall make all haste to the boxing saloon."

"I quite agree," responded the earl as he pulled up before the busy confectioner's. He jumped to the cobblestones and quickly moved to help Lady Mirthton descend from the carriage while his tiger ran to control the horses. Before she could take a decent breath, she was whisked inside and seated at the earl's favorite table with a cup of steaming tea in her hand. Two flaky meat pies appeared shortly after, followed by a selection of exotic fruits from various ports around the world. Lady Mirthton had just enough time to push the huge blue flower out of the center of her face when they were joined at their table by Lord Latham and his lovely wife, Katherine.

"Clairmont!" boomed the marquess over the bustle of activity in the room. "How good to see you!" He clapped the earl on his shoulder and grinned broadly. "Katherine and I have just come to Town. Saw Eversley earlier this morning and he said the two of you had sold out. Can't tell you how good it is to have you back."

"As good, I hope, as it is to be back," answered the earl as he stood respectfully. "Hello again, Katherine," he said with a smile. "May I present my companion, Lady Mirthton? My dear, the Marquess and Marchioness of Latham."

Lady Latham's eyes grew appreciably larger. "Oh, so you are she! How delighted I am to meet you, my dear!" she exclaimed. Lady Mirthton, who was tensed for the cut direct, sat staring at the ebullient woman, stunned into silence. "Tell me, is it true?" Lady Latham continued in conspiratorial tones. "Did you really walk through a country dance on a dare?"

"Well . . . I . . ."

"And did you truly wear a gown taken from Madame Tussaud's display of Queen Elizabeth?"

Lady Mirthton blinked rapidly, her eyes shading a more brilliant green. "Lady Latham," she began, "I do not . . ."

"La, how silly of me. Of course you do not wish to tell your secrets here in a public place," she laughed. "But say you will come to tea one afternoon and tell my friends and me all about it," she commanded. "I shall not take 'no' for an answer." With a delightful smile, she took her husband's arm, allowed Marc to kiss her fingers, and swept away in a cloud of lace and perfume.

Lord and Lady Latham had barely left their side when two other Pinks of the *ton* arrived asking Marc for introductions. No sooner had he complied and then scowled them away from his territory, than Lady Heatherton marched to their side.

"So nice to see you again, Clairmont," she uttered stentoriously, "and, of course, you as well, my gel," she added as she let her lorgnette droop against her jowl. "Delightful to have you both in attendance at my little affair." Then her majestic face grew slightly pensive. Lady Mirthton watched in fascination. "And so odd in Lady Peters to carry on as she did after you left, my dears," she began. "Not good *ton,* you know. No, not at all. Fairly flew into the ladies' withdrawing room and ripped my new draperies right off the windows." She sniffed disdainfully and slowly lumbered away.

Marc masked his explosion of laughter under a series of loud coughs. Lady Mirthton's sparkling eyes flew to his. "You should see to those throat problems of yours, my lord," she counseled with a grin, and then her mood shifted like quicksilver. "What do you know about all of this?" she asked suspiciously. "When I left the ball, I was a social pariah. What happened between then and now?"

Marc had been ready for her question. His answer took no time at all. "My dear," he answered, looking angelic, "I have no idea." The look Lady Mirthton drilled into his eyes let him know with absolutely no uncertainty that a quick change of subject was indeed called for. "Lady Mirthton," he said immediately, "I would like to talk more fully about the things your father said to you on the day he died."

"Very well," she replied as she lost her pique in the face of his return to her problems. "What would you care to discuss?" She lifted a wedge of sugared pineapple to her lips with her fork and waited for him to begin.

"I have been wondering about the list that your father mentioned," he said as he bit down on a wedge of his succulent pie. "It would be helpful if we knew what was on it."

"I have thought the same thing," she affirmed. "And, perhaps equally important, it would help to know why he had such a list in the first place."

"I agree," responded Marc with a smile of appreciation for her obvious intelligence. "Why would a man who, when on the verge of death had confessed himself a spy, still be compelled to speak of a list?"

"Its importance would have had to be overwhelming," said Lady Mirthton.

"Yes," agreed Marc softly. "Overwhelming enough to kill him because of it." He reached beneath the table and squeezed Lady Mirthton's cold hand.

She lifted her eyes and met his steadily, absorbing the strength she found there. "Could it have been a list of drop-off points?" she asked quietly.

"Possibly," he responded as he released her hand and sat back in his chair. "But drop-off points can easily be changed. A list of those would not be worth killing a man for."

"Unless the man was being killed instead for disloyalty. I do believe that my father was trying to change his life, my lord."

"And I believe you, Lady Mirthton," Marc replied warmly,

"but why, then, is whoever killed your father now coming after you? No, my dear, it is the list that is important. That is the crux of this whole havey-cavey affair."

"Then the list contained names, did it not?" she asked softly.

"That would be my guess," he affirmed. "I believe that your father was indeed trying to escape from his life as a spy, and that he made the list either to blackmail the others in his ring into letting him go or to turn over to the government in exchange for immunity."

"But something went wrong," she said, continuing his thoughts.

"Yes. I suspect that the list is not complete. Members of subversive groups like this rarely know each other. I imagine that your father had been working over a period of months to ferret out the others in his ring, but that before he could uncover all their identities, his activities were discovered."

"But the list, even though incomplete, is still damaging," she added as she took a calming sip of tea.

"Quite," said the earl.

Lady Mirthton's eyes suddenly filled with tears. Marc slipped her his pristine handkerchief and she caught the trickle of a tiny tear as it slid from the corner of her eye and started down her cheek. "Have no fear, my lord," she whispered. "I shall not become a watering pot."

"I have no doubt of that, my dear," responded Marc with a warm smile, "but perhaps you would like to return to my curricle so that you might compose yourself."

Lady Mirthton gave him a watery nod of agreement, and Marc quickly paid the shot. Shielding her discomposure from the others in the room with his large body, he soon had her settled beside him in the curricle and had moved into the traffic circling the square. He noticed that his handkerchief was quite damp now.

"I shall not make a cake of myself," she stated positively.

"Of course not," murmured the earl as he headed west around the north end of the square.

"It is just that sometimes . . .," she began, dampening the

handkerchief into sogginess, "it is all just the tiniest bit difficult."

Marc glanced at her and covered her two small fists with his free hand. Her courage pleased him mightily. He squeezed her hands gently and then turned into Mount Street.

Lady Mirthton watched as the sign for John Bailey and Sons, Poulterers, passed by. "You are going the wrong way again, my lord," she said, her tears forgotten. "Gentleman Jackson's is in the opposite direction."

Maddeningly, the earl merely smiled. "You must have time to compose yourself, my dear. You cannot expect to enter a man's domain with reddened eyes. You may gain a gentleman's sympathy, but certainly not his respect."

"Oh," she responded quietly. "Are they so very red, then?" she asked hesitantly.

"Oh, yes," lied the earl. "Quite blotchy, as a matter of fact. Clashes horribly with your gown."

"Oh," she repeated, as the earl turned left into Park Lane. "Where are you taking me then?" she asked as her gaze barely noticed the familiar mansions passing by on her left.

"For a drive in the park, of course," Marc answered. "We will take in the air and you will be recovered in no time."

He snapped his whip lightly and his horses picked up their pace. Soon they found themselves in a crush of carriages, all angling to pass through the entrance into Hyde Park.

"Lord Clairmont," said Lady Mirthton with growing apprehension, "what is the time? Why are all these people here?"

"Why, it is just now five o'clock, my lady," he replied with a very suspicious smirk. "Right at the fashionable hour, I believe."

Lady Mirthton's eyes narrowed into a brilliant green. "You have tricked me, my scurrilous lord," she seethed. "You never intended to take me to Gentleman Jackson's, did you? And now we are well and truly caught in this crush and will never be able to turn and leave. You are a bounder of the worst kind!"

"And you are quite lovely with your face all blotchy and your eyes such a magnificent green. It is rather like Christmas, looking at you," he teased.

"Oh!" gasped Lady Mirthton, thoroughly incensed. And then she burst into laughter. "I shall just go on my own tomorrow, you know," she chuckled as her mirth subsided.

"No you shall not," responded the earl mildly as he nodded to a passing acquaintance on horseback. "I am going to see Peter Babbington first thing tomorrow morning, and I want you to remain at home."

Lady Mirthton joined Marc in waving to Lord and Lady Latham as their landau passed by. "Lord Clairmont," she whispered with irritation, "I approached you last night merely to ask your advice. Why do you now think to manage my life?"

Mark turned suddenly and pierced her with a penetrating gaze. Lady Mirthton shivered slightly at the sight of it. "Because you are in danger, my dear," he replied in a deadly voice. "Can you have forgotten so soon? Perhaps I should be flattered that my presence puts you so at ease."

Lady Mirthton thought that if she had been standing, she would have staggered. The sudden glimpse that the earl granted her of the leashed power he held in check under his benign facade shook her to her very core. She wondered at it, felt herself desiring to lean into it; and suddenly, she felt very, very safe.

"Why do you go to see Viscount Eversley?" she asked in a somewhat shaky voice.

"He works for Lord Castlereagh," he replied with an immediate switch to a comfortable smile. He knew he had frightened her. He had done it on purpose. She just did not appreciate the seriousness of her situation. But now he needed to put her at ease with him again.

"But the note!" she gasped. "You would not tell them about me . . .?"

"Of course not, my dear," he reassured her, "but he may know something that would be of use to us. Do not concern yourself. I will be most discreet." Again his large hand covered hers and the warmth of it spread throughout her entire body.

Suddenly Marc stiffened. "Damme!" he muttered, and Lady Mirthton looked to see what was distressing him. Approaching them on a spirited chestnut gelding was Lady Peters. Lady Mirthton swallowed a very unladylike groan and smiled.

"Marc, darling!" cooed Samantha as she brought her mount into a walk beside them. She was dressed in a deep blue riding habit cut in the military style, and wore a matching shako perched at a jaunty angle on her lovely curls. "Naughty man! I expected you to call this morning."

"Indeed? But we did not dance, my dear," he responded a little too bluntly.

Samantha's eyes narrowed. "So we did not, darling," she responded with masked venom. She turned her attention toward the woman at his side. "And the most unusual Lady Mirthton is with you, I see," she said with a sweet smile. "How lovely you look, my dear."

"Good day, Lady Peters," she replied, knowing what was coming next. Conservatively, she calculated that she had been through this exact conversation four score times or more since she had been old enough to go about in society.

"How brave you are to take such fashion risks, my dear," she began. "Why, I myself could never think to be so creative."

Marc recognized the slur for what it was. His ire began to rise. "Samantha . . ."

"No, really, Marc," she continued, all but ignoring him, "simply consider all the colors our Lady Mirthton has managed to combine. It is quite as lovely as a spring garden. And she has set it all off with . . . the darling flower on that hat." Samantha could not help the slight curl of disgust that marred her pouting mouth.

"That is quite enough, Samantha," ground out Marc from between clenched teeth. It was one thing for him to moan about his lady's taste in clothing, but, by God, no one else had better criticize her!

"But I do so admire her, Marc darling," oozed Samantha. "She is indeed the Season's Original."

Lady Mirthton said the words before she could bite them back. "But how much better it would be to emulate you, Lady Peters, and be the Season's Incorrigible."

"Incomparable!" shouted Samantha. The eyes of every non-pareil in the vicinity swung toward her. She wilted under their blatant scrutiny. "I . . .," she began, and then her face hardened. "Good day," she uttered crisply, and then quickly rode away.

"I do beg your pardon," said Lady Mirthton when at last the dust had cleared and the carriages were moving again. "There are occasions when I cannot control my tongue."

Marc's eyes danced with humor. He looked at her and broke out in a soft chuckle.

"Incorrigible?" he repeated, and then laughed louder.

The corners of Lady Mirthton's mouth curved upward. "Yes, well . . . it was not very kind in me."

"You only gave her what she deserved," Marc said with a nod.

"But she was right." Lady Mirthton's response was so soft that Marc almost missed hearing it.

He glanced at her cautiously. "What do you mean, my dear?"

"Never say you haven't noticed, my lord? What a bouncer!" said Lady Mirthton as her eyebrows disappeared beneath the brim of her beehive hat.

Marc knew he was treading on very thin ice. How could he acknowledge the truth of Samantha's observations without hurting Lady Mirthton's feelings? She was a gentle thing. He would have to choose his words carefully, diplomatically.

"Very well, Lady Mirthton, why the deuce do you dress like one of the clowns at Astley's?"

Lady Mirthton burst into gales of heartwarming laughter. So caught up was she in her merriment, that just to look at her drew Marc to join in. Soon the two of them were leaning against each other helplessly, wiping their tear-filled eyes with any bit of fabric available.

Society in the park that day gave the earl and his Original a wide berth. He was smitten with her, of course, and from the looks of it, they were well suited. But it was most disconcerting to see what young people were coming to these days. Why, imagine one of the Four-in-Hand almost driving off the road!

"Oh, dear," gasped Lady Mirthton when she could finally

take a breath. She blotted her face and smoothed her skirts while she let the last of her chuckles die away. "I have never heard my plight put quite so succinctly."

"Have I embarrassed you terribly?" asked Marc as a bit of remorse began to set in.

"Oh, goodness, no!" she cried. "I have quite gotten used to it. And if you are to suffer the embarrassment of being seen in my company beyond this day, I do owe you an explanation."

"Only if you wish it, my dear," replied Marc with warm eyes.

"I do. I am afraid, my lord, that I have slid into the ranks of the genteelly poor. To be blunt, I haven't two coins to rub together and undoubtedly never will. The only reason I am in London at all is that my uncle ordered it. I was given this one Season in which to find myself an eligible *parti* and then my uncle would have considered that his obligation to me was discharged."

"What of your cousins?" asked Marc, hiding his anger at what his lady had had to suffer.

"They are of the same mind. I believe I mentioned that they were toads."

Marc gave her a wry half-smile. "Yes, I believe you did. And your clothing?"

"All of it belonged to my Aunt Beatrice. I have been wearing her cast-offs for years. And, before you say it," she added with and upheld hand, "I am quite well aware that my apparel is a mismatched hodge-podge."

"But, my dear, if you are aware of it . . .?" began the earl.

"Why do I not correct the problem?"

"Exactly," breathed the earl, relieved that he did not have to say the words.

"It is because of Plum," stated Lady Mirthton. "It is she who remakes all of my aunt's gowns for me."

"And she doesn't think to consult you, I take it," added the earl.

"No. She knows that I have more than I can do just to keep up with the housework. She tries to help by taking at least that one burden from me. She has been with me all of my life, you see. When she was very young, she was orphaned. Since she was the second cousin of my father and Uncle Boggs's stepmother, she came to live with them, growing up with them as if she were their sister. She was my nanny and my governess, and after my mother died, she did everything she could to take her place."

"I understand your devotion to her, my dear, but still, can you not say anything?"

"Oh, no, my lord. That would hurt her feelings," answered Lady Mirthton with a gentle shake of her head.

Marc was warmed by the goodness he saw revealed in the slender woman who had so entertained him over the past two days. He knew that he wanted her, and fully expected to one day possess her, but he was more than a little startled to find that she had also thoroughly captured his heart.

The sun was setting when Marc turned the curricle toward home. Just as his briskly trotting bays were passing a copse of poplars, Lady Mirthton reached out and touched his arm. She was staring intently at the trees. Immediately, Marc pulled over and brought his horses to a halt.

"What is it?" he demanded, thinking instantly of the ones who had threatened to kill her.

"My cousins," she said in a bewildered voice. "I would swear I had seen them over by those trees."

Marc signalled to his tiger and quickly got down from the curricle. In a matter of moments he had disappeared into the copse, not reappearing at the side of the carriage again until well after the sun had gone down.

"I found no one," he reported somewhat breathlessly as he climbed back up to his seat.

"I could not have been mistaken," replied Lady Mirthton in tones that suggested she thought exactly that.

Marc held her eyes captive in his direct gaze. "From this moment on, my dear," he said, lifting her chin with his finger, "we will assume that nothing we think we see is our imagination. Your life is at stake. If you think you see something, we will proceed on the assumption that you are correct." Grabbing the ribbons, he set the curricle in motion again.

"If that is the case, then, my lord," she said consideringly, "I did indeed see my cousins. But if that *is* the case, why are they here and not at Oxford?"

Chapter 5

"Good morning, Peter," greeted Marc as he stuck his head around the door of his friend's office.

"Marc!" smiled the viscount as he rose and extended his hand. "Finally come to your senses and decided to join us, have you?"

"What? And have you complaining all over again about the trials of saving my disreputable backside?" he replied as he shook the viscount's hand. "As a matter of fact, I was on my way to pick up a new cutaway from Weston's and thought I would pay you a visit first."

"Fribbles instead of epaulets," teased Peter. "What a colossal waste!" And then the viscount's voice took on a note of seriousness. "The service can use a man of your talents, Marc."

"Thank you, Peter," Marc replied warmly, "but my life of late has suddenly become more interesting. I am no longer quite so eager to abandon it."

"Ah, yes. Owing to the most unusual Lady Mirthton, so gossip has it," said Peter as he gestured toward a nearby chair.

Marc merely smiled. "She suits me, Peter," he said softly, then lowered himself into the chair.

"Then I am glad, my friend. But tell me, what brings you to the hallowed halls of the Foreign Ministry on this fine day?"

"Just a few questions," replied Marc with a casualness that belied his true feelings.

"What about?"

"Leaks."

Peter's eyes narrowed imperceptibly. He knew his friend well enough to know that this was no casual question. Marc had stumbled onto something, but he was not yet ready to confide in him. "It is a battle we constantly fight, as well you might imagine."

"And is it a battle you have been winning lately?" asked Marc as he leaned forward to rest his forearms on his muscular thighs.

"Eventually we always win. Except . . ."

"Except what?" asked Marc with an alert gleam in his eyes.

The viscount hesitated for a moment, and then his trust in his friend won out. "The matter is highly confidential, Marc," replied Peter. "You must not speak of anything I tell you outside this office."

"I understand. Do go on, Peter."

"I told you last night that the war was starting to turn in our favor. Napoleon is growing increasingly desperate. As a result, he is pushing his remaining operatives here in England for more and more information. The leaks we've been used to experiencing in the past have escalated alarmingly. Lord Castlereagh has just assigned me to look into the matter full time."

"But those very circumstances should make apprehending them much easier, Peter. With time running short, the operatives will have to take greater and greater chances. Even now you must have some men who are already at least under suspicion."

"None. Whoever has been passing the information this time probably has been in place for a long time; well past the time when any suspicion might be assigned to him. We suspect that these agents have up till now collected their data very subtly and carefully over quite a number of years, but that recent events have forced them into increased activity."

"With cover that deep, these agents would have had to have

been in place even before we went to war against the French, Peter.''

''Yes, exactly. Damme, Marc, they are probably just as English as you or I! Their dossiers are very likely unassailable. I am going to have the very devil of a time ferreting them out.''

Marc nodded his head thoughtfully. ''You have given me much to think about, my friend,'' he said as he at last rose to his feet. He smiled somewhat distractedly. ''Thank you, Peter,'' he said as he again shook hands. ''I appreciate your time, and good luck.''

''Marc,'' said the viscount as the earl turned toward the door, ''why? What is behind your questions?''

Marc was silent for a few moments before he spoke. ''I have heard a few things, Peter,'' he admitted, ''and I want some time to nose around a bit. I will keep you informed if anything comes to light.''

''Just be careful, Marc,'' Peter warned as his friend opened the door. ''Whoever they are, they have a nasty streak. We have already lost three men to them.''

Marc gritted his teeth, then nodded. The door closed quietly behind him.

''Dearest girl, is not the carpet threadbare enough?'' inquired Plum's sweet voice.

Lady Mirthton laughed and shook her head, setting the ruffle on her mobcap swaying. She was once again dressed in her drab gray gown and apron, having recently completed a morning of furniture polishing. ''In truth, Plum, I cannot sit still,'' she admitted as she finally settled and accepted a cup of reviving tea from her companion. ''The more I think on the matter, the more certain I am that I must try to find the whereabouts of Lucius and Willard, and that I must do so without delay.''

''Oh, no, my dear,'' countered Miss Plumley. ''You cannot. The earl quite distinctly told you to remain at home today. You told me so yourself. You did, you know,'' she affirmed as a moist, golden macaroon disappeared into her wrinkled, rosebud mouth.

"But that was before I saw my cousins," argued Lady Mirth-ton. "Lord Clairmont does not know those two worms as I do," she vowed with narrowed eyes, "and therefore cannot know the evil little tricks they can get up to."

"They are merely spirited boys," soothed Miss Plumley with an air of dismissal.

"Oh, yes, kindly souls who pulled the claws out of my kitten's paws when she shredded one of their neckcloths . . . and it was an old one at that!" cried Lady Mirthton in indignation.

The smooth roundness of Miss Plumley's plump forehead wrinkled into a slight frown. "I fail to see why you are getting yourself into such a pucker, dearest," she said with soft, bewildered eyes. "You do not need to go searching for the boys. If they indeed have come to Town, surely they will come to us. We are family, you know."

"Yet they have not," responded Lady Mirthton pensively. "Here we sit in a perfectly good townhouse, one that belongs to Lucius, I might add, and yet neither of my cousins has made an attempt to move in with us. It is most suspicious," she concluded with a slender finger astride her chin.

"That fact alone suggests to me that they are not even here, my dear," offered Plum.

"Oh, they are here all right," Lady Mirthton vowed, "and I have made up my mind. I am going to go ahead with my plan to find them."

"Oh, dear," sighed Miss Plumley as Lady Mirthton jumped to her feet and headed for her room. "Oh, dear, dear, dear."

"Hurry, Plum! You know I cannot go alone," she called as she scampered up the stairs. "Do bring your reticule, too, so we may see how many coins we have," she added from the landing. "We shall need to hire a hackney."

"Oh, dear, dear," sighed Miss Plumley in resignation as she toddled to the coat closet. By the time Lady Mirthton had returned, she was tying the ribbons of her black straw bonnet under her chin. As Lady Mirthton slipped into her brown wool pelisse, she opened the gathers of her reticule. "I cannot help but feel that this excursion is most unwise, dearest child," she warned as she dug around inside her reticule for her meager supply of coins. "I greatly fear what his lordship will say when he finds out what you have done. And where ever in this great city shall we begin to look?"

"Dear Plum," said Lady Mirthton with a warm smile, "do not worry so. I have been thinking the problem through all morning." She wrapped her arms around her companion's familiar softness and hugged her gently. "The key, you see, is to put oneself in Lucius and Willard's place. Now, if I were a young gentleman who had just come to Town, one who had no rooms or the homes of friends to accommodate me, what would I do?" She released Miss Plumley with an eager grin and took the supply of warm coins from her fleshy hand.

"I cannot imagine," replied Miss Plumley with an owlish blink.

"I would take a room at an inn or hotel, would I not?" offered Lady Mirthton proudly as she began to count their scanty wealth.

"I suppose so," agreed Miss Plumley.

"I would not choose the Pulteney, though," the lady continued. "That would relieve me of far too much of my blunt. Nor would I want to take a room in a posting house. Too much noise and contact with the lower classes. But what I would choose is an inn that catered to a gentleman such as I, one of modest, but independent, means." She pocketed the copper coins and escorted Miss Plumley through the door and into the street.

"... at the door again!" drifted out into the London air as they closed the door behind them.

"But do you know of such a place?" asked Miss Plumley, glancing at her charge. "No, never say so, my dear," she continued as she raised a hand in surrender. "I can see by your face that you do. How you come to be in possession of such information . . ."

"Do not overset yourself, dear Plum," laughed Lady Mirthton. "I learn a great deal while sitting behind potted palms. Come, let us look for an empty conveyance and we will be on our way to Limmer's."

"But dear Lucius and Willard would not go there," sputtered

Miss Plumley. And then her voice lowered to just above a whisper. "I have heard it said that it is a filthy place, and that sometimes women ... visit the gentlemen who are in residence."

"Oh, Plum, dear," chuckled Lady Mirthton as she raised her hand to hail a passing hackney, "gentlemen do not concern themselves about things such as that."

"Well, it is certainly distasteful to me, I can tell you," her companion uttered as she climbed into the carriage. "It is certainly distasteful to me."

Three quarters of an hour later, Lady Mirthton and Miss Plumley stepped from their hackney onto the cobblestones of Conduit Street and slipped quickly into a busy tea shop from whose window the entrance to the gentleman's inn could readily be seen. Lady Mirthton reluctantly gave an extra penny of her precious horde to the servant so that she and her companion might be quickly seated at the table nearest the soot-dusted panes.

"A bit of vinegar and water would certainly improve our view," sniffed Miss Plumley.

"Yes," replied Lady Mirthton with a smile, "but it would also improve my cousins' view of us. For once, the filth of London shall work to our advantage." Carefully she leaned toward the window and scanned both sides of the street, making sure that her cousins were not escaping before she realized it.

An unctuous servant placed a pot of steaming tea on their snowy tablecloth, and followed it with a small plate of cream cakes. "Will there be anything else, madam?" she asked, smiling deferentially.

"At the moment, no," replied Lady Mirthton, "but as we shall be here for quite sometime, we may need our pot refreshed later."

"Very good, madam," the servant replied, and then took herself off with a quick bow.

Four pots of tea later, and two trips to the necessary, Lady Mirthton clutched her companion's arm with a gasp. "There they are!" she cried.

"Where?" asked Miss Plumley as she pressed her nose against the smutty pane.

"There, just coming out of the doorway," answered Lady Mirthton as she pointed in their direction, "and look! They are slipping into that alley."

"Oh, my dear, are you sure it was them? They are so very far away. Could it not have been two other gentlemen?"

"It was them all right," vowed Lady Mirthton as she rose to pay their shot. "I would recognize their sneaky faces anywhere." She tugged on her reluctant companion's arm. "Do come on, Plum," she urged, "we must not let them get away."

"Why, what do you mean to do, my dear?" asked Miss Plumley, looking more than a little hesitant.

"I mean to follow them, of course," Lady Mirthton replied. "Why did they not just walk down the street like everyone else? Why scoot into an alley as if they had something to hide? I tell you, Plum, it is most suspicious."

"But . . . but you cannot chase down the street after two gentlemen, and I certainly do not wish . . . besides," she finally said in a firm whisper, "I cannot go anywhere until I have once again visited the necessary."

Lady Mirthton bit her tongue. "Very well, dear, but do hurry. I shall meet you outside. And, please, Plum, I do not wish for them to get away."

When Lady Mirthton stepped into the street, her eyes fastened instantly upon the dark orifice of the alley into which she had seen her cousins disappear. Quickly she walked to the entrance and peered down its length. It was, as she had feared, quite empty. She frowned slightly in disappointment and then glanced again up and down the street. Those two weevils simply had to turn up again somewhere. Her conscious mind absentmindedly absorbed the shops, vehicles, and bustling sounds that surrounded her as she searched the pedestrian traffic for any sign of her cousins. She noted Taylor's Apothecary, a brougham with the Torrence family crest, a matched set of grays pulling a yellow-wheeled curricle, Mason's Glove Emporium, Weston's, makers of gentlemen's fine clothing, a dark blue curricle with four matched bays, a linen draper's establishment. . . .

And then her mind snapped sharply into focus. A dark blue curricle with four matched bays! Instantly her eyes swung toward the carriage. Her heart plummeted into her toes and then swooped back up to hammer against her throat. It was him. *Oh, of all the perverse luck!* She watched as Lord Clairmont handed the ribbons to his tiger and stepped down onto the street in front of Weston's, and then, frantically, Lady Mirthton began to search her surroundings for a place to hide.

"Oh, there you are, dear," called Plum from the entrance to the tea shop. "I could not imagine where you had got off to." She waved her pudgy arm and began to toddle toward her horrified charge.

Devil a bit! thought Lady Mirthton, thankful for her reputation's sake that she had only thought it and not said it out loud. Again she sought out the earl's curricle, hoping against hope that he had not heard Miss Plumley's voice. But, with one glance, her hopes plummeted like yesterday's hemline. Her guilty green gaze swung straight into Lord Clairmont's glaring one, and Lady Mirthton knew in that mesmerizing instant what it felt like to be a rabbit in a snare. She swallowed hard as the irate earl started toward her and wondered fleetingly if it was possible to outrun him, but decided against it. Even wounded the dratted man would be upon her before she even managed to get turned around.

And then she had no desire to do anything but run toward him, for, from out of the alley closest to Weston's, two hooded men sprang toward the earl and fell upon him in a vicious attack. It happened so suddenly that Lady Mirthton gasped and hesitated, thinking that surely some passerby would come to his aid, but no one did. Instead, the busy shoppers either averted their eyes as they hastened on their way or began to gather around to watch the spectacle. Thoroughly incensed, she picked up her skirts and started across the street, but was suddenly stopped by Miss Plumley.

"My dear, what can you hope to accomplish by going to

him?'' the older woman cried as she held her arm in a tight grip.

"I can help him," Lady Mirthton asserted, trying to tug her arm free. She turned, then, and saw one of the hooded men slam his fist into the earl's abdomen. He dropped like a stone. *His wound!* she remembered with anguish. *He cannot fight them!* With a fierce jerk, she pulled her arm free, picked up her skirts, and hastened to cross the street.

Lord Clairmont quickly sprang to his feet and landed his fist against one of his assailant's jaws. He staggered with the effort, but his other fist found its mark, too, and the hooded man went down. As Lady Mirthton hurried toward him, she suddenly saw the other man appear behind the earl. She started to cry out a warning, but the sound died in her throat when her eyes caught the flicker of bright afternoon sunshine on polished steel. A knife! The other man had drawn a knife! And the earl was completely unaware of his danger.

Lady Mirthton did not take time to think. She screamed and broke into a run, rudely pushing aside the horrified spectators blocking her way. In a moment's glance, she saw that her scream had warned the earl but not given him time to position himself for the new onslaught. She did the only thing she could think to do. With her hands outstretched, she ran straight into the knife-wielding assailant, knocking him against the facade of Weston's mere seconds after he had buried his weapon in Lord Clairmont's broad shoulder. The stupefied man rolled his eyes in disbelief and then sank in a senseless heap upon the sidewalk.

"Oh, my lord," gasped Lady Mirthton as she immediately knelt to cradle his head on her lap. Quickly she rummaged through her reticule for her handkerchief. The earl lay quietly on his side with his head pillowed comfortably on her warm thighs and the knife still protruding at an odd angle from his back.

"Pull it out," he said in a husky whisper.

"Think you that I am a doctor?" she whispered back.

The earl's lips curved into a slight smile. His lady was letting her fear dissipate in the form of anger. He understood that. He had reacted the same way on the battlefield many times before.

"Dear girl," cried Miss Plumley as she finally gained their side. "Whatever possessed you to do such a thing! Why, you might have been killed!"

"I will not be scolded, Plum," she snapped. "I am much too upset."

"Pull it out, my dear," urged the earl more forcefully. "Please."

"And what if the tip has broken off, you mutton-head!" she exclaimed angrily. "What if the knife has pierced a vessel and your life's blood pours out right here in the middle of Conduit Street! What happens then?"

The earl slowly lifted a hand to rest upon the one she was using to support him on her lap. He squeezed it gently. "Let me put it this way, Lady Mirthton," he began, "as soon as I gain my feet I am going to shake you until you are silly for disobeying me. Then I am going to yell at you until my face turns blue. By the time I am through with you, you might very well wish you had brought about my death, my dear. Now, pull out the knife!"

"Oh, very well!" she cried, and, seizing the knife firmly in her free hand, she jerked it out of his body. Lord Clairmont gasped at the sudden searing pain, then relaxed against Lady Mirthton as a stain of new blood welled from his wound. "Never mind that I rushed to rescue you. Never mind that once again I have probably ruined my reputation, and all because of you. You are an impossible man!" Lady Mirthton quickly pressed her handkerchief against the seeping wound just as a warm tear dropped from the end of her nose onto the earl's cheek. She lifted a soiled sleeve to wipe the damp trail away, and looked up just in time to see the two assailants stagger to their feet and stumble into the alley.

"They're getting away," she cried to a cluster of young men still observing the drama. "You must stop them!" The young men were not so frightened of engaging the ruffians as were the others in the crowd. Immediately they spun about to go in pursuit, but ran straight into Miss Plumley, whose startled shrieks of dismay and frantic arm movements effectively blocked their path. By the time the young men had picked Miss Plumley up and gently set her aside, the two assailants had disappeared.

"Oh, Plum," wailed Lady Mirthton as she watched her flustered companion waddle near, "you have let them get away. Now how shall we ever discover their purpose?"

"Dearest girl, you cannot know how sorry I am. . . . Oh, but I have never. . . . But, dear, I am not used to such adventures!" Miss Plumley rooted around in her reticule until she drew forth her bottle of salts, then flourished it meaningfully beneath her nose.

"Of course you are not, dear Plum," said Lady Mirthton, biting down on her frustration. "Please forgive me for being so inconsiderate."

"Now would be a good time for a doctor, my dear," interjected the earl, coming to the conclusion that the two ladies had probably forgotten all about him. "It is most undignified for an earl to be seen lying about in the street."

"Oh, Lord Clairmont," gasped Lady Mirthton. "I am persuaded that I have far more hair than wit. Come, Plum, help me get his lordship into the curricle." She motioned to her companion and, between the two of them and the earl's tiger, they managed to set the wounded man back on his feet.

"As far as I can tell, my dear, you have no hair at all," murmured the earl, and then he felt his knees begin to buckle. Instinctively, he reached for his lady, falling against her and leaning heavily upon her shoulders. She smelled like lemon and beeswax.

"What?" whispered Lady Mirthton at the earl's astonishing comment. She took a few slow steps toward the carriage, struggling under his heavy weight.

"You have your mobcap on again, my dear," said the earl as he nuzzled close to her ear.

"Oh!" breathed Lady Mirthton as her hand flew up to her head. "I completely forgot . . ." If the earl hadn't been about to collapse, he would have laughed out loud at the expression of mortified horror that bloomed on Lady Mirthton's face. She bit her bottom lip and the little ball on the end of her nose dipped charmingly. "We must get you to safety immediately, my lord," she vowed with sudden determination, and, with amazing energy, she seized the earl tightly around his middle and almost carried him to the curricle.

The earl was nonplussed. What had suddenly gotten into her? When she had at last manhandled him into the carriage seat and commanded Plum to squeeze in beside them, he thought he understood. She was, of course, afraid for him. And that meant that she was coming to care for him. A smug smile of satisfaction widened his chiseled mouth. But as delighted as he was with this new development, he knew from the look of near panic on her face that he needed to ease the dear girl's fear for his condition. *And the sooner the better,* he thought as he studied the blush that was radiating a warmth even he could feel.

"The situation is not so desperate as it may seem, my lady," he said soothingly.

"It is past desperate, my lord," she cried with a wild look in her expressive green eyes. "It is intolerable!" She gathered the ribbons in her hands and made ready to set the team in motion.

"But it is only a shallow knife wound, my dear," he added kindly, perplexed by her continued agitation.

"Of course it is only a knife wound," she snapped. "I am well aware of that. Now if you will just let me concentrate, I shall drive you home in a trice and soon you shall be as good as new."

"Lady Mirthton," he responded, still smug that his wounding should affect her so, "since we are agreed that my shoulder will soon be better, why are you still so overset?"

Lady Mirthton gaped at him like a beached trout. "Because the most mortifying event of my entire life has just taken place, my lord, and the entire world was witness to it," she nearly shouted.

"And what event was that?" asked the earl in bafflement.

"I came to Conduit Street in my mobcap!" she cried, and slapped the ribbons against the earl's four matched bays with a resounding whack.

The curricle took off like a round from a cannon aimed straight at Bond Street. Lady Mirthton sawed back and forth on the ribbons, driving to an inch as she careened around lumbering landaus, bulky broughams, and the odd and assorted pedestrian. She sat forward on the carriage seat and drove so close to a passing freight wagon that the curricle was squeezed as tightly as she was to the earl's powerful legs.

"You have never driven before, have you?" shouted the appalled earl over the shrieks of Lady Mirthton's near misses.

"No," she responded, biting her lip in concentration. She swept around the corner into Bond Street, throwing Miss Plumley against the earl's tender shoulder. At his gasp of pain, she shrugged a rueful apology. "I suppose I should ask you where you live, my lord," she said, turning to look at him before nearly colliding with a red-faced, arm-waving beadle.

"Grosvenor Square," squawked the earl in a strangled voice as the beadle jumped to safety. "Turn left on Grosvenor Street."

Miss Plumley, who had been gripping the side of the curricle with both hands, smiled at the earl kindly and reached out to pat his hand with one of her plump ones. It was such a shame, she thought. She had never seen a living man look quite so white.

Soon the lathered bays clattered into the quiet residential square. The earl lifted a shaky finger and pointed to his home. Lady Mirthton nodded grimly and whipped the team around the eastern corner, bringing the bays to a halt in front of the earl's imposing mansion.

Lady Mirthton gave very little thought to the stately elegance of the earl's residence. As she jumped to the cobblestones and rushed to aid Miss Plumley, and then the earl, she barely saw the cream stucco facade accented with Cotswold stone and black wrought iron or the wide, sweeping portico that tastefully introduced the double mahogany doors. She cared only that she had been the cause of the earl's injury. If she had never gone to him for advice, he would not be suffering now.

She tucked her shoulder under the earl's arm and pulled him against her. "You must lean on me, my lord," she whispered. "I shall not let you be harmed further. Plum, please go up and knock on the door. Lord Clairmont's tiger has gone to take the curricle around to the mews."

"Very well, my dear," her companion responded, wafting her bottle of salts like incense before her as she started up the stairs.

"Am I too heavy for you, my dear?" the earl murmured close to her ear. He was only too glad to take advantage of his lady's proximity in order to scrutinize her further. His fine brow wrinkled into a frown. Surely after the madcap ride they had just taken at least one wisp of her hair would have come loose to poke out from beneath that ridiculous cap! But no, infuriatingly, there were none. Her skin was alabaster, though, and her lashes long and lovely. Wonderful things began to tighten inside him as he thought of exploring all that skin with his lips.

"War's over for you, Major," said a gravely voice that brought him out of his pleasant reverie. "Cain't you stop gettin' yourself wounded yet?" An enormous man, whose face split into an equally enormous grin, strode down the steps toward Lady Mirthton and the earl. Arms with the breadth of oak trees wrapped around the earl's frame and tossed him like a bale of cotton over the giant man's shoulder.

"Do be careful," cried Lady Mirthton as she finally overcame her stupefaction.

The huge man swung around. "Oh, he's safe enough with me, ma'am," came his rumbled reply. "I done et already today."

The earl chuckled from the height of his man's shoulder. "This is Mack, my dear. I helped him escape from a press gang a few years back and he has been tagging along after me ever since. He is an impudent American, as you have surely gathered by now, but he does brew a fine cup of tea. Mack, may I present Lady Mirthton and her companion Miss Plumley."

"How do you do, Mr. Mack," replied Lady Mirthton politely.

"Just Mack'll do, ma'am," the jovial giant urged. He turned toward the door, but again he halted. "Well, are ya comin' in?" he asked with a smile.

Lady Mirthton glanced at the earl, and then made up her

mind. "Indeed, I am, Mack," she answered, and then skipped ahead to hold open the door.

By the time the doctor finally arrived, Mack and Lady Mirthton had cleaned Marc's wound, sewn together the rough edges, and dressed it with basillicum powder. As soon as the doctor was shown upstairs, Lady Mirthton let one of the maids escort her to the drawing room where Plum awaited so that Mack and the doctor could bind the wound with clean bandages and help the earl into his nightshirt. Lady Mirthton thought that she probably should have stayed long enough to assist with the bandaging, but in truth, she was glad the doctor insisted that she not. The sight of the earl's bare torso had turned her insides into pudding. She thought that she might have been able to deal with her reaction given a little time, but the dratted man had purposely spent the entire time his naked chest was revealed to her staring at her and grinning like a drunken sailor. It was really too rag-mannered of him. The man needed a setdown and she would be the one to give it to him!

As soon as her insides stopped feeling like pudding.

The drawing room of Clairmont House was the loveliest Lady Mirthton had ever seen. The walls and ceiling were of pale yellow, as if the whole room stood in the shade of a huge tree. Hepplewhite furniture, upholstered in cream and gold, mirrored the gilded scrollwork edging the ceilings and gracing the wall above the marble fireplace. Two sofas sat near the fire upon an Aubusson carpet of cream, yellow and blue, while assorted other chairs and tables, a pianoforte, and a game table were clustered cozily throughout the room. As Lady Mirthton listened to the chime of a gilded ormolu clock she studied the portraits of the earl, his brother, and their parents. They had been a happy family. She knew that by the look Lord Clairmont's father was giving his mother. She understood then, the earl's penchant for laughter and could not prevent making a comparison with her own. His came from a life of security and joy; hers from an attempt to mask the fact that she had had so little.

The door opened suddenly and Mack filled the space.

"Oh!" peeped Miss Plumley as she looked up from her ever-present embroidery.

"The doctor's left now, ma'am," Mack began in his rough voice. "The earl'd be wonderin' if ye'd come to 'im now."

"Yes, of course," smiled Lady Mirthton as she immediately crossed the room. "Shall you come, too, Plum?"

"Oh, no, my dear. Indeed, no. I do so dislike stairs. Mack will leave the door open, though, won't you, my dear?"

"Yes, ma'am," said the gentle giant with a grin.

"How is he?" asked Lady Mirthton when they had entered the huge anteroom.

"In a powerful snort, ma'am," he replied. "Won't hardly abide staying bedded down for more'n a day, I'd wager." He tucked a hand under Lady Mirthton's elbow as they gained the stairs and steadied her as they made the climb. So supportive was he that Lady Mirthton was not quite sure her feet were even touching the treads. She kept moving them back and forth anyway. It helped to settle her kneecaps.

The earl was sitting up in bed, propped against a mass of pillows. He crooked a finger at Lady Mirthton when she entered his chamber and came to a halt just inside. Mack hurriedly placed a chair by the earl's bed and then left the room.

"Is that apprehension I see on your face, my lady?" he said awfully, crooking his finger again.

"No, it is not," replied the lady with as much bravado as she could muster. "I merely do not wish to sit down."

"Yes, you do," countered the earl, "for if you do not, I shall be forced to get out of my bed and come and get you."

"You would not! You must stay in bed," cried Lady Mirthton. "You have been horribly injured." And to the surprise of both of them, Lady Mirthton burst into tears.

The expression on Marc's face altered dramatically. His eyes filled with tenderness. "Come here, my dear," he said softly as he held out his uninjured arm.

Lady Mirthton needed no second invitation. She rushed across the room and climbed up the high mattress, then buried herself in the earl's warm embrace.

"This is all my fault," she sobbed into his neck. "I should

never have taken my problems to anyone else. If I had not you would never have been hurt."

Tears trickled steadily down Marc's neck and soaked into his clean nightshirt, but he made no attempt to stop them. He was far too content nestling Lady Mirthton's feminine softness close to his hard strength while he stroked her comfortingly. Mack appeared at the door with a tea tray and the earl casually motioned for him to place it on the table beside his bed.

"But then I never would have met you, my dear," Marc murmured as he rubbed his chin over the top of her mobcap. He felt a twist of hair under the soft fabric and grinned. At least now he knew she wasn't bald.

"What?" sniffled Lady Mirthon as her head bobbed up against the earl's chin, making his teeth clack together.

The earl hooked a finger under her chin and lifted her face to his view. Her eyes were red and swollen, and still streaming tears. Her lower lip was wedged beneath her overlapping teeth and as she huffed and hiccoughed her smooth cheeks billowed in and out. She was utterly adorable to him. He thought that the hardest battle he had ever fought was the one to keep from kissing her thoroughly right then and there, and then, of course, moving on to all the other delectable things his tightening body was urging him to do, but he battled himself with a will. It was too soon, he knew. And he had no wish to frighten her.

"I said that you are to stop enacting a Cheltenham tragedy," the earl lied. "We have matters of importance to discuss."

"We do?" sniffed Lady Mirthton as she gathered the remnants of her composure and looked around for a handkerchief.

The earl sighed. "Here," he said, lifting the already soggy folds of his nightshirt, "wipe your face with this." He took a handful of the fine muslin fabric in his fist and began dabbing at her eyes.

"This is your clean nightshirt," Lady Mirthton remarked, as his ministrations finally came under her notice.

"This *was* my clean nightshirt, my dear," he responded as he squeezed her nose dry.

"Oh," she sighed dejectedly. "I have been making a perfect gull of myself since the first day I met you, have I not?"

"An absolute cake," affirmed the earl with a teasing smile. "And since we both agree that you have frightfully scapegrace ways, I am now about to call you on the carpet."

Lady Mirthton couldn't stop the slow, rueful smile that crept across her reddened lips. "I suppose I do owe you a few explanations, my lord."

"A few!" cried the earl. "My dear lady, I could keep you here on my bed for the rest of the day and still not come to the end of this discussion."

"Your bed!" shouted Lady Mirthton, at last realizing her scandalous position. She struggled against the earl's hold, but he held her in an iron, if somewhat painful, grip.

"I would remind you of my shoulder, my dear," said the earl with a wince. "Besides, it is too late. You are compromised already."

Lady Mirthton's eyes grew large with shock. "Nonsense! There have only been the two of us in the room. No one else knows I was on your bed. We shall just proceed as if these last few minutes never happened." Again she struggled against him.

The earl's smile grew sympathetic. "Alas, my dear, you are quite incorrect."

"Incorrect?" shouted Lady Mirthton again.

"Incorrect," Lord Clairmont stated when at last his ears stopped ringing. Freeing one of his hands, he gestured to the table beside his bed. "Behold, the tea tray," he said with mock sadness.

"Mack was here?" questioned the lady in a quavery voice.

"Oh yes," responded the earl casually. "He watched you snuggle in my arms, on my bed, lying down, for quite some time."

"Oh," replied Lady Mirthton weakly.

"But we shall set all that aside for the moment, my dear," he said with a smugness he almost could not hide. "I wish to get back to the matter at hand, namely," he stated as his voice became a growl, "what the deuce you were doing today on Conduit Street!"

Chapter 6

"You will not approve," sighed Lady Mirthton as she once again relaxed against the earl's chest.

"Very likely, my dear, but tell me anyway," he replied gently.

"I was searching for my cousins. I reasoned that they most likely had lodgings in Limmer's, and I was correct."

The earl tensed slightly. "You saw them, my dear?" he asked with an unfamiliar edge to his voice.

"Yes, indeed. That is why I was in the street when you first noticed me. I had seen them leave the inn and duck into a nearby alley. I followed them there, but when I looked into the alley, they were gone."

Perhaps they disappeared into one alley only to emerge moments later from another one, thought Marc as he tightened his hold on the soft woman lying so snugly beside him. For her sake, he kept his thoughts to himself.

"It was not a robbery, was it, my lord?" asked Lady Mirthton in a voice barely above a whisper.

Marc looked down into her lovely green eyes and felt tenderness swell inside him. "No, my dear. They were set upon killing me."

Lady Mirthton stiffened. "Like my aunt and uncle, and . . . father," she breathed, tucking her face into his broad shoulder.

"Yes."

"But, why? You have no part in this," she cried.

"But I am helping you, and evidently those involved see that as a threat." Gently he pushed aside the flounce on Lady Mirthton's mobcap and rested his cheek against her forehead. She tensed momentarily, then relaxed again and sighed.

"This is really very improper, you know," she murmured against the folds of his nightshirt.

"In for a penny, in for a pound, my dear," Marc countered. "You are already compromised. What do a few more moments of impropriety matter?"

"Just the sort of thing a man would say," she chuckled, and then her face sank into sadness. "How shall I ever begin to solve this problem?" she whispered. "Where do I begin?"

"*We*, my dear," said the earl as he tapped a finger on the end of her nose. "*We* are going to solve your problem. I shall not allow you to attempt it on your own."

Lady Mirthton smiled tremulously. "But I cannot allow your continued participation, my lord," she said. "I will not have you killed."

"The idea is not very appealing to me either, my dear," smiled the earl, "but now I am forewarned. I will be ready should they ever so foolishly try it again."

Her appealing green eyes studied him. "One thing has puzzled me since the first morning you came to visit me. It is a question I cannot answer. Why would you help me? There is no benefit to you. I have nothing that I can give you in return."

Marc met her gaze evenly. "That is something I intend to discuss with you later, Lady Mirthton, but you may rest assured that you do indeed have something to give me, and I will most definitely exact payment when payment is due."

"But . . ."

"But now," interrupted Marc, "we need to apply ourselves to finding the solution to your problem." He sat up straighter and allowed Lady Mirthton to fluff and reposition his pillows, then pulled her back into his arms. "We must look at this as a puzzle, my dear," he began to expound, "and to solve a puzzle, one must look at all the pieces."

"And find the ones that are missing," she added.

"Exactly. Now you are getting into the spirit of the thing, my lady," he said, squeezing her slightly. "We know, for instance, that we are up against a number of spies."

"Because of the probability that there are several names on Father's list."

"Yes, and the fact that I was attacked by more than one man."

"If only Plum had not gotten in the way! We might have two of the ring members to question right now."

"It is probably just as well, my dear. We also know that the ring members are ruthless. Those young men who chased after my assailants had no idea what they were getting into. They could all be dead by now."

"Oh, my lord," she breathed, "I had not thought of that. It would have been as brutal and senseless a killing as was done to my family."

"Yes, my dear, but do not dwell on what never happened. Your young gallants are still quite healthy."

Lady Mirthton smiled. "Yes." Taking a deep breath, she asked, "Very well, my lord, what is the next piece of the puzzle that we know?"

"We know that your father mentioned 'the sign of the *sabot*.' It is still my view that this is the key to solving the whole puzzle."

"I do agree," responded Lady Mirthton. "If Father was indeed trying to uncover the others in his ring, there would have to have been some way in which he could have identified them."

"Yes, my dear," smiled Marc, "and it would seem that the image of a *sabot* is it."

"But there are no pictures of wooden shoes at Mirthton Manor," exclaimed Lady Mirthton.

"The sign could be anywhere, my dear," responded Marc. "Possibly on or in something that no one would notice. You could have been seeing the sign all your life and never even realized it."

Lady Mirthton's heart sank. "Then how do we find it?" she asked, looking up into Marc's warm eyes.

"Well, we certainly cannot discover it here in London," he replied with a half-smile. "We must make the trip to Mirthton Manor and do some searching ourselves."

"And now is the perfect time!" exclaimed Lady Mirthton excitedly. "My cousins are here in London and the Manor is now empty. If we are careful, they will not even know that we have left Town."

"I would not count on that, my dear," Marc replied somewhat hesitantly. "It is my feeling that you are being carefully watched."

Lady Mirthton went still. "Why do you think that, my lord?" she whispered.

Marc rubbed his warm hand up and down her arm soothingly. "Because how else would they know that I was helping you, my dear?" he asked softly. "Why not just assume that I was courting you in the usual way with visits to your home and rides in the park? Why see me as a threat if they were not well aware of what was really in our minds?"

The implications of what Marc was saying were too obvious for Lady Mirthton to ignore. "Then you think that the ones who sent me the note are somehow close to me?"

Marc gazed at her levelly. "I do not know it of a certainty, Lady Mirthton, but I think it is something we have to consider."

Marc was stirring cream into his morning coffee the following day when Mack bounded into the breakfast room and flourished a silver tray under his nose, disturbing some rather delightful daydreams about the pleasures of having Lady Mirthton cuddled next to him in bed. He smiled in remembrance. He had been loathe to let her leave even after the thuds of Miss Plumley's heavy footsteps sounded on the stairs leading to his chamber, and his lady had jumped from his embrace before her scandalous position could be noted by her negligent companion. But she would not be jumping from his arms for very much longer, he vowed. She did, after all, belong to him.

"Message for ya," rumbled Mack as he tipped the tray near the earl's empty plate and the delicate paper tumbled to the tablecloth.

Marc lifted his eyebrow and frowned, but the gentle reprimand had no effect on the exuberant American. He picked up the paper and soon was focused on its contents. "It is from Whitehall," he confided to his man. "They wish to see me as soon as possible this morning."

"Will ya be wantin' yer ride, then?"

"No, have my curricle brought round instead. I had better take care of this right away." He gently dabbed the corners of his mouth with a white damask serviette and rose to his feet.

"I'll put out yer drivin' clothes," offered Mack as he left to do his employer's bidding.

It was barely an hour later when Marc steered his curricle from Pall Mall into Cockspur Street. He was eaten with curiosity. Why would he be ordered to Whitehall? And he made no mistake about it, the message he had received was most assuredly an order. He might have understood it if the note had come from Peter. But it had not. It had come from the desk of Lord Castlereagh himself. *Well, I shall know soon enough,* he thought as he feathered a turn into Whitehall. He came to a stop in front of the Foreign Ministry and turned his team over to his tiger. Then, with a deep breath, he entered the building.

Lord Castlereagh's clerk escorted the earl into a pleasant, functionally furnished office with a view of St. James's Park. Bright sunlight gleamed against the window glass and set fire to the dust motes drifting through its warm rays.

"Lord Clairmont," said Lord Castlereagh as he rose in greeting. "Thank you for being so prompt. Do sit down, won't you?" He smiled and gestured toward a chair positioned in front of his desk. Marc crossed the room and shook the Foreign Secretary's hand, concentrating all the while on the powerful man's eyes. He had learned very early in his military career that a man's eyes would easily reveal not only what he was thinking, but what action he was about to take. Lord Castlereagh's eyes were blatantly calculating, continually assessing, as he watched Marc take his seat. Marc smiled to himself. He was now aware that the man did not trust him any further than the end of his arm.

"Good morning, Marc."

The earl's head pivoted toward this new voice directly behind him. "Peter!" he exclaimed, rising to his feet.

"Sit down, Marc," his friend urged with a hesitant smile. As Marc complied, he pulled up another chair and sat down beside him. "I imagine you know now why you are here."

Marc frowned slightly. "Obviously because of my visit to you yesterday."

"Lay no blame on your friend, Lord Clairmont," said Castlereagh sternly. "We are fighting a war. Any information which comes to light must be investigated. Peter only did what his honor required in discussing your visit with me."

"Marc," urged Peter, "if you have any information that will help us uncover these spies, you must share it with us. It is too important to our cause to keep to yourself."

Marc clenched his jaw against the indecision that twisted inside him. His need to protect Lady Mirthton was almost overpowering. He could not forget that she might very well lose her life because of what he might say today. Yet he could not in good conscience withhold information that might bring about a swifter conclusion to the war. In the end, he knew that he would have to reveal Collingwood's involvement in the spy ring, and then take every step possible to insure Lady Mirthton's safety.

"Very well," he responded, keeping his eyes locked on the Foreign Secretary's. He would be watching carefully to see how the man reacted to his words. "But what I have to reveal may cost the life of a young woman. I would be particularly upset should that happen."

A smile curled Castlereagh's lips. His cold gaze warmed slightly. "Your concern is duly noted. Nothing you say will leave this office."

"A few nights ago I was accosted by a young woman who

asked for my help. Peter was with me at the time, and can attest to that fact."

"Lady Mirthton?" asked Peter softly. Lord Castlereagh quickly scribbled something on a sheet of paper positioned before him.

"Yes. She revealed to me that she was under the threat of death if she did not recover a certain list that a certain group wanted." Beside him, Peter visibly straightened.

"Why would this group think she would be able to recover it?" asked Castlereagh as he leaned forward in his chair.

"The list was made by her father, Simon Mirthton, Viscount Collingwood."

"He was recently killed, was he not?" interjected Peter.

"Yes. And Lady Mirthton was with him when he died. Just before he passed away he told her that he was a spy and that there was a list, but he did not reveal its location. He only gave her a clue."

"My God, a gentleman of the nobility!" exclaimed Castlereagh almost to himself. "Did the man have no honor?"

Peter ignored Lord Castlereagh's comments and sat forward on his chair, his eyes gleaming with excitement. "This may be just the break we have been waiting for, Marc," he exclaimed. "What was the clue?"

"He said only, 'the sign of the *sabot.*'"

All three men relaxed back into their chairs. "It means nothing to me. Does it to you, Peter?" asked Lord Castlereagh.

Peter shook his head and looked at Marc. "Have either you or Lady Mirthton figured it out?"

"No. But we had planned to go to her country home and search regardless. The answer is there, I am certain."

"We will send men with you," stated Castlereagh quickly.

"My lord," said Marc as he shook his head, "Lady Mirthton was specifically told not to involve the government." He shifted his gaze to Peter. "That is why I said no more than I did when I saw you yesterday, Peter. If these operatives know that I have spoken to you, they will go after her. I have already been attacked because of my involvement."

"Attacked?" questioned Peter.

"Yes, I was knifed in the back yesterday morning," gritted Marc from between clenched teeth. "You were right, Peter, they are a vicious group." Peter blew a gust of air out of his mouth and looked at his friend with sympathy.

"I agree that we must be careful to keep our knowledge of this affair secret," said Castlereagh, "but you must also understand, Clairmont, that I cannot simply turn over the fate of these spies into your and Lady Mirthton's hands."

"And you must understand, my lord, that I will not have Lady Mirthton's life jeopardized."

The two men stared at each other like combatants in a ring, until each became fully aware of the other's strength of will. Then they smiled, Lord Castlereagh because he was now confident that within a matter of days he would have his spies, and the earl because he had finally detected the warmth of trust in the Foreign Secretary's eyes.

"This is what I propose," said Castlereagh finally. "I will have operatives assigned to you, Clairmont, but they will be placed so discreetly that no one will be aware of them, not even you. When you and Lady Mirthton travel to her country home, some will be sent on ahead and the rest travel by various routes, so that no one will suspect you are being followed. Is this agreeable to you?"

Marc considered the plan for only a moment and then nodded.

"The only drawback," added Peter, "is that in order for our operatives to remain unobtrusive, they will have to remain at a distance. If you find yourselves in trouble, they might not be able to reach you in time."

"Then we will just have to hope Lady Mirthton knows how to scream," replied Marc with a grin, and he stood to bid the two somber gentlemen good day.

The matter of Lady Mirthton's protection occupied Marc's mind most of the way down St. James's Street. No matter what assurances the Foreign Ministry gave him, there was still the very real possibility that someone connected with the spy ring would know of his visit to them. It had suddenly become too dangerous for Lady Mirthton to be alone, especially if what he suspected about her cousins was true. The two men had easy access to her, and she would never suspect their perfidy until it was too late. No, he could not let her stay alone in that decrepit townhouse a moment longer. She would have to move in with him.

He started to direct his team into Piccadilly in the direction of Half Moon Street when he remembered the Latham's ball that was to be held that evening. He had given his old friend his word that he would attend, even knowing that the reason for soliciting his promise was probably a fluffy pink debutante that his wife wanted him to meet, but he could not back down from his word. The solution came to him quickly. He would simply escort Lady Mirthton. And then he remembered her horrible turban and winced. She would definitely need something to wear. And that decision solved the problem of where he would head next. He turned right into Piccadilly and whistled happily all the way to Madame Felice's. Once again she would give him ease. But he would not be asking for the warmth of her this time, only her skills as a modiste.

Beedle beat Lady Mirthton to the door. It was not a difficult task to accomplish, though, since his mistress was in the kitchen up to her elbows in blackberry jam. With a creaking of ancient joints, he pulled the heavy door open and regarded a rather scruffy-looking messenger. Wordlessly, he stretched out his cadaverous hand and received into it an envelope, soiled near the bottom corner by the dirt on the messenger's fingers. Then, securing the door and turning with painstaking steps, he slowly shuffled down the dark hall toward the kitchen.

By coincidence, Lady Mirthton arrived on the other side of the swinging green baize door at exactly the same time. She pushed against the familiar surface and, oddly, met wavering resistance. She pushed again, but still the door would not give way. Finally, exasperated, she leaned against the soft felt and bumped it with her hip.

"Madam," came a resonant voice from the other side resembling the lofty tones used by vicars at important funerals, "I have a note for you."

The sudden voice made Lady Mirthton jerk with surprise, but soon she chuckled with amusement. "Then let me out, Beedle, so that I might have it," she said. In spite of her words, the steady, stubborn pressure remained against the door.

"I was on my way *in* to give it to you," returned her obstinate retainer in deep, vibrating tones.

"But if you do not let me out, then you also cannot come in," she teased, trying hard not to laugh audibly. After long moments, she heard a loud, heavy sigh from the other side of the door.

"It is indeed difficult to know the ins and the outs around here," the old man replied as Lady Mirthton gripped her stomach to hold back the laughter. "I shall instead slip your note under the door."

After considerable popping and creaking, the envelope appeared on the floor beside Lady Mirthton's foot. She picked it up readily, tore open the seal and began to read. The color blanched from her face.

"What is it, dearest?" asked Miss Plumley, who had been observing Lady Mirthton's exchange with Beedle from her chair by the kitchen door.

"It is another note," she said faintly.

"Oh, dear," exclaimed Plum as she hurried to her charge's side. "What does this one say?"

"It demands that I stop accepting help from Lord Clairmont and find the list on my own. If I do not comply, his death is promised, too."

"Oh, dear, dear," murmured Plum in an agitated voice, "all this talk of death! My dear, what will you do?"

"I shall comply, of course. Lord Clairmont has already received a knife wound because of his involvement with me. I tried to talk him out of continuing then, but he would not hear of it. Now I have the reason I need. I must end his feelings of responsibility for me, and I must end them today."

Lady Mirthton calmly tucked the note in the large pocket of her apron and began to arrange the cooling jars of jam where they might catch the morning air. Her hands, she discovered, were trembling. *He could die,* she realized with growing horror, and knew also that she could never let it come to that.

How had it happened, she wondered, that she had fallen in love with him? Was it his smile, or his sense of humor that so easily matched hers? Or was it the thoroughly enjoyable way he tried to bully her and never quite succeeded? Or was it the incredible comfort of his arms around her? She did not know. She only knew that the thought of him lying dead somewhere made her stomach shake.

"But how will you find the list, my dear?" came Plum's question, breaking into her reverie.

"The same way I would have had I never spoken to the earl," she answered with growing resolve. "We shall travel by ourselves to the Manor and search for it. Plum, dear, go upstairs without delay and pack your things. I shall inform Beedle of our plans. The poor old dear must stay here, I am afraid. We shall be traveling by stage and the discomfort of that might be too much for him."

In less than an hour Lady Mirthton and her companion were climbing into a hackney and making their way down Piccadilly to the Bull and Mouth posting house where they intended to buy tickets on the next stage to Brighton.

Brighton, however, was not their final destination, though it was the quickest way to get there. The estate of Mirthton Manor lay instead approximately fifteen miles along the coast to the east not far from where the rolling downs of East Sussex met the craggy cliffs of Eastbourne. The Manor was situated near a timber weald that skirted the River Cuckmere and contained some of the richest land in East Sussex. It was Lady Mirthton's intention, since she was without a carriage of her own, to do as she usually did and talk a friendly farmer into giving her and Plum a ride on the back of his cart from Brighton to the Manor.

"Do you have the tickets, dear?" questioned Miss Plumley

as she looked up from her embroidery. Lady Mirthton had seated her earlier at a table in the busy posting house and had plied her with lemonade.

"Yes," the lady replied, "and they were quite dear. I am not sure that even if we come upon the list we will have the blunt to get back to Town again."

"There, now, dearest," said Plum as she patted Lady Mirthton's hand. "Things always have a way of working out. Will the stage be along shortly?"

"Yes, in just a few minutes. Finish up your lemonade, dear, and we will go outside to wait for it."

"You are doing the right thing, you know," said Miss Plumley gently.

"Yes," responded Miss Mirthton. "You were always adamant against involving Lord Clairmont. It seems you were quite right."

"It comes with the years, my dear. Comes with the years. Now," she said as she took Lady Mirthton's elbow, "let us go and wait for that stage."

The Earl of Clairmont was a satisfied man. In the space of a few short days, he had found the woman he would make his wife, completely alleviated his boredom, and made a rather stunning inroad into the sad state of Lady Mirthton's wardrobe. Of course, he would much prefer burning every stitch of clothing she had and buying everything for her new, but that would have to wait. For now, he would be content to see her in the lovely gown he had purchased from Felice for the Latham's ball.

It was perfect for her; a soft yellow confection in shimmering silk with an overskirt of sheer pastel yellow tissue that teased over the bodice's low *décolleté* to gather at the neck under a narrow, pearl-studded band of the yellow satin. A matching band of yellow satin embellished with similar pearls drew the gown's high waist together just beneath the bodice. It was demure and yet extremely provocative, and with its matching gloves and slippers, had cost the earl a small fortune, but it was money he was happy to spend. He counted himself fortunate that some woman had ordered it made, but not been able to pay for it, for he could not have chosen better.

He had taken the gown from Felice's shop to his mansion in Grosvenor Square, and then set out again for Half Moon Street. As his bays took him swiftly down South Audley Street and into Curzon Street, he wondered what sort of difficulty he would have convincing Lady Mirthton to come live with him. It would not be a totally unheard of suggestion, he reasoned. Miss Plumley would be in residence as her chaperone, after all. And it would only be for one evening, since he had every intention of leaving for Mirthton Manor the following day. Lord Castlereagh had informed him earlier that a number of his agents had already left for the Manor and that several more had begun their surveillance of both Lady Mirthton and him. He saw no reason for delay. In truth, he wanted to get this whole havey-cavey business behind them as soon as possible. Then he would be free to direct his energies toward a much more delightful conquest.

He rounded the corner into Half Moon Street and pulled to a halt in front of Number Eight, jumping to the cobblestones almost before the curricle had stopped moving.

"Keep them warm, Jem," he called to his tiger as he bounded toward the door, "I shall not be long." Buoyed by pleasant expectations, he rapped soundly on the door.

There was no response. He frowned slightly and knocked again more forcefully. Flakes of paint swirled to the tops of his mirrorlike Hessians, but there was still no answer. And then he did what no earl surely had ever done before. He leaned forward and pressed his ear against Lady Mirthton's door. The earl smiled another smile of satisfaction. The shuffling sound he heard on the other side was unmistakable. He leaned back on his heels and waited. And waited. Finally, with a groan of neglected hinges that matched the joints of the ancient butler, Beedle opened the door.

"Good day, my lord," said Beedle stentoriously. "You have paint in your ear."

"What? Oh," began the disconcerted earl as he brushed a

flurry of chips off his skin. When he was satisfied that he was
again pristine, he continued. "Please tell Lady Mirthton that I
am here."

"I cannot, my lord," Beedle responded, looking down the
length of his wedge-shaped nose.

"And why is that, my good man?" asked Marc with a twinkle
of amusement in his fine eyes.

"Her ladyship is not at home."

The earl was in a happy mood. He suddenly had the urge to
tease. "Do you mean not 'at home,' as in 'not wishing to see
me,' or not 'at home,' as in 'not on the premises?'" questioned
the earl.

The elderly butler's eyes crossed slightly. "I have not yet
got the 'ins' and the 'outs,' my lord. Do you require the 'at
homes' as well?"

Marc began to look a bit wild-eyed himself. He thought he
should really try to get more sleep. He took a deep breath
and seized the old retainer's frail shoulders. "Beedle, is Lady
Mirthton anywhere in the house? Simply answer yes or no."

"No," complied the butler.

"Ah, now we are getting somewhere. Then where is she?
Answer in one word, if you please."

Beedle's shaggy eyebrows rose, fell, and twisted as he tried
to figure out how best to comply with the earl's request. At
last he came up with a solution.

"Manor," he said succinctly.

"She went to the Manor!" exploded the earl.

"How very astute, my lord."

Why? thought Marc as panic threaded through him. *She is
alone and unprotected. Has the woman no sense?* "When did
she leave, Beedle?" he asked.

"Several hours ago, my lord," the butler replied. "She will
be on the Brighton stage."

The earl gave the elderly man a tight smile. "Thank you,
Beedle," he said with intensity. "I am going to go after her.
While we are gone, keep your doors locked."

"Is there danger afoot, my lord?" asked the butler with
widened eyes.

"Yes, Beedle, so stay on your toes."

The earl drove to an inch as he maneuvered his curricle through the busy streets of Mayfair toward his home. He needed to change both his clothes and his carriage. He fully intended to yank his headstrong lady off the Brighton stage and bring her back to London, but, as he was certain that Miss Plumley was with her, he knew he would need his larger phaeton. It was only a short while after he arrived at his home that he was ready to leave again, resplendent in a deep brown many-caped drab-coat and curly-brimmed beaver. He had chosen his horses this time not for elegance but for stamina. He would need to drive them hard if he intended to overtake the stage.

The trip through the city was frustratingly slow, but soon Marc was clattering across Westminster Bridge and heading for the Kennington turnpike and the Brighton Road. He kept his pace steady and unrelenting and soon both Brixton Village and Streatham Common were behind him. It was only a few miles further to Croyden, where the stage made its first stop at a posting house called the Bear. He checked on the state of his cattle, noting with satisfaction that he had chosen well. Their endurance was going to make the difference between getting his hands on that impudent little chit and missing her altogether.

At last he guided his phaeton past a deep rut and round a gentle hill, and the town of Croyden came into sight. Marc stood to his feet and strained to see ahead into the town, then relaxed and blew out a gust of air in relief. The stage was still at the Bear. He swore then and there that if fate was with him and he found his lady still unharmed, he might just have to ruin her reputation all over again and kiss her. After, that is, he had wrung her beautiful, slender neck.

Chapter 7

Upon occasion, Lady Mirthton wondered why someone did not just shake her when she got daft ideas like going to the Manor alone into her head . . . and then, shockingly, someone did.

The journey to the first stage stop in Croydon had been abominable. Lady Mirthton had found herself wedged between Plum and an enormously fat farmer's wife whose last five meals undoubtedly consisted of nothing but onions. She had a headache, a queasy stomach, a crick in her back, and, to add to it all, the young dandy wedged just as tightly into the seat opposite her had been nudging her knees with his silver-buckled ones over the course of the entire trip. Why, the looby had even tried to use the larger jolts of the carriage to duck down and peek under her beehive bonnet! It was not to be borne!

But just when she had thought that she could tolerate no more, the coachman had sounded his horn and the stage had pulled mercifully in at the first stop. Immediately, ostlers had surrounded the carriage, quickly working to exchange the exhausted horses with fresh ones, while the innkeeper had strode across the dusty yard and had opened the stage door so that this new batch of cramped customers could alight.

"Welcome to the Bear," he had greeted jovially as he gave the ladies his hand.

Lady Mirthton had waited patiently for the farmer's wife to descend, watching as she squeezed her vast bulk through the narrow doorway and hanging on for dear life when the woman finally gained the ground and the stretched coach springs sprang violently back into place. But she had no sooner taken the innkeeper's hand herself and stepped to the ground, than she was roughly seized by two pairs of masculine hands and dragged several feet away from the cluster of weary passengers. It was moments more before she could determine that her captors were her own cousins.

"Lucius!" she had cried when the shock of their actions had finally passed. "Willard! What has come over you? Release me at once!"

"I should beat you," Lucius had hissed into her ear.

"Yes, indeed," Willard had added, "Lucius should beat you."

"Why? What am I supposed to have done?" she had questioned as his fingers bit into her arm.

"You will not be successful, dear cousin," Lucius had continued with narrowed eyes, "no matter who you find to help you. You will not be successful." And then he had grabbed her shoulders in a painful grip, and had begun to shake her.

"Lucius, stop this instant!" cried Plum as she finally noticed her charge's plight and began to make her way toward them.

Lady Mirthton's head was bobbing on her shoulders to such a degree that she feared it would fly off at any moment. She was undecided about what to do first. Should she try to hold on to her bouncing beehive bonnet, or should she try to break the viselike grip on her slender shoulders? In the end she tried to do both, thus did neither very effectively.

"Here, now!" called the frowning innkeeper as he realized what was happening to one of his more prosperous-looking customers. Lucius only gave him a quick glance and a dismissing sneer, then went right on with his shaking.

By then, however, Lady Mirthton's situation had caught everyone's attention. A dozen or so of the gentlemen idling away their time in the inn yard heard the innkeeper's cry and started forward behind him, ready for any kind of mill that would give them an afternoon's entertainment. The dandy stood near the stage trying to make a bet with several of the ostlers on which direction the lady's bonnet would fly, but no one would take him on. No one that day, in fact, found any satisfaction, for, within minutes of starting their eager advance, one by one they were tossed aside by a large, thoroughly enraged nobleman, until only he was left to make his way to the lady's side.

Marc's heart had ceased beating when he had pulled his phaeton into the inn yard behind the stage and seen what was happening to Lady Mirthton. His mind had muddled with instant fear for her safety, and then just as quickly had cleared, leaving him with only one objective: to get his hands on the bounder who had dared to touch what belonged to him. The men who stood in the way were no problem. They moved readily enough when he gave them a gentle nudge. But the carrion who was abusing her, that was another matter entirely. He would be lucky to live.

From her wobbly disorientation, Lady Mirthton heard Willard squeak with fright. She attempted to turn to see what he was gaping at, but instead saw Lucius's hands fall from her shoulders, sag to his sides, and then follow his body through the air to land with a resounding thump against the stagecoach door. She staggered as her abused equilibrium spun her in ludicrous tilts and weaves, but then felt herself being pulled into a pair of warm, familiar arms just as she was about to fall.

"Lord Clairmont," she breathed with a relieved sigh against his very Mathematical neckcloth. The contents of her cranium were still doing somersaults behind her slightly crossed eyes and she clung to the earl's immaculate lapels with humble gratitude.

"Are you all right, my dear?" he quietly asked as he lifted her chin and peered at her face. His own was tight with anger.

Oh, dear! thought Lady Mirthton, realizing quickly that she would have to deflect his ire or murder might be done. "Yes, my lord. I am only a bit dizzy."

"You will need my salts, dearest," stated Plum as she came up beside her and began rummaging in her reticule.

"No, Plum, I am fine," said Lady Mirthton as she laid an

arresting hand on her companion's arm. Then, turning toward the earl once again, she gave him a rueful smile and gestured toward the crumpled figure at the foot of the stage, "Lord Clairmont, may I introduce you to Viscount Collingwood and his brother, Willard, my cousins."

The earl's eyes widened considerably. "These two scoundrels are your cousins?" he asked with a look of incredulity.

"I believe I mentioned that they were toads, my lord," whispered Lady Mirthton behind her soiled glove.

A flush of anger once again mottled the earl's face. His gaze raked over the cousins as Willard helped Lucius stagger to his feet. "Well, gentlemen," he began in the best of his lordly tones, "I cannot say that meeting you is much of a pleasure. What have you to say for yourselves?"

Lucius was trying to think quickly, no easy task since his head had connected quite solidly with the stagecoach door. He knew he must appease the earl and try to deflect his suspicions or all his plans would go for naught.

"I would most humbly beg your pardon, my lord," he began with a contrite smile. "I am afraid that I allowed myself to become a trifle overset."

"Your apology is due to your cousin, sir," said the earl sharply, "not to me."

"Of course, of course. And you have it, dear cousin. Surely you of all people know how difficult it has been for Willard and me, losing our dear parents so suddenly as we did." He moved to stand closer to his cowering brother and put his arm around the younger man's shoulders in a show of comfort.

"Why were you so angry with me, Lucius?" asked Lady Mirthton. The earl glanced down at her softly spoken words with their undertone of sadness, then hugged her closer to his large body.

"Surely, cousin, you must understand," he pleaded in a hurt voice. "Life for Willard and me is at sixes and sevens. We have our education, our estate, and our grief to contend with." And then his voice turned petulant. "We gave you only one task to help lift our burden, my dear, and that was to marry. Yet you have done nothing to further your cause. Far from it, in fact. From what Willard and I can determine from the latest *on dits,* you have consistently behaved in your usual rag-mannered way."

"A regular antidote," added Willard with a sneer.

"Correct me if I am mistaken, gentlemen, but are you saying that you were abusing your cousin for not marrying?" summarized the earl as his blood bubbled.

"Her unwed state is just one more burden to bear, my lord," reasoned Lucius with an oily voice. "Add to that my need, nay, my right, to claim *all* my estate, including my London townhouse, and I think that you might admit I had some small justification for losing control of my temper."

"But why did you not simply move in with Plum and me?" asked Lady Mirthton before the earl could sear her cousin with a blistering setdown.

"Really, cousin! I cannot think that such a thing would be at all proper," replied Lucius with a supercilious air. "I am quite surprised, in fact, that you would suggest such a thing."

"Lucius, dear boy," interjected Plum, "you are forgetting that she is under my care. I am quite offended that you think I would allow any impropriety to occur."

Remembering the long minutes Lady Mirthton had spent in his bed, the earl cocked a disbelieving eyebrow at this bald statement and almost rolled his eyes.

"It is not the fact but the perception that we must guard against," answered the young man righteously. "My cousin must be above taint if she is to find a suitable *parti.*"

Marc thought that the young man's excuses were as thin as the hair on his head, but he kept his opinion to himself. There was too much to lose by rushing his fences. He did not yet wish the two cousins to know of his suspicions. But there was still a certain matter which must be settled, and settled quickly.

"Reputations and living arrangements aside, Collingwood, there is never justification for abusing a woman," snapped the earl, "and you will never do so to this one again. Touch her just once, and I shall have my seconds on your doorstep within the quarter hour."

Lucius visibly blanched at the earl's tone of command. He

controlled his anger. There was nothing this powerful man could do to stop what was planned, but he could make his bothersome cousin suspicious. Sensibly, he remained silent.

"As to the townhouse," continued Marc coldly, "Lady Mirthton nó longer has need of it." Beside him, he felt his lady stiffen. "She and Miss Plumley will be residing with me."

Lady Mirthton gasped with surprise, but before she could raise any objections the earl whirled her around and slipped his hand under her elbow. Then, without a further word, he escorted her out the posting house gate and down the dusty road toward the outskirts of town.

"Where are you taking me?" she finally asked, a bit breathless from the quickness of their pace.

"I need to cool off," stated the earl as he trod relentlessly on. He led her unerringly toward a copse of beech trees that hugged the banks of a curving, lazy stream, then seated her on the textured surface of a crumbling, hollow giant. She immediately began to study the hands she had fisted on her lap while he paced back and forth, studying her until his fury was spent. Finally he sat down gingerly on the log beside her. "All right, my dear," he said, "tell me what else is wrong."

"I have just had my teeth rattled by my cousin. Is that not enough for a somewhat somber mood? What makes you think there is anything else wrong, my lord?" she asked, tipping her head back as far as it would go in order to see him from under the brim of her beehive bonnet.

"Because you are far too quiet," he replied, "and your lovely emerald eyes have gone all mossy on me, and you have not said one outrageously amusing thing since I arrived, that is what."

Lady Mirthton grinned. "You are coming to know me too well, my lord."

"Please, my dear, you offend me," he responded. "I never take women to my bed that I do not know well. Now, tell me what is wrong."

Lady Mirthton cast a disconcerted glance at the earl, then began to smooth her skirts to cover her lovely blush. "I was just puzzling over what Lucius said to me before you arrived, my lord," she began. "He said that I would not be successful no matter who helped me."

"Indeed," replied the earl as he noticeably tensed. "Did he say nothing to explain his words?"

"No. I am persuaded after hearing his explanation to you that he must have been speaking of my lack of success in finding a husband," she said, looking up at him, "but he was in the veriest rage. I cannot see that my single status should merit such ire."

Privately, Marc agreed. If his suspicions about her cousins were correct, then Lucius's statement to Lady Mirthton undoubtedly meant something far different . . . her success in finding the list, in all likelihood. And if that was indeed the case, what he told Lady Mirthton was tantamount to an admission of their involvement in the spy ring. And then Marc's heart began to beat faster. Collingwood's words also implied that the two men planned their cousin's death whether she found the list or not. Marc's concern for his lady doubled instantaneously. Without further thought, he reached over and enfolded her two icy hands into the warmth of his.

"Whatever his meaning, you are not to worry, my dear," he said with a soft smile. "I will not let either of your cousins approach you again."

Lady Mirthton returned his smile with one so sweet Marc's heart began to throb against his ribs. "No," she whispered in denial.

The earl's smile faded. "No?" he queried in a tight voice.

"No," she affirmed. "You will not be there to stop them." She squared her shoulders and turned to face him fully. "You are going to go back to London, and I am continuing on alone to the Manor."

"The deuce you are," Marc said softly as his eyes narrowed.

"The deuce I am," she stated in rebuttal.

The earl was silent for a moment while he studied his rebellious lady. "Suppose you tell me why you have made this momentous decision after going to such lengths to procure my help in the first place," he finally said.

"If you recall, I only asked you for lessons in self-defense, which, I might remind you, you refused to give me." She tugged her now-warm hands away from his grip, but he tugged them right back again all the way over onto his own lap.

"It won't fadge, my dear. If *you* recall, we more or less agreed to work together while snuggling in my bed."

"Must you continually bring that up?" she groused.

"Must you continually change the subject?" he countered with a smug smile. "Now, my dear, what is this all about?"

"I do not know what you mean," she said thinly.

"Yes, you do. Something happened to make you leave for the Manor without me, and I want to know what it was."

In Lady Mirthton's eyes, she had one glaring fault. She could not dissemble. The fault was working against her now, and she was so provoked she wanted to kick the log in frustration. "I received another note," she finally grumped.

Marc went still. "What did the note say?"

Lady Mirthton took a deep breath and let it out slowly. "That I was to cease asking for your help or you would be killed," she answered in a small voice.

Marc's smile belied the tension in his eyes. "Be at ease, my dear. They have tried that already," he soothed, trying to lighten her worry.

"Well, they shall not again!" she shouted. "You are going back to London!"

"*We* are going back to London," the earl calmly corrected as Lady Mirthton gaped at him, "and we are going to do so now. If we leave immediately, we will have just enough time when we get to my home to eat a light supper, change our clothes, and be fashionably late for the Latham's ball." With a broad, confident smile, Marc pulled the spluttering woman to her feet and started toward his awaiting phaeton.

Marc slipped his arms into his new bottle green cutaway and twisted his torso slightly as Mack adjusted the form-fitting garment over his white silk waistcoat and matching inexpressibles. His hair was still damp from his hasty bath, and as Mack did battle with his neckcloth, he combed his fingers through it, liking the feel of its cleanness.

"There ya be, yer fine and noble lordship," said Mack with satisfaction as the intricacies of the Oriental fell into place. "Will ya be wantin' yer emerald stickpin?"

"Yes, Mack," answered the earl. "Do you suppose Lady Mirthton is ready yet?"

"A bit worried how the lady'll take to her new ball gown, are we?" chuckled the all-too-perceptive man.

"It is somewhat different than her usual style," admitted the earl with a wry smile.

"Never fear, yer earlship," said Mack as he nested the thumb-sized emerald in the folds of the earl's neckcloth, "our Sara'll have the lady lookin' like one o' them Incomparables."

"She has no need of Sara for that, my friend," grinned the earl as he gave a final check of his appearance in the cheval glass. "She is incomparable. There is no one else on the face of the earth like her."

And she is mine, thought the earl with pleasure. She gave him such joy. He thought that he had laughed more in the last few days than he had in his entire life. She had no idea what a rare treasure her honesty and lack of self-centeredness was. And then Marc's handsome face grew stormy. She was the last person in the world who should be made to feel fear. Even worse, she should never have been made to experience that fear from those who should be giving her love. He itched to tell her about Whitehall's secret involvement, to give her just that little bit of comfort, but he knew that he must be very careful of that information. Whoever was threatening her had too intimate a knowledge of her for him to be able to share that confidence. He alone, therefore, would be able to benefit from the knowledge that they were being guarded and that they had that secret edge. Meanwhile, it would fall to him to give her the reassurance that she needed. And he would do it gladly. He would protect her like the precious jewel that she was because she needed him, and because she belonged to him, and because he had always taken good care of what was his.

The lady who so filled Lord Clairmont's thoughts was at that very moment thinking of nothing at all. She was standing before the cheval glass in her own room so stunned by the vision she saw before her that her mind was refusing to function.

"Sara?" she breathed in question.

"Yes, my lady," answered her maid with a beaming face, "it is indeed you."

"But I am . . . rather . . . passable . . . would you not say?"

Sara laughed aloud at that understatement. "You are lovely, my lady," she assured the awestruck woman.

And every square inch of the glass spoke that what Sara said was true. The gown fit her perfectly, provocatively accentuating her small, high bosom, and hinting at the gentle, womanly curves hidden beneath its flowing skirt. The warm glow of the pearls covering the satin band circling the base of her neck enhanced both its delicate arch and the peach-hued blush of her shell-like ears. Her face glowed with excitement, sending wave after wave of soft, warm color to her cheeks and lips as her eyes sparkled like the emeralds they so closely resembled.

But the most wondrous sight of all was Lady Mirthton's hair. A soft, waving mass of honey-gold, Sara had known the instant she had removed the lady's ridiculous hat that as long as she was in Lady Mirthton's service, she would never allow it to be obscured in tight twists and coils, but let it hang gloriously free. She had washed it carefully and rinsed it in lemon water to bring out the golden lights, then, after it had dried, had arranged it in a curling, cascading fall that ended midway down Lady Mirthton's back. The effect was startling, giving the lady a look of sophistication and innocence all at the same time.

The maid let her mouth curve into a knowing smile. She made up her mind right then to follow her lady when she descended the stairs. Far enough, at least, to be able to see the earl's face when he caught sight of her. The earl would probably cock up his toes at his first full glimpse of her startling beauty, and Sara couldn't wait to tell the whole of it when she took tea later with Cook belowstairs.

"Fustian!" laughed Lady Mirthton. "I have no aspirations beyond 'passable,' Sara. If I have managed to gain that lofty pinnacle, then I will have succeeded as never before. I am in your debt, and I thank you for all your efforts.''

"Say no more about it, my lady," responded Sara. "Here now, let me help you slip on these gloves and you will be ready to join his lordship. If I know my master, he is pacing a groove in the floor waiting for you."

Lady Mirthton suddenly experienced a jolt of apprehension. "Sara, I . . ."

"You are lovely, my lady," replied the maid with a reassuring smile, and before the lady could voice another objection, the wise woman whisked her nervous mistress out the door.

Sara knew her master very well indeed. Marc was already in his black evening cloak, impatiently fidgeting with the frogs on the one he had purchased to match Lady Mirthton's gown, when he heard the first of her soft footsteps on the stairs above him. He looked up, and the soft silk of Lady Mirthton's cloak slithered to the floor.

He could not speak. Not one word. His breathing seemed to cease altogether. As she glided toward him, his body reacted with a violence he had not thought possible. He could not take his eyes off her hair . . . her glorious, incredible hair. He had never dreamed that it would be so lovely. His fingers tingled to touch it. And then he almost laughed. No, he did not want to touch it. He wanted to crush it, stroke it, wrap it around his hands, run his fingers through it, smell it, kiss it, bury his face in it. . . . *Damme!* he thought as he fought to control his runaway desires.

She was standing in front of him now, looking at him like a frightened fawn. A frown rippled across his brow and then was gone. He never wanted her to be afraid of anything again. He took her hands into his own and lifted them to his lips as his eyes bored into hers. "You are beautiful, my dear," he whispered.

"Oh, no," answered Lady Mirthton softly as her heart began a strange rhythm against her left breast. "The gown is beautiful, and I do thank you for the use of it this evening, but, dear me, my lord! I have never been beautiful in my life. Sara said I was lovely, but I think that is still too strong. I have decided upon 'passable,' my lord. I have never been passable either, you see, so it is a great delight to me that I have at last attained that goal.''

''Have you finished with your self-evaluation, my dear?'' asked Marc as he shook his head and fought to hold back his laughter.

Lady Mirthton thought for a moment, and then nodded. ''Yes. I do believe that I am not stretching the truth too far to say 'passable.' ''

Marc did release his laughter then. ''You are indeed passable, my lady, but I am afraid that you have forgotten something. You have neglected to include the most important part of the word.''

Lady Mirthton looked up at the earl questioningly. ''What part is that?'' she wondered with her bright eyes sparkling appealingly into his.

''The prefix that changes the word into 'unsurpassable,' my dear,'' he murmured as he touched a gloved fingertip to her chin, ''for that is exactly what you are. Never doubt it for a moment. Now, hold still while I fasten your cloak around you and we will be off.''

The Latham's mansion was located almost directly across Grosvenor Square from Clairmont House, a pleasant walk through the wooded park that filled the central square on any other day. But on this occasion Marc's carriage was brought around from the mews and stood waiting when the earl and Lady Mirthton stepped out into the night. Almost instantly Marc felt the dirt of the evening air settle upon his skin and immaculate clothing. He grasped Lady Mirthton's arm more securely and hurried her down the recently scrubbed steps to the carriage, then bundled her inside before the soft yellow of her gown turned to a dismal gray.

Lady Mirthton settled herself into the soft squabs of the earl's carriage as he took his place on the opposite seat with his back to the horses. He knew that although the short trip around the square took only minutes during the day, the crush of carriages jockeying for position to drop off their passengers for the ball would prevent them from reaching the Latham's door for the better part of an hour. He decided to use the time to discuss his plans for the following day. Besides, he needed a good, safe subject. Anything that would keep him from grabbing Lady Mirthton and dragging her across the carriage to lie against the length of his throbbing body.

He brushed at the sleeve of his coat and then looked at his white-gloved fingers distastefully. Hiding a smile behind three of her gloved fingers, Lady Mirthton watched as the earl stripped off his soiled glove, followed by its partner, and laid them on the seat beside him. Then he took a clean pair from a box he had carried with him from the house and put them on instead. He looked up then to see her eyes dancing with merriment.

"You find my actions amusing?" asked the earl with one eyebrow raised and a look on his face that dared Lady Mirthton to admit it.

A soft, pleasant laugh bubbled from Lady Mirthton's throat. "I was just thinking, my lord, what a pair we make."

The earl's other eyebrow rose to meet its partner. A slight smile began at the corners of his mouth. "Indeed. How so, my lady?"

"We are rather like those gloves of yours . . . one soiled and the other spotlessly clean. I do not own even a single pair of bright, new gloves to keep clean, Lord Clairmont, yet you take an entire box of them to a single ball. We are so very different, you and I. And no matter how hard I consider it, I cannot understand why I am in your company at all. I do sometimes have a compelling urge to tip myself a settler just to make sure I am not dreaming all this." Lady Mirthton sighed softly and let her gaze flow over the plush interior of the carriage.

The earl smiled at her tenderly. "You are not dreaming, my dear," he said with a warm intensity, "and you are quite wrong, as usual. You are exactly where you ought to be. And you do own a pair of bright, new gloves. You are wearing them."

Lady Mirthton looked at her hands, and then back into the earl's eyes. "These are merely borrowed, my lord, and well you know it. They match the gown you have allowed me to wear."

"Which is also yours, my dear. I bought them all for you."

"Oh," breathed Lady Mirthton as her hand rose to the pearl-studded band at her throat. Tears sprang into her wide, expressive eyes. "Oh, dear," she gasped, swallowing hard. "Never fear, my lord. I shall not become a watering pot," she said as she struggled with her emotions. She gulped two or three more times and the earl rolled his patient eyes.

"I believe I have heard that before," he murmured as he passed her his soft linen handkerchief.

"Well, this time I truly shall not," she vowed through a throaty giggle. She dabbed gingerly at the moisture brimming in her emerald eyes. "But I cannot accept the gown, you know. It would be most improper."

"Today, perhaps," replied the earl with an unfamiliar gleam in his eye, "but in a few days, a week at the most, it will not be, my dear. I will keep it for you until then." And before the lady could open her mouth to voice the question that sprang into her wide-eyed gaze, the earl quickly changed the subject.

"We shall be leaving for the Manor first thing after breaking our fast tomorrow, Lady Mirthton."

"Yes," she agreed, a bit startled by the abrupt change in their conversation. She tossed a wayward golden wave back over her shoulder. The earl watched the innocent movement with the concentration of a mongoose watching a cobra. "I suppose there is no reason for delay. But I had hoped to make the trip in relative secrecy."

"I fear that there is no chance of that, my dear," the earl replied, still letting his eyes caress her hair. "I fully expect your cousins to be in residence when we arrive."

Lady Mirthton nodded. The errant curl slipped forward again and came to rest against the soft swell of her breast. "And angrier with me than before, if that is possible. Do you think they will deny us entry?"

The earl fisted his tingling fingers, then looked up as the carriage came to a halt outside the Latham residence. Though the door of the carriage was immediately opened by one of the Latham's footmen, Marc did not descend. Instead, he captured Lady Mirthton's two hands in his and looked intently into her eyes. "You are not to worry about a thing, my dear. If your cousins try to keep us out, I will not let them."

Lady Mirthton's lips curved into a wry smile. "My cousins will have every tenant on their land blocking our way. How do you think you can stop them?"

The earl pulled himself militarily erect and assumed an injured air. "I am hurt, my lady. Devastated, in fact. Do you think I mean to charge into an unknown situation unprepared?"

Lady Mirthton's eyes sparkled with mirth. "Do you have a secret weapon?" she whispered conspiratorially as her lips twitched.

"Indeed I do," replied the earl with his nose at a haughty angle in the air.

"But my cousins may have dozens of weapons, my lord," cautioned the lady.

Marc let the suggestion of a smile form at the edges of his mouth, and his eyes grew warm with a mischievous gleam. "They may have a dozen eight pounders, a hundred rifles, and a whole battalion of cavalry, but they do not have what I have," replied the earl.

"And what is that?" asked Lady Mirthton, thoroughly caught up in the earl's playfulness.

"They do not have Mack, my dear," said the earl, and his wicked grin spread from ear to ear.

Chapter 8

Lady Mirthton's fingers were clutching Marc's arm in a death grip as he escorted her up the wide marble stairs leading to the Latham's ballroom. He smiled at this evidence of her discomposure and glanced down pointedly toward her legs. When his eyes met hers and his brow rose in question, she burst into delightful laughter.

"You are too bad, my lord," she scolded with a gurgle of mirth.

"Well?" he insisted.

"Oh, very well, I admit it," she grinned. "It is pointless to deny it, is it not? My kneecaps are banging away at my petticoat and I am astonished that no one has asked me yet if there is a mill going on down there."

The earl joined her laughter and covered her hand with his own. "You look perfectly poised, my dear," he said. "No one would guess that the battle of Leipzig is being waged beneath your skirts."

Lady Mirthton blushed prettily. "This is a very improper conversation, my lord," she chided as they reached the top of the stairs.

"Ah, but then I have very improper thoughts about you, my

dear," whispered the earl just as the Marquess of Latham took her hand.

And so it was that the marquess and marchioness handed Lady Mirthton very gently down the receiving line, carefully shifting her ruddy hand from one family member to another, anxious to do nothing to cause her further pain. It was such a shame, they thought. What could she have been thinking to allow it to happen? She would have been in splendid looks, too, they all decided privately, if it had not been for that disgraceful sunburn. A soft "tsk, tsk" followed the lady down the length of the line. It was such a shame.

"The Earl of Clairmont and Lady Mirthton," announced a tall bewigged major-domo at the ballroom's entrance.

Lady Mirthton was certain she was imagining it, but it seemed as if a hush fell over the assembly at the servant's pronouncement. She gripped the earl's arm more tightly and felt him squeeze hers in reassurance. She wondered why he was not moving forward. Surely there were others behind them who wished to gain entrance. She jiggled his elbow slightly and questioned him with her wide green eyes, but he only smiled at her warmly.

Marc had no intention of rushing Lady Mirthton into the room. He wanted every eye to feast upon her, to see what they had so blatantly snubbed only a few evenings before. He let his gaze of possessive challenge slowly sweep the room, letting every man present know that they could look, but they could not touch. She belonged to him. And then, when he knew that his point was made, he led his lady forward.

Almost immediately he heard a delicate laugh trip lightly down the scale. His shoulders sagged and he just caught the groan that was squeezed past his throat before it became audible. Of course. He should have realized it. Lady Latham was her godmother, after all. He had not been coaxed into attending this ball in order to meet some nubile bit of pink fluff, but for her. He forced a thin smile onto his lips and turned, his chest narrowly avoiding her barely covered breasts.

"Samantha," he stated.

"Darling, you have finally come," breathed Lady Peters, ignoring Lady Mirthton altogether. "Godmama assured me you would. I have been waiting ever so long." She draw her rosebud mouth into a pretty pout and slipped her arm through his.

"You remember Lady Mirthton, do you not?" asked Marc as he attempted to draw his lady forward.

Lady Peters would have none of it. "Of course," she replied, letting her eyes rake over Lady Mirthton's form. Then once again her attention centered on Marc. "Darling, Peter is in the game room. He has been asking for you. I am sure he wishes a private conversation," she added, glancing pointedly at Lady Mirthton, "so I will take you to him now if you wish."

Marc frowned slightly, reluctant to leave his lady so soon after their arrival, but he thought that Peter might have uncovered further information for him that might prove important in their search. "Thank you, Samantha," he replied, "I do have a need to speak with him. Will you excuse me for just a moment, my dear?" he asked as he turned toward Lady Mirthton.

She was not in the least fooled. She knew very well that Samantha Peters would do all in her power to keep the earl by her side for the entire evening. And in view of her considerable charms, Lady Mirthton did not think that would be a difficult thing for her to do. But she was not one to mourn over things that could not be changed. She would instead rejoice over the good that had befallen her. She was, for instance, and for the first time in her life, dressed in something besides an outdated hand-me-down. She was also present at the most important ball of the Season; and, for the space of a few hours or so, she was passable. She smiled at the thought, oblivious to the sweet beauty the smile brought to her face.

"Of course, my lord," she said softly. "Give no thought to me. I shall do quite well on my own."

"Not too well, I hope," murmured the earl with a half smile, "or I shall begin to feel quite unnecessary."

Lady Mirthton laughed. The earl found himself wondering how that marvelous sound could affect his groin so intensely when Lady Peter's laugh rubbed against his nerves like a metal file. "What a hum, my lord," she said with a grin. "You would move in and make yourself necessary whether I wished it or not."

"True," he grinned in return as he tapped a finger on her nose. "Do not go too far away while I am gone."

Lady Mirthton smiled and nodded, and the earl followed Samantha into the crowd.

It did not take Lady Mirthton long to locate the perfect potted palm. She allowed herself just the slightest bit of arrogance at her expertise. It could not be a palm that was too much in the thick of things or her status as a wallflower would come under an embarrassing amount of scrutiny. Yet the palm must also not be in an isolated corner, either. There was nothing more frustrating to the unapproached than a mass of chattering nonpareils blocking one's view. Observation was, after all, the only occupation left to a wallflower with which to ward off an attack of the screaming fidgets during the interminable hours of boredom suffered at a ball.

But this palm was perfect. It was located near enough to the punch bowl so that Lady Mirthton could eavesdrop on the occasional interesting conversation, yet far enough so that no one would notice her doing it. Perfect. She smiled a secret smile of success, then hurried toward her chosen hideaway.

The Latham's ballroom was swathed in soft rose silk. Lady Mirthton spent the next half hour trying to calculate how many yards of the costly fabric hung in lavish drapes from the ceiling alone, but stopped when she began to get a crick in her neck. A quick glance around told her that Lord Clairmont was not yet back from his meeting with Lord Babbington. She noticed Lady Peters, though. She turned gracefully in the arms of her partner, and then looked directly at Lady Mirthton with an arrogant smile. Lady Mirthton sighed softly and then smiled at the pang of envy that stabbed into her heart. She supposed that she ought to try to get used to it. She knew that in spite of his flirtatious teasing, she was far too much of an Antidote for the earl to consider her seriously as a wife. She would have to get used to the idea that there would always be another

woman who held the earl's heart. She also knew that it would
be many long years before she could accept it, and think about
this time that she was spending with the earl without a sense
of deep loss. *But I have not lost him yet,* she thought as her
spirits rose. *And I am the veriest cocklehead to begin missing
him before he is even gone!*

Lady Mirthton thought, then, that a bit of conversation might
help to pass the time, so she began to focus on a few of the
on dits that were being passed like sugar wafers around the
punch bowl. She learned to her amazement that Lord Hurley's
mother had followed him all the way to a mill in Leeds, then
proceeded to drive him from the crowd of spectators with the
point of her umbrella because he had wagered the scullery
maid's virtue on the outcome of the fight. She learned that
Lady Burston-Smythe had had the audacity to set up her own
rooms in Soho where she daily entertained a variety of gentlemen at one of her "salons for the discussion of ways to improve
both mind and body," and had improved hers to the point of
now being *enceinte.* And she learned that Lord Billingsgate,
gambler and reprobate that he had always been, had recently
married a commoner, given up his title, and done the unforgiv-
able. The scapegrace may have done wonders to improve his
character, but he had actually gone into trade!

Soft music swirled around Lady Mirthton, setting her toes
to tapping. Couples dressed in the highest stare of fashion
moved in regimented form past her parlor palm, barely noticing
her wide-eyed gaze. Lady Peters and her partner stepped closer
as well . . . so close, in fact, that Lady Peter's foot ground into
the top of Lady Mirthton's toes as she danced gaily by. Lady
Mirthton inhaled with a hiss and almost cried out from the
pain. Then she reacted without thinking. Quickly she hooked
her bruised toes around Lady Peter's ankle and sent her stum-
bling into her startled partner. Like dominos, the line of Roger
de Coverley dancers bumped into each other until the final one,
a lecherous earl arrayed head to foot in purple silk, fell into
the widespread, maidenly arms of Miss Penelope Prangle, who
laughed with such delight at having finally caught herself a man

that she squeezed the hapless earl until the buckram wadding padding his narrow shoulders popped out and fell upon the floor.

Lady Mirthton clamped a hand over her mouth to hold back a very impolite giggle. She watched as Lady Latham hurried over to help the earl stand only to have her soft, white hands swatted away as she tried to replace the earl's wadding. Lady Mirthton hunched her shoulders as laughter threatened and bit a groove into her bottom lip. She noticed the black dancing slippers then. They were directly in front of her and attached to a pair of rather long, muscular, silk-clad legs. Which stopped at the edge of a gleaming white waistcoat. Which set off an immaculately tied white neckcloth. Which framed the earl's face. Lady Mirthton swallowed the walnut that had formed in her throat and attempted a smile.

The earl's eyebrow rose to uncharted heights.

"I see that in future I shall not be able to let you out of my sight, my dear," he said awfully.

Lady Mirthton blushed furiously and would have sought to dig herself under the protecting palm if she had not seen the twinkle of amusement that enlivened the earl's eyes. "Fustian," she said bravely. "I have been sitting here with all decorum the entire time you have been gone."

"Hmm," responded the earl as he flipped out his tails and sat down beside her. Beyond him the remnant of the dancers were being helped to their feet by several of Lord Latham's more burly footmen. "Such innocence."

Lady Mirthton's green gaze peered smilingly into his, but there was wariness as well. "Have I ruined my reputation yet again, my lord?" she asked quietly.

"Without a doubt, my dear," grinned the earl. And then he shook his head and sighed heavily. "Ah me, I suppose I shall just have to get you out of the suds once again."

"And how will you help me escape my fate this time, my lord?" she asked with mock humility.

"We shall do it together, my dear," he replied decisively. "I shall be seen delighting in your company on the dance floor, and you shall deny everything. Come," he said as he rose to bow over her gloved hand, "they are playing a waltz and it has been a whole day since I held you in my arms." With a grace that belied his size, Marc escorted Lady Mirthton to the dance floor, took her hand in his, and placed a warm palm at her waist. His smiling eyes captured hers, and, with gentle pressure, he led her into the graceful sweep of the dance.

"Oh, this is wonderful!" she breathed as they circled the floor. She closed her eyes lazily and leaned against Marc's hand. The earl's lips parted as he watched her pleasure, knowing without a doubt that she would look exactly like this beneath him in his bed. His body tightened with desire, and, without realizing it, he pulled her slightly closer.

"I have never been asked to dance before, my lord," she said, gazing up at him once again. She turned, then, to watch Miss Penelope Prangle sail by with her lecherous lord. When she turned back, Marc was grinning at her. "If I had known how exquisite it could be, perhaps I would have contrived to trip a man into my lap instead." Lady Mirthton's eyes glittered with merriment.

"You would not," Marc vowed. "Any number of gentlemen would ask you to dance, my dear, if you did not bury yourself beneath palm fronds all evening. I searched for you for more than a quarter hour before I found you, you know." Just to accentuate his pique, the earl pulled Lady Mirthton a little closer.

"Oh, but I did not always hide behind parlor palms, my lord," she said softly. And then she laughed. "But it did not take sitting in the open at too many balls before I concluded that for some reason I lacked a certain appeal. I have puzzled it out, though."

"Indeed," replied the earl, not at all pleased with his lady's self-assessment.

"Yes." She looked at him steadily. The earl's heart thumped in an odd rhythm. "I believe it is my front teeth, my lord," she began with a serious nod to her head. A honey-gold curl fell forward onto her shoulder and the earl felt a compulsion to brush it with his lips.

"Your teeth?" he questioned softly.

"Yes. They overlap, you see. Surely you noticed?"

"Not at all, my dear."

"What a plumper! You are the most frightful tease, my lord. My two front teeth look like gentlemen too foxed to stand up straight," Lady Mirthton vowed.

The earl stifled a blossoming chuckle. "I assure you, my dear, your front teeth are most appealing . . . certainly not a great enough flaw to keep gentlemen of the *ton* from asking you to dance."

"Then it must be my nose," said Lady Mirthton thoughtfully.

Both the earl's brows rose this time. "What is wrong with your nose?" he questioned as he tried to keep his laughter at bay.

"It has a ball on the end of it," she replied.

"But I like the ball on the end of your nose, my dear," said the earl.

"Wait until winter," stated Lady Mirthton vehemently. "The ball turns red with the cold and I look for all the world like a trained seal."

"Surely not," stammered the earl with a strangled voice.

"Oh yes, indeed," replied the lady. And then a mischievous gleam crept into her eyes. "But perhaps I am mistaken after all. Perhaps my lack of success has nothing to do with my looks." She eyed the earl with a sweet, elfin smile and batted her eyelids. "Perhaps gentlemen simply do not care to dance with ladies who dress like clowns from Astley's."

The earl could hold it back no more. His soft chuckles came like the sound of a brook tumbling over age-rounded boulders. "You minx!" he said through his mirth. "You have me running from one end of England to the other, get me stabbed, and now you have the gall to throw my own words back in my face. I should give you a thorough hiding."

Lady Mirthton flushed to the roots of her hair. Instantly her face grew somber. Marc could have kicked himself, but he knew he could return her to good spirits with another dose of humor.

"I am being a great deal of trouble to you, am I not?" she asked softly.

Mark smiled broadly. "Oh, yes, my dear, you are." When Lady Mirthton's face took on a decidedly crestfallen appearance, he laughed out loud. Lifting her chin with one tapered finger, he continued. "But it is quite the most curious thing, my lady. Ever since you sailed across that crowded ballroom and into my life, I have not been the least bit bored."

Lady Mirthton's eyes brightened considerably. She thought that was something, at least. And his smile was so warm as he spun her around the floor that she hardly noticed the tightening of his palm as he moved her just the tiniest bit closer to the heat of his body.

"Well, I am gratified that I have proved to be entertaining to you," she sighed. "Did you learn anything from Lord Babbington this evening, my lord?" she asked somewhat dreamily.

"Marc," replied the earl.

"I beg your pardon?" asked the lady.

"My name is Marc. I wish you to use it from now on."

"Oh, no," Lady Mirthton said hastily.

"No?" responded the earl in surprise.

"No, I cannot do that, my lord," she stated emphatically.

"Yes, you can. I have just given you permission to, my dear," he said with a smile.

"No, I cannot."

The earl's brow wrinkled into a frown. "Then you are going to have to explain why not, Lady Mirthton," he said tightly.

"Because . . ." she began nervously.

"Yes?" he prompted as he twirled the breath out of her.

"Because I cannot allow it, my lord."

"Keep going, Lady Mirthton," badgered the earl.

"Our . . . our association will only last for a short time, my lord. I . . . I do not wish for the intimacy of first names." Lady Mirthton's face flamed and her head dropped to hide the evidence.

The earl was silent for a moment, considering what her words had revealed. When he finally spoke, his words were a soft caress. His lips were so close to her ear that his warm breath sent chills of delight racing over the surface of her body. Lady Mirthton shivered in response.

"There is already far more intimacy between us than the use of our given names suggests, my dearest lady. Have you forgotten? You shared my bed."

Lady Mirthton gasped at the earl's creative manipulation of the facts. And she would have scolded him soundly for it, too, if she had not been trembling so badly from his nearness. She felt the earl's supporting hand tighten once again over her spine and felt his strong legs moving against hers through the thin fabric of her gown.

"My lord," she whispered as the hum of censure surrounded her from the other dancers, "you are holding me far too closely."

"Marc," the earl repeated evenly. His arm tightened.

Lady Mirthton's eyes flew to his. The determination she saw there caused her heart to sink like one of Plum's dumplings. "You do not understand," she pleaded.

"Marc," he again repeated, narrowing his eyes stubbornly.

"You do not know what you are asking!" she hissed, noticing as she glanced around that more and more of the others present were watching them with avid curiosity.

"Of course, I do," said the earl mildly. "I am asking that you use my given name."

"You are not asking that at all, you odious man," she sputtered. "You are asking me to use your name so that you can get me to give you permission to use mine. And I will not, I tell you. I will not!"

The earl was more than a little stunned. It seemed that his lady had finally gotten to the real reason why she refused to call him by his given name, but her objection was so bizarre that he found he could not credit it. And yet, as he thought back on it, he had never heard anyone, not even those closest to her, use her given name. And if a courageous, bright, spirited woman like Lady Mirthton refused for her name to be known, it must be horrible beyond belief. Incredible. Mortifying. The earl's eyes widened at the implications, but he quickly controlled his thoughts when he saw the rigid tightness of his lady's lovely face. He decided to work on one thing at a time.

"I am only asking that you call me Marc," said the earl

coaxingly. "Is that such a difficult request?" His thumb began a slow, soothing journey back and forth across her warm spine. He smiled when, after a few seconds, Lady Mirthton began to relax.

"No. It is just that I know you will want to know my name, too."

"Only if you truly wish to tell me," he said softly.

"I will not wish to tell you, my lord . . ."

"Marc."

Lady Mirthton looked at the earl with eyes as soft and green as sunlight on the sea. She smiled in resignation. "Marc," she uttered, barely above a whisper.

Desire pounded through Marc's body. He was lost in her sea-green eyes. "My name on your lips feels like a kiss," he said with no little amount of wonder. His heart was pounding the breath right out of him. He was sure that was why he was feeling so light-headed. He pulled her just the slightest bit closer. "And now I wish to know your name, my dear," he murmured.

"I knew it!" she snapped, drawing away from him. "I knew you would say that, you jackanapes! But I will not tell you."

"Very well," Marc replied calmly, drawing her back into his arms, "I shall call you by a name that I shall give you." He smiled broadly and swerved to miss another couple.

Lady Mirthton eyed him suspiciously. She had seen the conniving earl turn things to his advantage once too often, so when she spoke her voice was wary. "What name do you intend to call me, my lo—Marc," she said.

"Hmm," responded the earl with his eyes on the billowing folds of fabric lining the ceiling. "It should be a special name, of course. One that the *ton* will readily recognize. Nothing too fancy, I think. But certainly one that will catch every gentleman's ear." He swayed to the music for a few more seconds, and then released her hand with a snap of his fingers. "I have it!" he said brightly. "I shall call you Ladybird."

"What?" squeaked Lady Mirthton as her jaw dropped into an appalled "O." "You would call me a name that would label me as a lightskirt? Why not just climb up to the dome of St.

Paul's and shout to all society that I am your mistress? There is no truth in either statement, but that is not what the *ton* will believe.''

"Then tell me your name," said the earl softly.

"That is blackmail," said Lady Mirthton through her teeth.

"Yes, it is," returned the earl.

"You are not a very nice man, my lo—Marc," said Lady Mirthton softly.

"As it happens, my dear, I am a very nice man. I am also persistent. Tell me your name."

"Oh, no," she sputtered.

"It cannot be that bad," he coaxed, hoping with all his heart that he was right.

"It is," she responded as her shoulders began to shake.

"My dear," said the earl with alarm, wondering if he should take her from the floor before she broke down completely. Why, oh why had he insisted that she tell him in the middle of the dance floor? "Surely it cannot be that bad?" He hooked his finger under her chin and lifted her face toward his.

She was struggling to hold back her laughter. The earl blinked in amazement. Would she never stop surprising him? As his own lips curved into a smile, he fervently hoped not.

"It is appalling," she gurgled. "It is the most ridiculous name ever given. It does not suit me at all. And I cannot tell you."

"Oh, yes, you will," demanded the smiling earl. "You are not going to leave me wondering after a statement like that. Now tell me your name."

"Merrily," she whispered as tears of laughter slipped from her eyes. She was shaking with so much mirth that her head dropped to the earl's shoulder and stayed there.

A gasp of alarm spread over the dance floor. All eyes were centered on the brazen couple who were locked in a most improper embrace. One simply did not hold one's partner in such close proximity during a waltz in the ballroom.

"Merrily?" whispered the earl in his lady's ear. "But, my dear, what is so . . .?" And then it came to him. The earl threw up his dignified hands and burst into gales of laughter. "It does not suit you, you say," he laughed as he wiped his eyes with his handkerchief. "I would say it is the perfect name for you, Lady Merrily Mirthton," he wheezed, and then was lost in laughter again.

The earl's words were whisked around the crowded ballroom with the speed of a cricket ball. Rumbles of chuckles broke out in various places, followed by the ladies' descending scales, until the entire room was filled with merriment. No one could remember attending a ball quite as entertaining as the Latham's had become. Knees and backs were slapped, and fans were waved, until the folds of rose silk hanging from the ceiling actually billowed.

But Merrily had ceased to be amused. She poked the earl's shoulder as he bent beside her, resting his hands on his knees in the weakness of his hilarity. "You have made me a laughing-stock," she said with irritation.

"W-what," stammered the earl over the shouts of the others' laughter.

"You have made me a laughingstock," repeated Merrily in a shout.

"Marc had no need to, my dear," tittered Lady Peters as she strolled by. "You have done a very good job of that yourself."

It was the outside of enough. Slowly the irate woman turned toward Lord Clairmont. She felt her hands clenching into fists. The earl found her anger even more amusing. He straightened and placed his hands on his hips, then threw back his head with his chuckles. "Never say you are angry, Lady Merrily Mirthton," he teased.

"Very well, I shall not say so," she responded as she advanced slowly toward him.

It finally came to the earl's notice that his lady was not only not laughing, but had a rather belligerent gleam in her eye. "Now, Merrily, my dear," warned the earl as he backed into the punch table.

"Lady Mirthton to you, you bounder," she hissed as she continued to bear down on him. "I told you my name in confidence, and you have managed to assure that it will be bruited about all London before morning."

"Look on the bright side, my dear," cajoled the earl, still not quite able to control his hilarity.

"What bright side?" Merrily ground out against her teeth.

"They could have been calling you a ladybird." He tried, but he could not hold it back. Out came another spate of rumbling laughter as he leaned weakly against the table.

Merrily's eyes narrowed with fury. She would have to be her own champion this time, she realized. It was not the thing, of course, and she knew that after she did it, she would be ruined socially for the rest of her life. She rolled her eyes. That was certainly nothing new. But her honor demanded that she stand up for her good name, ridiculous as it was.

If Marc had been watching her instead of wiping his streaming eyes, he would have been prepared. He would have seen her carefully bunching the fingers of her right hand and tucking her thumb safely out of the way. He would have seen, too, the measured way she pulled back her arm and aimed just before she planted him a facer that sent him crashing back into the punch bowl and down onto the floor. But he didn't see, and so the *ton* had something else to laugh about that night: the sight of the sodden Catch of the Season chasing across the ballroom after the Original Merrily Mirthton as she stormed like a Channel gale out into the night.

Chapter 9

It was late afternoon of the following day before Marc spoke to Merrily again. By the time the earl had caught up with the outrageous hoyden after she had fled the ball and stuffed her like a sack of grain into his carriage, nothing under heaven could have induced him to talk to her. He could never remember being so angry. Blister it, she had struck him! He gave her grudging admiration, though. The lady tipped a mean settler. He could feel the bruise darkening on his jaw even as the carriage jolted its way around the square.

Yet by the time they had reached Clairmont House, Marc's temper had for the most part dissipated. He was not one to lie to himself. He had been forced to acknowledge that none of it would have happened if he had not embarrassed Merrily so terribly, laughing at her as he had. *She had every right to be overset,* he had thought as he had taken her gloved hand when the carriage had come to a halt and helped her down the hastily placed steps onto the cobblestones at the front of his gate. In the light of the flambeaux that had gleamed beside his door, he had forced himself to look at her fully for the first time since they had left the Latham's. Her face had been bleak. The lively, joyous light had gone out of her eyes. And the earl's heart had shattered. *Ah, Merrily, have I ruined it for us?* he had thought wrenchingly, and then his gaze had dropped to the steps leading to his door. *Damme, woman! You do cut up my peace!*

When they had arrived in the anteroom, Mack had taken their cloaks and whisked them efficiently away. Marc had never felt so awkward. He had wanted desperately to say something to set things right between them, but his mind had been moving like syrup in the snow. And when Plum had toddled toward them from the drawing room, seen the look on her darling charge's face and had enfolded her immediately in her pillow-soft arms, Marc had known that the time for a private apology was past.

But tomorrow was another day, and they would be spending it and the days following together. Marc had found himself counting on that. He had understood his lady well enough by then to know that she could not stay angry forever. It was contrary to her bright nature. He would just have to wait for the appropriate moment, catch her in the right frame of mind, and then he would make everything all right again. Gleaning hope from that thought, he had given Plum a terse statement that they would be departing early and traveling by way of Tunbridge Wells instead of Brighton in order to throw any pursuers off the scent; and, having said that, he had given Merrily one last glance and taken himself off to bed.

Marc had not seemed angry, Merrily thought, when he had helped her and Plum into his brougham late the following morning. In truth, she would have been happier if he had been. She could deal with his anger. But, instead, he had seemed subdued, contained. She had never seen him like that before, and it had worried her. She had been certain of the reason, of course. Her behavior at the ball the night before had put her beyond the pale even for the open-minded earl. And she had struck him in front of the entire *haut ton!* Just the thought of what she had done appalled her.

Merrily sighed and sank back into the soft squabs of the earl's carriage. There could be no doubt now that he was regretting his involvement with her, but Merrily was sure that his honor would not allow him to withdraw. Worse still, she did not know what to do about it. And so she had allowed him to hand her into the carriage earlier that morning with barely a nod of thanks, hoping that by her unobtrusive silence she could in some way make up for the embarrassment she had caused him.

She hated him. God in heaven, how could he have been such a knuckle-wit as to laugh at her in front of all those people? And how the deuce was he supposed to make it up to her? Marc ran his fingers through his blond locks and replaced his beaver back on his head. He had been certain that by the bright light of morning, she would have been well on the road to forgiving him. But she had barely looked at him when he had handed her into the carriage. It had been his intention to ride inside the coach with Merrily, having positioned three of his footmen to act as outriders and put Mack at the ribbons, but one look at her face as she had come down the stairs that morning had him quickly ordering Barbary to be saddled instead. The last thing she had appeared to want was his company. But then, how could he blame her? He had made a fool of her in front of the entire *haut ton*. Just the thought of what he had done appalled him. Worse still, he did not know what to do about it. And so he kept his silence, hoping that by doing so he could in some way make up for the embarrassment he had caused her.

The carriage rolled over deeply rutted, dusty roads, tossing its occupants about like flotsam on an earthen sea. Merrily felt her stomach roll in completely different directions from her bouncing body.

"Do you mind if I draw back the curtains, Plum?" she asked when she thought she could take no more.

"Are you feeling bilious again, my pet?" responded Miss Plumley solicitously. "You know I cannot like the dust pouring in upon me, but if you need the fresh air, my dear, by all means draw the curtains."

Merrily did so with alacrity. And found her gaze connecting electrically with the earl's troubled eyes. "I . . . I needed a breath of air," she said hesitantly.

Marc stared at her fiercely, wanting, but not knowing quite how, to apologize. He swallowed, concluding that the time was not yet right. "Then I shall not block your view," he said softly and then immediately spurred Barbary forward in a cloud of dust to take up a position well to the fore of the carriage.

Merrily's heart sank. He could not even stand the sight of her. What was she to do? She took a deep breath of the dusty air and let her gaze wander over the countryside. The road traveled alongside an ancient cherry orchard that had probably been planted in the days of the Tudors. Thick, twisted trunks stood in neat rows behind a crumbling stone wall, their tart, red abundance having been harvested weeks ago. Beyond the orchard lay acre after acre of hops fields, stretching as far as the eye could see over the rolling hills. Conically shaped oasthouses with kilns for drying the hops dotted the fields, testifying to the land's fertility. But Merrily barely saw them. What she saw instead was the frown of disapproval that hovered above Lord Clairmont's dark blue eyes.

It was near dusk when Marc signalled the carriage to pull into the inn yard of The Three Crowns near Tunbridge Wells. Dismounting quickly and giving terse instructions to the ostlers about the care of Barbary and the coach cattle, he strode with a purposeful step toward the inn and disappeared through the door. Merrily watched his movements with a sadness that sat upon her heart like a heavy stone. In a short time the earl returned, crossing the inn yard with a lithe gait before opening the carriage door and helping the ladies to descend.

"We have a bit of a problem," he began, as they stood in the dusty courtyard. "The town seems to be in the midst of an annual celebration of sorts to honor Lord North, the man who discovered the spring that feeds the spa here in the town. The inns are quite full, I fear, although I have managed to bespeak a small garret room here for you ladies. Unfortunately, the private parlors have all been reserved, but the innkeeper has promised to screen off one of the tables in the common room for our use."

"But where will you sleep, Marc?" asked Merrily softly.

At the unexpected, and wholly unhoped for, use of his name, Marc's blood seemed to swell and flow out of his veins. Instantly his eyes flew to hers, and his look seared her with a hot hunger that forced Merrily to step back a pace. "I will sleep with Mack and the footmen in the stables."

Tears blossomed in Merrily's eyes. Not only had she shamed the earl, but now he was having to give up his comfort for her. Yet she knew that she could not offer to take his place in the stable. She could not even offer to sleep in the carriage. No woman, lady or not, could put herself in such a vulnerable position without terrible repercussions to her reputation. And so she remained silent.

Marc was stunned by her tears. He could not account for them. Was she sorry that she had come, that he could not provide better accommodation for her? No, she was not so self-serving as that. What then? Could it possibly be his accommodation that discomfited her? Might she have forgiven him enough to care? Hope soared in Marc's heart. He had to know her thoughts. He could not go through another day like he had today. He would not let another night pass without settling what had gone wrong between them once and for all. Even if it killed him. And considering the condemnation she was likely to heap upon his head, it probably damn near would.

"Very well," said Merrily in a whisper. "I have some money. I would like to pay for our accommodation, Marc."

The earl's eyebrow rose alarmingly. "The deuce you will," he said between gritted teeth. He took an elbow belonging to each of the ladies in his firm grasp, then turned them toward the thatch-covered inn.

"Why ever not?" she replied without heat. "It seems a very sensible suggestion to me. You shall not be using the room, only Plum and me. So why should you pay for it?"

Marc firmly escorted first one woman and then the other through the wide inn door and on into the common room. "Because," he answered tightly as his eyes searched the smoky haze that had settled over the clamorous room for any signs of either Merrily's cousins or men they might have hired to attack them.

"Are you aware that you always say that when you do not have a good argument?" challenged Merrily as they crossed the crowded room.

Marc shielded her from the other patrons' view with his big body until they came to a halt beside the welcoming fire. Immediately the innkeeper brought a folding screen to conceal the earl's party, while his wife set a tray filled with cups and a pitcher of warm mulled wine on the table nearby. Plum sighed with pleasure and busied herself with filling the cups and passing them out.

"Very well, I shall be more explicit," replied the earl, relaxing a little as he concluded that the others in the common room looked harmless enough. "It is because I am the man, and the man always pays the shot." Marc took a purposeful sip of his wine and promptly burned his tongue.

"Fustian."

"Are you aware that you always say that when *you* do not have a good argument, my dear?"

Merrily's eyebrow rose to a height that matched the earl's. A small curl appeared at the corner of her mouth. She masked it beneath a sip of wine. Delight glistened in her green eyes. He was speaking to her again! No, more than that. He was teasing her! Hope soared in her bruised heart. Perhaps all could be made right again.

"Then I shall pay for our meal," she said decisively.

Marc's eyes gleamed with admiration. He would never tire of sparring with her. Not in two rollicking lifetimes. "Oh, you will pay, all right," he murmured, "but not now, and not with your meager guineas."

Merrily's mouth dropped open, but before she could sputter out a scathing reply, a serving girl carrying a tray laden with a huge joint of beef, two roasted chickens, a pork pie, and three dishes of vegetables slipped behind their screen and made her way precariously toward their table. Just as she was about to reach her goal, she jumped a foot into the air, shrieking in counterpoint to a tiny squeal as she juggled the dishes back and forth in her deft hands and struggled to regain her balance. Finally, she dropped the tray with a crash on the table.

"A pox on that rummy cat!" she bellowed in distinctly unladylike tones as she gave a tiny calico kitten that had gotten tangled between her feet a kick that sent the creature crashing into the wall. The kitten lay stunned for just a moment, then mewed pitifully and began struggling to regain her wobbly feet.

"For shame," cried Merrily as she rushed to take the kitten in her arms. "How dare you treat this baby so cruelly?" She held the tiny ball of fluff close to her breast, much to Marc's envy, and began to soothe it with tender words and soft strokes. Then she turned toward the hapless servant with a glaring gaze that might easily have melted metal.

"There be dozens of 'em, my lady," murmured the girl defensively. "Me master keeps 'em to catch mice, 'n they be always underfoot."

"But that is no reason to abuse them, my girl," declared Lady Mirthton, "and as long as I am in residence, this kitten stays with me."

"Dearest, all that fur . . .," reminded Plum as she backed away as far as the screen would allow.

"I shall not keep her, Plum," replied Merrily firmly, "but I would see her safe for one more day."

"You may leave us," interjected the earl to the serving girl. "And make sure your master is the one who brings us whatever is left to be served." As the blushing girl took her leave, Marc's eyes once again sought out Merrily. "Come, my dear," he said, gesturing with his hand, "our meal grows cold. Wrap the kitten in my cloak and set it near the fire. She will be quite comfortable while we eat."

Merrily smiled at Marc, thankful for his understanding. She laughed with him as the kitten caught the delicious odors of the steaming food and lifted her moist, pink nose up and down, flaring her tiny nostrils in insatiable desire.

"Oh, no, you little bounder," laughed Merrily as she folded the earl's large cloak around the kitten's wispy body. "You shall have to catch your own food tonight." She carried her wriggling bundle over to the fire and nestled it on the warmth of the hearthstones.

The common room of the inn grew increasingly boisterous as the earl and his companions finally sat down to eat. Marc frowned slightly, knowing that it was only a matter of time before the revelers who had filled the room after spending the day at the fair that had been set up on the town green grew worse for their drink, and dangerously unpredictable. He had not even eaten half the food on his plate before his prediction became reality. With a loud burst of profane shouting, a fight broke out at one of the tables set up for gaming, and in moments the entire room was galvanized into frenzied fisticuffs.

The screen crashed against Marc just as he was about to lift a fork full of pork pie to his tantalized lips. He rose with a bellow of outrage and instantly moved to get out from under it in order to protect the ladies. Miss Plumley screamed with fright and flattened her bulk against the wall, but Merrily hurried to help lift the heavy screen off the earl's back.

"Get over next to the wall," he shouted to her as he raised his arm to fend off an eager combatant. In two swings he had polished the man off and shifted to take on the next comer.

Again and again he planted himself between the brawlers and the two ladies, fighting like a man possessed to protect them. When one heavyset man stumbled up behind the earl and raised a chair over his head, Merrily rushed forward, grabbed the pitcher of wine from their table and smashed it over the brute's thick skull. The earl grinned at her gratefully, then swung around to take on the next man.

Suddenly, bodies began to fly through the air. Heads began to crack against other heads, or walls, or overturned tables. Marc sent the man he was punching down onto the ale-drenched floor, then straightened to rest his fists on his hips as he gasped for breath and grinned. Merrily rushed from behind the tilted screen and headed straight for his side.

"What is happening?" she cried as she stumbled over one of dozens of prostrate bodies. She grabbed his arm and looked about her in disbelief.

"Mack is happening," grinned the earl. "He must have decided to come and join the fun."

"Oh, dear," gasped Merrily, feeling a little weak in the knees. She watched in awe as the huge man flicked work-hardened men aside as if they were annoying flies.

"Fun," scoffed Mack as he strolled leisurely up to their

side. "Tweren't nothin' more'n a little exercise. Like a dawg scratchin' his fleas."

Merrily looked at the giant man with awe. He had cracked the heads of an entire room full of drunken revelers and hadn't even broken into a sweat!

"Come on, then," laughed the earl as he clapped the large man on his back. "Sit down at our table and you can exercise your jaw a little, too. We may not have knocked everyone senseless, but at least Lady Mirthton and I saved your supper." He moved, then, to set the screen back in place before walking around the table to seat the ladies.

And then Miss Plumley screamed.

"Oh, dear God," breathed Merrily as she stared in horror at the table.

Marc was at her side instantly, pulling her face into the warmth of his neck. She was shaking violently. He countered that by crushing her tightly against him, squeezing away her fear in his powerful arms. In truth, his blood was running a little bit cold, too; for there on the table lay the tiny calico kitten, her lifeless head looking strangely peaceful as it nestled on top of the earl's helping of the savory pork pie.

"She must not have been able to resist the food after all," said Lady Mirthton in a trembling voice. "She must have jumped up on the table during all the commotion. I did not see her, Marc," she said as she lifted her misted eyes to his. "I would have stopped her else."

"Shh," murmured Marc against her forehead. "Her misbehavior saved our lives, Merrily. Do not grieve."

"Dearest, I am going to faint," stated Miss Plumley as she began fumbling around in her reticule, once again seeking her salts.

Reluctantly, Merrily pulled away from the earl's embrace and went to Plum's side. "Gammon, Plum, I shall not allow it," she said with quickly mustered spirits. She put her arms around her companion and turned her toward the stairs. When she had reached the first riser, she turned back toward Marc. "I shall be but a moment, Marc," she said with iron in her tone. "I shall get Plum settled in our room and then I shall return." Her eyes moved lingeringly over the tiny ball of fur, and then again sought his. "There are things we need to discuss, and I wish to do so without delay."

"No," responded Marc in a voice filled with tension. This latest incident had changed his plans instantaneously. "Mack and I will come to you."

"You cannot come to my room, Marc," she said with a half-smile. "Must I forever be reminding you what is proper?"

"Hang propriety!" said Marc vehemently. "I would rather you be compromised yet again by me, my dear, than for you to be dead."

The smile faded from Merrily's face. There was little to be said after the earl's words, so she nodded in resignation and continued on toward their room.

The tiny garret room that was tucked under the sloping eaves of the inn roof was barely big enough to contain the narrow bed that took up most of the lower wall, but the innkeeper had cleverly managed to place a candlestand nearby and a small, but functional washstand under the single dormer window. The room looked clean, to Merrily's delight, and a bright, warming fire had been laid in the fireplace opposite the bed to welcome them.

"I declare, my dear," began Plum as she entered the room and immediately hung her cloak and reticule on a peg near the door, "this entire experience has me in quite a pucker. Quite a pucker. It is not the thing for me to become so overset, my dear. It is not good for my nerves, you know."

"Yes, I do know, dear Plum," comforted Merrily as she hung her cloak and crossed to light the candle.

A light scratching sounded at the door, and Merrily opened it to allow a chambermaid with a pitcher of hot water to enter. Merrily smiled at her and accepted the clean towels that were hanging over the maid's forearm before following the woman toward the hallway and closing the door softly behind her.

"Lord Clairmont will be coming up soon," said Merrily, taking up the conversation where she had left it. "Why do you not wash now and change into your nightgown, and then slip into bed. The others of us will talk quietly so that you can rest."

"Oh, never say so, my gel," cried the plump woman with horror. "I will not allow you to be in the same room with two gentlemen without a proper chaperone."

Merrily chuckled softly, remembering from the time she spent wrapped in Marc's arms on his bed just how lax her stalwart chaperone could be. "Very well, dearest, but wash at least. The water will not be warm much longer."

"I shall comply, my dear," responded the older woman, "but this whole havey-cavey affair has me ready to fly into the boughs."

As Plum proceeded grumblingly to go through her nightly ablutions, Merrily added another log to the cheerful fire. She was feeling a distinct need for cheer at that moment. She had been thinking over the events leading up to the kitten's death, and was filled with worry over their implications. Plum had just fastened the last button on her wrinkled, but fresh, black bombazine when another scratch sounded at the door. Merrily checked to see if Plum was ready and then turned to allow Marc and Mack entrance.

Their masculine presence rendered the small room miniscule. Marc strode through the doorway, filling it with his broad shoulders, then quickly crossed to the candlestand where he placed a bottle of porter next to the single candle and poured himself a drink.

"I could find no one in that litter of insensate humanity who looked remotely familiar," he said after taking a hefty swallow.

"Couldn't find no one we reckernized, neither," added Mack with a twinkle in his impudent eye.

Marc shot him a quelling glance. "It galls me to have to admit it, Merrily, but I do not know how the bastards got to you." He began to pace back and forth in the tiny space in front of the narrow bed like a caged tiger.

Miss Plumley gasped. "Your language, sir!" she reprimanded.

"Your pardon, ma'am," he offered absentmindedly.

Merrily smiled. "I do not believe that I was the target, Marc," she said as she sat on the bed beside Plum.

Marc stopped his pacing instantly. He gazed at her intently. "Go on," he urged.

"The kitten died with her head resting in your pork pie."

"So?"

"So, I had already eaten a good part of my own portion, and so had Plum. Yours was the only portion that had not been tasted."

Mack crossed to the hearth and seated himself in the warmth of the fire while Marc resumed his silent pacing. Seconds later, the earl stopped again.

"The kitten could have eaten from another of the dishes and wandered close to my plate before the poison took effect and killed her."

"Except for the fact that I had tasted something of everything that was on my plate. That means that the dishes themselves could not have been tainted or I would have been poisoned, too." She turned, then, toward Plum. "Dearest, had you eaten something of each dish as well?"

"Well, I . . . yes, well . . . I suppose. . . . Oh, this is such a pother! Such a pother. My nerves are quite overset." She fanned herself rigorously with her hand, and then in spite of the shocking impropriety of her actions, rolled herself to the opposite side of the bed facing the wall and pulled a downy pillow over her head.

"I think we can assume that she did," said the earl as he blinked at the rotund woman's black-clad back.

"So we are left with the fact that the poison was only in your food, my lord," she stated evenly, "and therefore, you were the sole target." Carefully she eased from the bed and moved to join Mack on the floor by the fire, then watched as acceptance cleared the earl's deep blue eyes.

"How'd they get it in your feed, d'you suppose?" asked Mack, stating the question aloud that they'd all been wondering.

"Merrily has proven that it could not have been in the food when it was brought to us . . ." began the earl.

"So someone had to have added it after it reached our table," concluded Lady Mirthton. "But when?"

"It had to have been during the fight," reasoned Marc. "Merrily, did you see anyone approach the table while the fighting was going on?"

"Oh, Marc, it could have happened anytime," she cried softly. "My attention was on you. I was so afraid you would be hurt."

Marc's eyes suddenly sparkled with tenderness. He immediately crossed to the fireplace, then folded his long legs and sat down next to Merrily. "Were you?" he murmured, gazing at her intently.

Merrily's heart began to flutter under the scrutiny of the earl's warm eyes. "Yes," she replied softly. Then her eyes began a slow sweep down Marc's chest to his abdomen. Fire coursed through his already throbbing veins. "Your wound . . ." she said, stretching her hand toward him slightly.

Marc caught her hand in his and began to slowly draw it toward his puckered scar. He was aching for her touch, eager for the heat of her hand against his body. He drew her nearer . . . nearer . . .

"Ahem," rumbled Mack as he cleared his throat like the sound of distant thunder.

Marc blinked and drew back instantly. "Yes, well . . . the point is that I do not intend to leave you alone, my dear. Not now. Not after this. And certainly not until we know who is behind all these incidents."

Merrily broke into soft laughter. She drew up her knees and wrapped her arms around them, then lowered her head to rest in the nest she had made. When she finally raised her eyes again to his, her smile was tender and wistful. "So you will stay the night in my room, propriety be hanged. Do you intend to actually sleep with me this time, my lord?"

Mack had a sudden attack of coughing, and Marc looked pleasantly startled. "Would that be so horrible, my dear?" he teased.

Merrily ignored him. "Let me see now. The first time I lay with you, Mack there, felt quite free to wander in and out, bringing us tea and sandwiches, if I recall correctly. And this time you suggest that we do it with my chaperone in our bed. I am becoming most concerned over certain aberrations in your character, my lord."

Marc chuckled heartily. "What do you know of such things, my innocent?" he asked.

"That I never thought to have so much company when I was compromised, my lord," she replied with a grin.

Behind him, Mack rumbled with laughter. "You will have my company, you little nodcock, but not in your bed," Marc said as he tapped her nose. "You and Miss Plumley will share the bed, and I shall sleep here on the floor by the fire."

"And Mack?" she asked as she peeked around Marc to grin at the gentle giant.

"I'll be a-hunkerin' down in front of the door, ma'am," he replied.

"It is still a very improper arrangement, Marc," she said as she smoothed her skirt.

"Gammon. We will all stay mumchance. Who is to know?"

Merrily shrugged her shoulders. She supposed that it would not matter significantly if anyone did know. It changed nothing as far as she was concerned. Her reputation was still in shreds. She did take some comfort in the fact that she was no worse off now than she was when she first met the earl. She was still unmarried, homeless, and socially ruined, so why did his staying in her room under questionable circumstances again bother her? Why should one more item on the list of her improprieties matter? Yet somehow it did. Merrily's mother had wanted so much for her only daughter, and had tried so hard to overcome the taint her husband had visited upon them. Merrily shuddered to think of what had become of all her mother's hopes. Her daughter had certainly come to a fine end, she thought, sitting on the floor of an inn garret with two men, each of them wondering if they would be the next to be murdered. A shiver trailed down her spine.

"Are you cold?" asked Marc, breaking into her thoughts with a voice of tender concern.

"A little," she replied with a soft smile.

"Then why do you not retire? Mack and I shall do quite well on the floor, believe me." He placed a warm palm on the center of her back and gave her a gentle nudge.

Merrily nodded and rose to her feet. Then she crossed to the bed, kicked off her shoes, and slipped beneath the quilts. She watched as Marc rose to his feet and crossed to the table near her bed. He watched her intently for several seconds, and then poured himself another measure of porter before leaning down to blow out the candle.

"Good night, Merrily," he whispered, touching a finger to her soft cheek.

From the depths of the covers, she answered, "Good night, my lord."

An ice blue moon rose in the early morning hours and shone through the dormer window, casting pale shadows over Merrily's sleeping face. She squinted slightly in the unaccustomed brightness, and then awakened, disoriented at finding herself in a strange place. She remembered then, and cast a glance about her, smiling as she noticed the large male humps that lay on the floor nearby. She looked, then, at the soft disk that floated just outside the window and answered the compulsion to rise and move toward it. It was a melancholy moon. Merrily felt its power as she placed her hands on the icy windowpanes and let the moonshine wash over her.

Suddenly strong arms reached out to surround her, pulling her gently back into their warmth, but she was not afraid. She sighed sweetly and let her head drop back against a broad, firm shoulder. "I did not even hear you approach," she said in a whisper.

"A necessity for a soldier," Marc murmured in reply. "Could you not sleep?" His lips were close to her ear. Each word reached her on a wash of warm air that sent pleasant sensations skittering over her skin like butterfly wings.

"I did a little," she returned as she lifted her arms to cover his, "but I shall not be able to go back to sleep now."

"Nor will I," he said, and then he fell into silence. When at last he spoke again, his voice was hesitant. "Merrily . . .," he began, "I wish to apologize."

"Do you?" she responded. Marc could tell from the sound of her voice that she was smiling. "Let me see. Could it be for agreeing to help me when you had no earthly desire to do so? Or perhaps for taking my part when my cousins thought to castigate me? Oh, no, it must be for taking days out of your life to come to my home, at deadly peril to yourself, I might add, and search for a list that might save my life. Oh dear, my lord, you have been most remiss, have you not? This apology is far too long in coming."

"Minx!" whispered the earl in her ear. "This is serious. And I have never been so tongue-tied in my life. I have been trying to apologize to you ever since the Latham's ball for embarrassing you so badly. Will you forgive me?"

Merrily turned slowly in Marc's arms. She lifted her hands to rest on his chest. The moonlight shining on her features showed Marc her amazement. "Forgive you?" she whispered. "But I have been trying to find a way all day to apologize to you!" The earl began to chuckle. "It is not funny, Marc," she insisted. "I boxed you right into the punch bowl."

"Can you imagine the sight we must have made?" he said, still chortling.

Merrily beat upon his chest with her tiny fists. "Stop laughing, you ninnyhammer! We shall neither of us be able to show our faces in Town again."

"Of course, we shall, my dear," he said, squeezing her tighter. "By the time we return to Town again, something else will have happened to take our well-earned places."

"Oh, Marc, you take this all so casually," moaned Merrily as she dropped her head against the earl's chest. "It is not so easy for me. No one will have me now, do you not see? Where will I go? No one will want a rackety hoyden like me."

Marc's arms tightened fiercely. The words were dancing on the end of his tongue, fighting to be said. But he could not declare himself yet. It was too soon, too soon. He did not know of her feelings for him yet, and as certain as he was that she would soon be his, he still needed to know that she cared for him. And so he held her, and suffered the torture of the unsated as he did, giving her what reassurance he could.

"It will be all right," he murmured against her thick, curling hair. "Trust me, Merrily. Trust me."

Thus, clinging tightly to one another, they improperly passed the remainder of the night.

Chapter 10

The road Marc chose for the remainder of their journey after leaving Tunbridge Wells skirted the Weald and played tag with the river Cuckmere as it twisted its way south through a gap in the Downs at Alfriston. It was an ancient road, better suited to carts and farm wagons than a stylish nobleman's carriage, but to Marc's way of thinking, it was perfect. In all likelihood, any cutthroats who might be following them wouldn't think they'd be addlepated enough to come this way. And if it was difficult for them to traverse the road's muddy ruts and wash-outs, certainly the brigands who might be on their trail would be having just as much trouble as they. But just the same, Marc's eyes scanned the surrounding countryside like a harbor beacon, watching with hawk's eyes for any sign of danger.

They had stopped for a light meal at midday, turning off the road at a nearby tenant farm to buy bread, cheese, apples and ale from the farmer's jovial wife and then moving on a little farther down the road to eat their repast *al fresco* under a huge oak which for centuries marked the corner boundary of a deserted hops field. Merrily had shivered as the chill autumn wind sliced through her brown wool pelisse, and the men had immediately formed a warm, male windbreak around her and

Plum. She had smiled her gratitude, but the days were growing shorter, and the knowledge was in all of them that they needed to hurry on.

It was nearing dusk when Merrily called to Marc from the carriage and pointed out a weed-choked drive leading off to the right of the rutted road. Immediately he signalled to Mack to halt the carriage and rode up to her side.

"The Manor lies at the end of this drive," Merrily informed him. "There is a wrought iron gate about a mile from here. If my cousins have deployed men to stop us, my guess is that they will be stationed there."

"Yes, I would agree," Marc responded as he removed his beaver and slapped it against his thigh. A cloud of dust drifted up from his pantaloons and momentarily obscured Merrily's vision. "But I dislike leaving anything to chance. Mack and I shall go ahead on foot to see if we have guessed correctly."

"I shall come, too," said Merrily as she placed her hand on the door of the carriage.

"Absolutely not," replied the earl severely. "Mack and I will be sneaking. I have never known a woman yet who could properly sneak. Always chattering or rustling petticoats or squeaking because they stepped on something squishy. No, my dear, you and Plum will remain here."

Merrily swallowed her indignation and her hot retort, but her green eyes had brightened considerably. She quickly lowered her eyelids so that Marc would not notice the change. The dratted man would spot her intentions immediately if he thought to look at her closely. She waited instead, watching surreptitiously as he dismounted and then signalled Mack to skirt one side of the road while he slipped behind the concealing trees on the other. In moments they were both lost to Merrily's sight in the cool, misty denseness of the forest.

All of Marc's senses hummed with tension as he moved stealthily forward. He was not certain how far he had come or even if, in constantly shifting to avoid the huge trees, he had lost his sense of direction, but soon the unfamiliar surroundings were no longer a problem. He heard the murmur of voices long before he saw the men gathered to the side of the double gates that sealed off the road, and turned to head directly toward them.

He scanned the forest across the road from him but was not concerned by its emptiness. He might have lost sight of Mack as the mist thickened in the deeper recesses of the woodland, yet he knew that he was still there. Slowly he inched forward, working to keep the flame-colored leaves that littered the spongy forest floor from crackling under his booted feet. With catlike stealth he crept from tree to tree, keeping himself concealed as he moved in a half-crouch through the soft gray mist. At last he saw the diffused glow of the fire the men had built by the side of the road to keep themselves warm while they waited. Marc crept as close as he could and then began to reconnoiter.

Just as he had finished counting their number and was concentrating on a study of their weapons, one of the men, a burly brute with auburn hair, turned at the crunch of gravel on the road before him and raised his cudgel menacingly. He took a step forward, then stopped abruptly, breaking into the widest, most gape-toothed grin Marc had ever seen.

Out of the mist and straight down the center of the road strode Merrily. Marc straightened so rapidly that his skull came into resounding contact with a thick branch that had sprouted, perversely, just above him. *The deuce!* he thought as he gingerly touched the rising bump on the top of his head. *So much for military tactics. Now what is she about to get me into?* Keeping himself concealed behind the tree, he listened as he mentally shoved the lid back onto his rising blood pressure.

"Thomas!" cried Merrily brightly as she stepped out of the mist and seized both the beaming man's coarsely calloused hands in her soft, small ones. "How is Betsey? Did she get over her influenza?"

"She's right as rain, m'lady," said the powerful man. "Nothin' short o' the final trump'd keep my woman down for long."

With smiles of recognition breaking out all around, the others crowded around her, and Merrily greeted them all, shaking their hands and asking after their families as if none of the men

were sporting a bevy of deadly weapons and had been sent
there specifically to harry her. Marc was tensed to race to her
defense, but the stupefying scene of her reunion with her former
tenants kept him motionless. He began, muscle by clenched
muscle, to relax. He saw Mack, then, on the opposite side of
the gate and shook his head slightly in a silent message to
watch and wait for a while longer.

"You shouldn't ought to be here, m'lady," said one of the
other men whom Merrily had called Andrew.

"Aye," affirmed another called Paul. "Th' new master's
given us instructions to have at yer men an' stop ye from goin'
through th' gate."

"I know, Paul," said Merrily gently. "What do you intend
to do?" From his vantage point near the side of the road, Marc's
eyes widened at her open trust in these work-hardened men.

"Why, nothin', o' course!" said Thomas as his huge chest
wheezed with laughter. "Ye an' yer ma were th' only ones who
treated us right, m'lady. There's not a one o' us who'd turn
agin ye. But ye mustn't face them two alone. We've all decided
t' come along wi' ye. Somethin' foul is in th' mind o' the new
'my lord.' "

"Aye," interjected Paul. "None of us knows what it is, but
ye can count on it not bein' good."

Merrily was silent for a moment, and then she nodded. "I
have no idea what my cousins might be up to either," she
said more firmly, "but you must not come with me. If Lord
Collingwood sees you in my company, he will turn you out
without a second thought."

"Nay, m'lady," argued Andrew. "Ye're no Daniel t' be
walkin' into the lion's den alone. We'll be goin' w' ye."

"But I am not alone," she smiled. She turned then, at looked
directly at the place where the earl was hiding. Marc burned
away a good portion of the enveloping mist with his returning
glare. He had done his best sneaking, after all. How the deuce
had she known he was there? "You may come forward now,
my lord," she called gaily. "No harm will come to anyone
here today."

Marc was not so sure about that. He thought that he could

happily ring Lady Mirthton's slender neck. In the next moment he was quite sure about it, for, as he stepped from behind the tree and began to walk toward her, she flashed him a mischievous smile that would have looked quite at home on one of the devil's own imps.

"You were supposed to stay with the carriage," he said in a low voice between gritted teeth.

"Ah, but you issued a challenge that stung my woman's pride," she whispered as he reached her side. "I had no choice but to take up the gauntlet. To my everlasting shame, though, I fear that you were right. I have no talent for sneaking." She pursed her lips and blinked with abject humility.

"But not for being sneaky, my little witch," countered Marc with a smile that promised repercussions later. "Why did you not tell me the tenants would be on your side? That little bit of information might have saved me from stalking through the forest like a demented poacher."

"You are embarrassed," stated Merrily in surprise.

"Never say so, my dear," replied the earl haughtily. "Earls simply do not embarrass."

"Yet your face is suspiciously red, my lord," teased Lady Mirthton unmercifully.

"You have proved my point for me, my dear," replied the earl as his nose rose to new heights. "The blood of English nobility runs through my veins. If I were to become embarrassed, my face would turn blue." And then he turned toward the silently observing tenants. "I am Lord Clairmont. You have my gratitude for your care of Lady Mirthton today."

"It weren't nothin' but turn about for what she's done for us," answered Andrew boldly as he swept his hat off his head and clutched it to his abdomen beneath a low bow. A ruddy blush stained his rugged features.

Marc's gaze shifted slowly to each man, learning the faces of Merrily's champions. "Your loyalty is a rare thing," said Marc, "and should not go unrewarded. There will be places for you on any of my lands should you ever be turned off here.

You have only to mention the events of this day and employment will be yours."

Merrily was just as astonished as the gape-jawed tenants. "Thank you, my lord," she said softly after a glance at the stunned looks on the men's faces told her that they were beyond answering for themselves.

Marc smiled in understanding. "It is my privilege, my dear. Andrew, perhaps you would be so good as to walk back to the main road and have one of my men drive our carriage up to the house. Miss Plumley is inside, and I am sure she is wondering what has happened."

"Aye, my lord," responded the man with a bow. Immediately he turned and set off at a trot.

"Now," continued Marc as he took Merrily's arm, "we have only to open the gate." His eyes scanned the staves of tooled, rusting iron, noticing immediately the bright, new chain that held the gates closed against them.

"Have you a key to the padlock, Thomas?" asked Lady Mirthton.

"Nay, m'lady," he replied. "Lord Collingwood has th' only one."

"No matter," said Marc calmly. And then he nodded toward Mack, who was leaning negligently, and totally unremarked, against a nearby tree. "Well, Mack. Have at it, if you please."

"Have it open in a whisker, yer uppity-ship," the giant man replied. His face was split with its usual good-humored grin.

The farmers gaped again as they watched Mack roll his back away from the deeply creased trunk and saunter forward. He stopped before the rusted iron and let his eyes roam over its surface. Then, not even considering the thick, padlocked chain, he strolled over to the side where several rusted hinges secured the gate to a tall brick gatepost. He placed his powerful hands against the eroded metal, tested the strength of the rusted bolts with a few harsh rattles, then reared back and slammed his open palms against the hinges. With a grinding crash they gave way, their severed bolts allowing the gate to swing away and to teeter lopsidedly against its twisted companion. Just as the carriage pulled into sight, Mack lifted both heavy gates off the road and leaned them against the opposite gatepost.

"Pon my soul," murmured Miss Plumley as she hung out the window of the carriage and stared at the tangled metal.

"Guess ye truly won't be needin' our help, will ye, m'lord?" grinned Thomas as he shook his head at the ruins of the gate.

Marc laughed at the expressions of awe on the farmers' creased faces. "Thank you, men, but no. I brought my own army. Besides, Lady Mirthton was quite correct when she warned you that it will go badly for you if you go against your lord to any greater degree than you already have. My offer to you will always be open, of course, but I'll wager most of you have lived here all your lives. Your families might not be so anxious to tear out their roots and move to new land."

"Aye," responded Thomas as his round face sobered, "we'll take ourselves off then. But if ye need us, send out th' word. Roots or no roots, we'll come."

Marc nodded his gratitude, then took Merrily's elbow and turned her toward the carriage. "In you go, my dear," he said, motioning to one of the footmen to lead Barbary before helping Merrily climb inside. "We may as well arrive in grand style. I fear that we have lost the element of surprise, though. Babbington probably heard that gate crash back in London."

An impish gleam brightened Merrily's green eyes. "Just as long as we do not have to sneak anymore, my lord," she responded as she pursed her lips into a teasing bow. "Of a certainty, I am no good at sneaking."

Marc raised his eyebrow, shook his head, and let a smile of resignation spread across his face.

Not long after the carriage passed between the gateposts, Marc got his first glimpse of Mirthton Manor. He could not help the feelings of regret that stole over him as he viewed its decayed glory. He could only imagine what Merrily must be feeling. The drive wound its way through what once must have been a beautiful park laid out in a natural style which had all the earmarks of having been designed by the famous Lancelot "Capability" Brown, a man who got his name from seeing the land he was working as being filled with "capabilities."

The house itself was set on a slight rise, and was constructed of warm brick in the shape of an "H." It was a beautiful pile with a facade of genteel simplicity, displayed to perfection in its tall elevations and long sash windows whose panes were even now being set aflame by the gentle pastels of the waning sunset. The Manor's roof was hipped and was decorated with pedimented dormer windows. A cupola, whose copper-clad dome had weathered to a soft verdigris, perched midway across the roof, giving the house balance and no small degree of whimsey. Marc was lost in thoughts of what the house might have once looked like when Merrily's hand rested lightly on his arm.

As his eyes met hers, she nodded toward the wide steps that framed the entrance into the Manor. Lucius and Willard stood in the doorway, their rigid stance making them look like a pair of polished marble statues some Pink of the *ton* might have brought home from his Grand Tour.

"Hmm, the welcoming committee," stated Marc as he spotted them.

" 'Welcome' is not a word I would readily use in reference to my cousins, my lord," said Lady Mirthton warily.

"What? You are not afraid, are you?" asked Marc lightly. And then his eyebrows rose knowingly and he placed a warm hand on her knee.

"Lord Clairmont!" gasped Plum as she batted his hand away.

Marc laughed. "Your pardon, Miss Plumley, but once again our lady is betrayed. Her kneecaps are clacking like the castanets I once saw in the hands of a Spanish dancer in the Peninsula."

A wave of pique overrode the tingling sensation Marc's wholly improper caress aroused in her. *Spanish dancer!* she thought with ire. "I have heard of such women," she said in a cool voice. "They wear skirts that are rather short, do they not?"

Marc sighed long and loud. "Very short indeed," he replied with a far away look in his eyes.

Merrily's eyes darkened and narrowed. "And how long did you observe this dancer?" she asked with deceptive softness.

"Oh, all evening if I remember correctly," answered the earl casually. "She was quite good."

"What else was she good at?" growled Merrily.

"That, my dear Lady Mirthton," replied the earl with a victorious smile, "would be impolite to say."

The carriage came to a halt before the Manor just then, and Marc was thankful for Mack's timing. Merrily was glaring at him as if she would like to clack a few castanets on top of his head, but at least by responding to his teasing she had gotten over her fear. And he had to admit that he was just the tiniest bit pleased by her show of jealousy. Tiniest bit? The deuce! He was ready to do cartwheels all the way back to London.

As soon as one of Marc's footmen opened the carriage door, though, he controlled the grin that kept trying to spread across his face and helped Miss Plumley and Merrily climb down onto the ungraded gravel drive. Taking an elbow in each hand, he then escorted them up the crumbling steps toward her two cousins.

Merrily hadn't realized how difficult it would be to see Lucius standing so proprietarily on the steps of what had once been her refuge. She lowered her eyes at the pain of it and unconsciously moved closer to Marc's side. He squeezed her elbow consolingly and she brightened somewhat, certain, though no words had been spoken, that he understood her dismay.

"We have been expecting you," said Lucius coldly.

"We thought as much," answered Marc with a pleasant smile. "So kind in you to provide such a happy reception for Merrily."

Lucius's scowl deepened. So the tenants still gave his cousin their loyalty. Her removal was now not just desirable. It was a necessity. He stepped in front of the advancing earl and put up his hand. "You are not welcome here, Clairmont," he said acidly.

"Indeed?" responded the earl in a soft voice that belied its intensity. His gaze turned quickly to iron. "Your lack of hospitality toward a fellow peer who happens to find himself in the vicinity is not at all *de rigueur,* Collingwood. What will you do, then? Toss us out on our ears?"

As Lucius opened his mouth to utter a sharp retort, Mack, with his usual impeccable timing, rose from his seat on the carriage, jumped with a thunderous thud onto the ground, and strolled in a loose-limbed, rolling gait to stand protectively on the other side of Merrily.

"I'm gettin' powerful hungry, yer la-de-da-ship. Is them two fellas the ones 'at's puttin' on the feedbag?"

Lucius and Willard winced and visibly shrank from the huge man who stood grinning down at them. "Plum and our . . . our cousin, o-of course, can stay f-for a short time," blurted Willard. His contribution to the confrontation only earned him his brother's glare.

"I am only thinking of my cousin's reputation," said Lucius piously.

"Cut line, Collingwood," said Marc as he tired of the sparring game. He was concerned for Merrily, who was practically digging herself into his side in her anxiety. He imagined that her kneecaps must be about to fly off her legs about now. That thought amused him enough to temper his anger somewhat. "We are not here on a social call." *As I am sure you are well aware.* "When our business in the house is finished we will leave . . . but not a moment before. Have I made myself clear?"

Willard began to sputter indignantly just before Mack stepped forward to emphasize the earl's point. Within moments, both cousins were nodding heartily.

"Very well, then. Step aside and show us to our rooms." Marc took the ladies' elbows and steered them past the gaping cousins and into the chill of the Manor.

"Such a pother," said Plum as she passed them by. "Such a pother. I have been traveling for two days over the most wretched road and I wish to seek my bed. For shame, Lucius, to keep me standing on the steps. For shame."

Thoroughly chastised, Lucius and Willard glanced meaningfully at one another and then followed their unwanted houseguests into the Manor.

The hall into which Marc and Merrily entered was large and sparsely furnished. Pillars of gray marble topped with scrolled plasterwork which had at one time gleamed with gilding sup-

ported a high domed roof decorated with oval paintings that
were framed by complementary plaster mouldings. Marc
noticed several empty pedestals spaced in between the marble
pillars and wondered at the absence of their statuary. A curved
stairway rose to the second level at the side of the hall and a
large doorway stood just opposite the entrance leading into the
grand saloon.

"Your coat, sir," said a deep voice from behind. Marc turned
just as a middle-aged man approach from what looked to be
the drawing room. "I am Grimes, sir. I will see to your things."

"Thank you, Grimes," responded Marc as he lifted a questioning eyebrow to Merrily.

Her silent answer was a slight shrug. "He is new," she
whispered when the butler had taken their cloaks away.

"Then we must be wary of what we say around him, I think,"
responded Marc. He turned, then, as Plum drew up to their
side.

"Dear me, I am fatigued," she lamented. "Have you seen
any sign of a maid, dearest? I vow, I would like nothing better
than a light repast in my room and the comfort of my own bed
this evening. Would someone bring me a tray, do you think?"

"I shall bring it, dear," answered Merrily with a hug and a
smile. "I shall show Lord Clairmont to his room and then see
if a bath can be had for you."

"Oh, no, dearest, you are well aware of my feelings on that
score. I shall bathe on the day before Easter services, and not
a moment before."

Merrily rolled her expressive eyes at Marc and noted the
amused gleam in his. "Very well, then," she responded
patiently, her tone suggesting that they had had this argument
many times before, "I shall bring you a can of warm water
for your washing and then see about a tray for you."

"Thank you, my dear," said Plum as she turned toward the
stairs. "Try not to be too long, though, dear one," she added.
"I shall not be able to keep my eyes open much longer, but I
do wish to dine before I retire. You know how sensitive my
digestion can be if I miss my meals."

"Yes, dear. Go along now and I will see to everything." She turned, then, in time to watch the approach of her cousins. "Lucius," she began as they were about to pass her by. Lucius halted a flicker of irritation and gave her his attention. "Is there a maid in residence? Plum was hoping for water in which to wash and a light meal on a tray."

"There is one maid, a girl named Lucy," he responded. "I shall have Grimes send her to Plum." He turned to go, but Merrily stopped him again.

"When is the evening meal to be served?" she bravely ventured to ask.

Lucius's eyes narrowed a fraction. "In one hour. I trust that will give you time to dress?" His eyes raked over her dusty pelisse with distaste.

"Yes. Thank you, Lucius," said Merrily softly. "I . . . I am truly sorry to cut up your peace, cousin," she apologized. "I know you are not pleased to see us here, but we do have an important reason for coming."

"And what might that be?" asked Lucius in icy tones.

"We will be looking through Simon Mirthton's personal effects," replied Marc before his trusting Merrily could say any more.

"How long do you anticipate you will be staying?" inquired Lucius.

"As long as it takes," challenged Marc in a steady voice.

"Then you will get no support from me," Lucius hissed, and before either Marc or Merrily could respond, he strode after Willard into the drawing room and slammed the door.

Marc immediately motioned for Mack to join them. "I want you to go into the village," the earl ordered. "We will need a temporary maid for Lady Mirthton and a cook to see to our needs. Offer them twice what they would normally be paid. You will also need to see the local merchants about supplying whatever foodstuffs and other necessities we will want while we are here."

"I have some money, Marc . . ." began Merrily.

"The gentleman always pays," interrupted Marc dismissively.

"And the lady always pays him back," muttered Merrily with heat.

Marc's eyes swung to hers. His sensual mouth spread into a lascivious grin. "Absolutely," he whispered as his fingers stroked her cheek.

Merrily was so startled by the wave of tingles that washed over her at the earl's softly spoken promise that she totally missed the next ten minutes of her life. She came back to reality, feeling inordinately foolish, in the middle of her own room as the sound of splashing water dissipated her dream. She turned, then to see a young girl she assumed to be Lucy pouring warm water into a hip bath that had been placed nearby.

"Thank you," she said as the maid emptied the container. "Have Miss Plumley's needs been attended to?"

"Oh, yes, m'lady," said the girl with a smile. "Th' old dear's likely asleep already. Will ye be wantin' one o' yer gowns laid out, m'lady?"

"No, thank you, Lucy. I shall see to that myself. You may go now."

Merrily waited until the maid had left and then quickly slipped out of her dust-covered clothing. She eased herself into the warmth of the water and sighed with pleasure. She reached, then, for the linen cloth Lucy had provided for her and lathered it generously with rose-scented soap, then smoothed the cloth over her shoulders. Shivers of pleasure raced over her pebbled skin, not unlike those that inundated her whenever the earl touched her.

Now there was a mystery. What was it about his nearness that made her body react so oddly? She trailed her hands down over her slender body, delighting in the sensations the touch provoked. She wondered what it would feel like if the earl touched her like that. An arrow of sensation pierced her abdomen. She sat up abruptly. *Goodness!* she thought in amazement. *I'd best think no more on that subject!*

It was almost an hour later when Merrily joined the earl and her cousins in the drawing room before going in to dinner. The earl winced as she entered the room and released a long sigh.

She was dressed in a frightful gown of heavy damask covered with a tangle of huge cabbage roses. So overpowering was the display of ruby-colored flora that it was next to impossible to distinguish her fine, soft features among all that riotous verdure. He blanked his pained expression with a will, then walked to her side.

The earl thought he really should try to be more understanding about her wardrobe. He knew the reason, after all. Actually, he thought her quite wonderful to wear atrocity after atrocity just to spare Plum's sensibilities. If looking at her just didn't cause his head to hurt so, he thought he could be much more tolerant. But she was determined to cause no hurt in her companion. He felt his heart go fuzzy with the depth of emotion her sweetness aroused in him. She had such tenderhearted feelings. He would make sure he was always near to protect them. With the power of his burgeoning emotions strong in his mind, he raised her hand to his lips and regarded her tenderly.

"You look like an explosion at a garden party," he murmured with avid warmth.

Merrily broke into joyous laughter. "You will turn my head with such tender sentiments, my lord," she replied when she had finally caught her breath.

"You should expect no less from me," he responded with a brisk military bow. "I am tender to a fault."

"Hmm," she responded with a raised eyebrow. "Perhaps I should ask the opinion of those two cutthroats we met in Conduit Street."

"Do so if you like," he grinned. "I have no doubt they will tell you I poked my fives in their faces very tenderly."

"And Lucius?" she asked.

"I merely gave him a companionable pat on the back."

"Ah," she replied with a nod toward her approaching cousin. "Perhaps you would care to discuss the subtle nuances of your touch with the one who received them?"

Marc's blue eyes blazed. "A discussion of my more subtle caresses will only be held with you, my dear," he whispered, "and you will be the only one who is receiving them."

Merrily's eyes widened in surprise. "I . . . I think perhaps we are not talking about the same thing, my lord," she breathed.

"You may be sure of it, my dear," replied Marc as his eyes feasted on hers. He stepped back then as Lucius and Willard arrived at their side.

"Would you care to take my arm, cousin?" Lucius asked as he extended his elbow. "Dinner is ready, I believe."

"Yes, thank you, Lucius," she replied as she moved hesitantly toward him.

She glanced back at Marc and he gave her a sudden wink. Her cheeks flamed and she shook her head in reproach. He meant none of it, of course. But for a while, just for a few days, she thought she might let herself pretend that he did. It would hurt later, after he was gone, she knew, but it would undoubtedly be the only taste of romance she would ever know. Would it be so wrong? she wondered. Just once, couldn't she lower the guard she had erected around her feelings and simply let her heart sing?

"After you, cousin," said Lucius in a flat voice as he pushed open the door to the saloon.

Merrily's imaginings shattered with the sound of her odious cousin's voice. Immediately her eyes sought out Marc. He was there, close beside her, his smile reassuring her with a power she could barely comprehend. She took comfort in it, as she knew he had intended, and allowed her cousin to escort her inside.

Willard saw the thin line of light escaping from under the library door and released some of the tension that was making his head throb. It was well past midnight and the Manor was as quiet as a tomb. Everyone had long since retired for the night, but he knew his brother would be waiting for him. So much depended on the next few days. He cast a wary glance over his shoulder, but the single candle that wobbled in his hand barely penetrated the thick blackness of the hall. He shook himself in his irritation. There was no one there. He had checked each room himself. He knew that they were all fast asleep. Yet, as he crossed the chamber in silence, a feeling of impending disaster trickled through his veins. He did not let it shake him, however. Lucius was awaiting him, and Lucius would take care of everything.

He turned the handle of the door with a soft click and entered the barrel-vaulted library. Row upon row of empty shelves lined the walls, and except for a few items of furniture, the large, once lovely room was bare. Lucius sat behind an ornate walnut desk with a glass of brandy in his hand. He had turned so that his outstretched feet extended for warmth toward the fire, and as he swirled the dark liquid around in his glass, he stared into the mesmerizing flames unseeingly.

"You are late," he commented flatly as he took a long pull on his brandy.

"I wanted to make sure no one would be listening," responded Willard as he eased himself into a chair across from his brother. "Wh-what are we going to do now, Lucius?"

"Get rid of her, of course," replied the young man evenly, "just as we planned."

"But how are we going to do that?" queried Willard nervously.

"Be at ease, brother," soothed Lucius. "The way has not presented itself as yet, but it will. We must be patient. If we are to be successful, we must wait until Merrily is apart from that brute of an earl and his giant friend. We will not have many opportunities, though, so when the time is right, we must act quickly."

"How will we know when they are not together?" asked Willard, irritating his brother with his show of simple-mindedness.

"We will watch them, of course," Lucius snapped. "We will lead them to believe that we are frequently away on estate business, but we will be observing them instead."

"Like bugs under a glass?" asked Willard with dawning understanding.

"Precisely," uttered his brother as the firelight gleamed in his eyes. "And when the time is right . . ."

"We will tear off our cousin's wings!" finished Willard with a cry of delight.

"I believe you have it at last, dear brother," murmured Lucius, and, as Willard stretched his own feet toward the warming fire, he let his wandering thoughts play tag once again with the shimmering flames.

Chapter 11

"I hardly know where to begin," said Merrily the next morning as she and Marc stood in the middle of her father's room.

"We begin by being thankful that it has not yet occurred to Lucius to move into the master suite," responded the earl with a grin. "The room looks relatively undisturbed."

Marc's gaze traveled the spare, but well-appointed chamber. It was not large as master bedrooms went, but was tastefully decorated in the Chinese style with fine painted wallpaper and several lacquered pieces enhanced with exotic designs. A relatively new half-tester bed with an ornately fringed pelmet buttressed one wall, and just beyond the bedside table stood a door which opened into the adjoining dressing room. Marc crossed to the door and looked inside, noting the dressing table, Cheval glass, tall chifforobe, and, fitted into the small space between the door and the corner of the dressing room, a narrow, lacquered, many-drawered cabinet with a small picture hanging above it.

"I do not believe that Uncle Boggs used the room either," added Merrily as her gaze shifted about the room. "Aunt Beatrice seemed to prefer waiting until they could afford to redecorate before she took over these rooms. Unfortunately, they were both killed before that could happen."

Marc gave her a supportive smile. He knew what she was thinking . . . that her aunt and uncle would rather have lived in the discomfort of a cramped guest room than to soil themselves by using her father's things, but he kept silent. She needed his strength now, not his anger.

"I fear you have been mistaken about the cause of their deaths, my sweet," he said with a perfectly straight face.

Merrily whirled around to face him. "Whatever do you mean?"

"I have only moments ago finished, if you recall, sampling one of Lucy's breakfasts."

"I recall it well. I watched you, if *you* recall, force it down," she responded as her eyes took on a lovely sparkle.

"I also, if *you* recall, recall it well. After the first spoonful, your skin color matched your eyes."

Merrily grinned broadly. "A most unfashionable color . . . but what does all this have to do with my aunt and uncle's deaths?" she asked.

"That is obvious, my dear," he answered as he tested the softness of the bed with his long fingers. "It was the porridge that did them in."

"Oh, Marc," said Merrily as she shook her head and laughed softly, "you are the most appalling man."

"No, indeed," he replied staunchly, "I am above all things a practical man. That is why I have sent Mack off to the village on an errand of mercy. He is not to return until he has procured for us a culinary Rembrandt."

"In our village?" asked Merrily in surprise. "I think not, my lord."

"Hmm," he responded with a finger on his chin, "no Rembrandt, you say? Not even a Tintoretto?"

Merrily was giggling now. "I very much doubt it, my lord," she gurgled in reply.

"Ah, well," he sighed, "I shall settle for someone who can boil eggs. Will Plum be able to help us search?"

"I have never known her to rise much before noon, Marc, and I doubt my cousins would care to lend a hand. They will not be here anyway," she continued. "Lucius informed me

earlier that he and Willard had business to attend to somewhere
on the estate. They shall be gone all day."

"No matter," the earl replied easily. "The fewer who are
involved, the better. If you would care to begin your search
with your father's desk, my dear, I will empty the lacquered
chest at the foot of his bed."

"Very well, Marc," Merrily responded, and she turned to
begin her task.

As the hours of the morning drifted by, Marc and Merrily
labored over every inch of her father's room in their effort to
discover the whereabouts of the list. Nothing escaped their
notice. They searched every drawer, checking with infinite care
for hidden compartments or latches. They did uncover one such
compartment in Simon's desk, but it contained only a packet
of letters that Merrily had sent him as a child. Merrily did not
allow herself the tears that threatened to spill. There was simply
too much to do and so very little time.

They ran their fingers over every surface of the walls, knocking as they went, hoping to discover a hidden panel somewhere
that would contain the list, but their search proved fruitless.
They checked the dressing room just as thoroughly, searching
every drawer, every surface, every drape, even the silvered
back of the Cheval glass, but to no avail. They found a small
lacquered box in the top drawer of the narrow chest in the
dressing room and opened it excitedly, but it contained only
Simon's ruby ring, a cameo of Merrily's mother, and a picture
she had drawn at age five. Merrily carried the box to the bed
and spread the meager horde upon the coverlet.

"Nothing," she murmured dejectedly. "There is nothing. I
was so sure . . ."

"Do not give up yet," said Marc as he sat down on the bed.
"This was only one room."

"But the most likely to contain a clue," she whispered.

"Perhaps," he said, looking warmly into her swimming eyes.
"But there is a clue here that you should not miss, Merrily. It
is one that is more important than the clue leading to the list,
I believe. Did you see it?"

"What are you talking about?" she sighed.

"What were the personal items your father thought important enough to save?" he asked gently.

"There were hardly any," she said with a questioning frown. "Just my letters, a picture I drew, a cameo of my mother, and his ring." And then her eyes widened with joy. "Oh!" she breathed.

Marc grinned. "Exactly," he said. "The proof is right here on the bed. Your father may not have spent much of his life with you, Merrily, but he loved you dearly."

"Yes," she whispered as she swallowed her tears. "I see that he did. But that particular clue gets us no closer to finding the one we are looking for."

"No," replied Marc smoothly, "but it does get our digestive organs in better shape to tackle Lucy's luncheon. Come, my dear," he said as he rose from the bed, "let us stop for a while and see if we can discover a clue as to what Lucy has piled upon our plates."

Mack was waiting for them in the saloon. Marc had never been so glad to see someone in his life. He strode forward and slapped the huge man on his back.

"Is it safe to ask for something to eat?" he inquired with a grin.

A chuckle rumbled low in Mack's throat. "Aye, yer uppityship. Found me the purtiest gal I ever did see. Made her fix somp'in, too, so's I could taste her vittles." He sighed contentedly. "Like honey in a gum tree, it was. Grabbed her right on th' spot."

The earl smiled in relief. "Then have her serve us, man," he ordered eagerly. "I could eat the whole gum tree."

In only a few moments, the three of them were relishing a savory stew, fresh-baked bread, and fruit tarts with sweetened cream, prepared by the competent hands of a maid from the village named Charlotte. Marc took one bite of the delicious stew and sent Grimes scurrying into the kitchen with his compliments.

"Did you happen to see my cousins when you were about, Mack?" Merrily asked later over a fork full of tart.

"Nay, my lady," answered the large man.

Marc looked up from his plate and gave her a searching look. "What is it, Merrily?" he asked gently.

"Nothing, really," she responded. "I suppose I am a bit nervous about what Lucius will say when he sees the untidiness of my father's room. I shall ask Lucy to help me straighten it up before we continue our search, I think. After Father sold so many of the household goods to pay his debts, I am persuaded that Lucius will be quite overset if he sees that what little is left has been trifled with."

Merrily's concerns reminded Marc of the missing statuary he had noticed upon his arrival. His eyes automatically scanned the saloon. It was indeed bare. Bright patches of wallpaper stood out from their surroundings, marking the places where dozens of pictures once stood. Something began to nag at the back of Marc's mind. Pictures! That was it. He had been in enough of the rooms to realize that none of them contained any pictures. Yet there was one . . . Suddenly he sprang to his feet.

"Come with me," he ordered as he grabbed Merrily's hand and pulled her after him. Mack stared after them in consternation, then shrugged his massive shoulders and slid another tart onto his already groaning plate.

"Where are we going?" inquired Merrily as she half-ran, half-stumbled to keep pace with the earl.

"To look at every room in this house," answered Marc purposefully.

"Why?" gasped Merrily.

"To see if there are any pictures," he responded.

For the next half hour, they burst into room after room, slamming the doors open and quickly scanning the walls until, with no letup in his pace, Marc dragged Merrily up to the second level. Again they repeated their hasty searches, striding from room to room until Marc had satisfied himself that there were no pictures hanging in any of them.

"What about the attics? The servants' quarters?" asked Marc as he gripped Merrily's shoulders.

"They are empty. Their contents were sold long ago. And whatever servants we have had since then have slept in a small area off the kitchen." Merrily seized Marc's hand in her own then. "Marc, what is this all about?"

"Come. I will show you." He took her hand in his, more gently this time, and led her back into her father's room. Quickly, he crossed to the dressing room and pulled her inside. Then he placed his hands on her shoulders and turned her to face the narrow chest of drawers. "Merrily, there are no pictures in the entire house," he said, and then he pointed to the wall, "except that one. There must be a reason for it."

Merrily liked the way the heat of the earl's large body warmed her back. She instinctively leaned against him, resting her soft curls against his broad shoulder. "There is a reason for it," she responded with a sigh of pleasure. "My father told me he would never get rid of that picture. He said the little girl in the scene looked like me. Besides," she added, nestling closer as Marc's arms slid around her waist, "I have no idea where he purchased the painting. The author is unknown, so who would have bought it even if Father had wanted to sell it?"

Marc shook his head. "There is more to it than that. I feel it in my bones. And I have learned to follow my hunches. They have never led me astray." He moved Merrily forward, then, absentmindedly rubbing his chin against her fragrant hair as he studied the painting. The slight, rasping motion of his whiskers against her delicate skin sent swirls of sensation rippling over Merrily's nerve endings and she instinctively tilted her face up for more. But the dratted earl was not paying attention. He was leaning forward instead, squinting slightly to get a better look at the painting's detail.

"Look, my dear," he said at last as he lifted the painting down from the wall. "Look at the painting closely."

Merrily took the picture from the earl and began to study it. It was no bigger than a piece of writing paper and had been worked with a fine brush so that small details were readily evident. The painting portrayed a young girl sitting on an island in the middle of a small stream. Floating on the rippling water were five toy boats. Behind the girl was a field of grain bent by the will of a warm summer breeze. The girl was dressed in a mobcap, out from under which a few strands of honey-gold hair had escaped, a peasant's gown of soft blue, and a white, lace trimmed apron. And there, embroidered on the apron's bib, were five tiny . . .

"Wooden shoes!" gasped Merrily as her eyes rounded.

"Precisely," laughed Marc as he squeezed her tightly.

"This is the clue, is it not?" cried Merrily as she turned in his arms and hugged him joyously. "Oh, Marc, you have found it!"

"Lord Clairmont!" shrieked Miss Plumley from the doorway. "Unhand that girl! The two of you . . . alone in a bedchamber . . . embracing! Dearest, come away at once. You have been compromised!"

Marc burst into laughter. "How many times is it now, do you suppose?" he whispered with a mischievous grin.

Merrily groaned and dropped her forehead against Marc's chest. "I have lost count," she sighed in reply. "Well, my lord, how am I going to get out of this one?"

"Simple. We shall ignore it," he answered as he nuzzled her ear. Merrily thought her skin might just shiver itself right on down into a puddle on the floor. "Plum!" cried the earl in the very next second. "Come and see what we have discovered."

"Discovered? Why, but I just saw . . . and your arms were . . . discovered, you say?" Immediately Miss Plumley toddled closer. Marc held out the small picture to her and she gazed at it indifferently. "Why this is just that silly painting Simon did," she uttered in dismissal.

"My father painted it?" asked Merrily.

"Oh, yes, dearest," Plum replied. "He took a notion one day to paint. Hadn't lifted a brush since he was in leading strings either, mind you. But it was one of those rare times when he was home for a few weeks and he seemed to want to capture you in oils."

"So the girl in the painting truly is Merrily," concluded Marc. "I wonder why your father would tell you otherwise."

"To hide its significance, perhaps," offered Merrily.

"Yes, I believe you are right, my dear," agreed the earl. "Plum, we have concluded that this picture is the clue that will lead us to the list."

"Never say so," responded Miss Plumley as her eyes narrowed slightly. "How have you come to this conclusion, my lord?"

The earl pointed at the young child's pinafore. "There are wooden shoes here, do you see?"

"Yes indeed," marveled the elderly woman. "Oh, dear me, yes indeed!" She lifted her pudgy fingertips to her lips in her growing excitement. "But what does the painting tell us, my dears? What is the clue?"

"We were just at the point of trying to figure that out when you joined us, dear," answered Merrily.

"I think we can say with some assurance that the number five is significant," offered Marc.

"There are five shoes," cried Miss Plumley.

"And five toy boats," added Merrily. "Boats might indicate a harbor or a port of some kind."

"Just so," agreed Marc, "and the number five must indicate that the place we are looking for is one of the ancient Cinque Ports, but which one?"

Together, three avid faces studied the picture in silence.

"The grain in the background, Marc," exclaimed Merrily excitedly. "It is rye!"

"And Rye was one of the Cinque Ports!" cried Plum. "Oh dear, dear, dear. I shall need my salts. The excitement, my dear . . ."

"Fustian," smiled Merrily as she hugged her companion. "Oh, Marc, this is wonderful," she breathed as her eyes sparkled with enthusiasm. "We know that we must look in Rye."

"But where?" asked Plum in a bewildered voice.

Marc took the painting from her and searched the pebbled surface, studying not only the picture, but also its frame. Then he turned it over and began to scan the back.

"Here is something," he said suddenly. "Some words have been inscribed on the back of the frame. The writing is very small and the ink has faded badly, but . . . let me take it into better light."

Merrily and Plum followed Marc as he left the dressing room and crossed to the long windows that looked out over the park.

He rubbed his thumb back and forth over the writing and turned the frame toward the light.

"My . . . Saintly . . . Merry," he read slowly. "My Saintly Merry."

"My Saintly Merry?" questioned Plum.

"My Saintly Merry," repeated Merrily.

And then suddenly the answer came. Their eyes widened and their jaws dropped open and they clutched at one another in sheer gladness.

"St. Mary's!" all three chorused together. "It has to mean the Church of St. Mary's!"

"You are saved, my dearest," breathed Plum with such joyful relief on her round face that Merrily caught her up in an enveloping hug.

"Let us not go into alt prematurely," cautioned Marc. "I will not rest easily until the list is in my hand and the perpetrators of this plot are known to me."

"You are right, of course, Marc," said Merrily more soberly. "There is still much ahead for us. Will we go to Rye soon?"

"Tomorrow," Marc responded. "You will, of course, want to accompany us, Plum," he added with a grin. "Under no circumstances must Merrily be compromised."

"Never say so!" huffed Miss Plumley. "The very idea that I would allow such a thing to occur is the outside of eno— Why, Lord Clairmont," she tittered suddenly, "I am persuaded that you are jesting with me!"

"Never say so!" parroted the rag-mannered earl as he led the ladies from the room.

A light rain began to fall shortly after the carriage pulled out of the drive the following morning. The sky clung low and thick to the tops of the trees, funneling a chill wind over the outriders as they pulled up their collars against it. Marc was riding Barbary and once again had assigned Mack the ribbons. Merrily could hear the low grumbles of the footmen as they complained about the turn in the weather, and was grateful for Marc's provision of the carriage. She smiled encouragingly at

Plum and tucked her hands under the thick traveling shawl for extra warmth.

She had not seen her cousins before they had left the Manor. Merrily thought that rather odd. She had wanted to inform them of her plan to return the next day, but had had to be satisfied with giving that information to Grimes. She knew very well what the demands of running an estate could be, but could not understand her cousins' unusual absence. She remembered Marc's warning, then, that the ones who were threatening her were very likely people who were close to her. Could it be Lucius and Willard? No, it was impossible. They were too young to be involved in a spy ring whose members, like her father, must have been participants for a long time. But might her Uncle Boggs have been involved as well and recruited his sons later? If so, it would mean that he would have had to be the one who killed her father. Could he have hated his own brother enough to destroy him? Merrily shuddered at the thought.

"Are you cold, dearest?" inquired Plum solicitously.

"No, Plum. I was merely thinking."

"Well, if you are, dear," responded Plum, not attending to a word Merrily had said, "signal Lord Clairmont for a fire to reheat our bricks." She settled against the soft squabs once again and soon drifted into a light sleep.

Merrily continued her contemplation. It could not have been Uncle Boggs. Someone had killed him as well, after all. And his wife. Could Lucius and Willard have killed their own parents? Merrily's heart began to pound at that horrible thought. No. They were hateful creatures, she knew, toads if one were totally honest about it, but she could not believe they would stoop to murdering their own flesh and blood. What would have been their reason? Still, she must not let her feelings cloud her judgment. She would have to be very careful around them. They were not acting normally. And as even Thomas had warned, they were indeed up to something.

The carriage pulled into the innyard of The Black Crow near Hastings close to the noon hour. Marc dismounted quickly and, after giving instructions for the care of his cattle, helped Plum and Merrily to descend.

"Something is wrong," he said when he saw lines of worry furrowing across Merrily's brow.

"Not really, Marc," she replied. "I have just been considering my circumstances."

Marc led her toward the inn, leaving Mack to escort Miss Plumley. "You do not have any circumstances, my dear. They belong to me."

Merrily stared at him in astonishment. She was just about to sputter an indignant reply when she realized that she was oddly comforted by the earl's overbearing arrogance. She laughed softly instead.

"You are the most incomprehensible man I have ever met, my lord."

"Just so," replied the earl smugly. "Tell me what you have been thinking."

They entered the inn then, and Merrily delayed her answer until the innkeeper had brought a delicately seasoned kidney pie, sliced mutton, warm whole-grain bread, and a tray of fresh fruit into the private parlor Marc had bespoken. As Merrily poured the ale, she continued.

"I have been considering who might be involved in this plot, Marc," she said softly. "I am afraid of the conclusions that could be reached."

Marc sensed that she did not want to be more specific. His inclination was affirmed when he saw her glance toward Plum. She was protecting her companion, well aware of the strong ties the elderly woman had to each of the family members. He reached beneath the table and took her hand.

"You are not alone," he said softly, thinking of the entire English Foreign service that was aware of her every move. "Everything will be well, Merrily. Please try to trust me."

Merrily's eyes glowed sea green. How she loved this funny, arrogant, tender man! "I do, Marc. Completely," she whispered.

He smiled at her then, and just for a moment, though she was sure she had imagined it, she saw the warmth of love in his eyes. He squeezed her hand gently. "I have taken a room, my dear," he informed her. "There is time for you and Plum to rest a bit and still allow us to be able to reach Rye by nightfall."

"Thank you, Marc," Merrily replied. "The rest will be welcome, especially for Plum. Will you stay here in the parlor?"

"Yes. Mack and I have some things to discuss. Go along now, my dear. The innkeeper will show you the way."

"Very well," she responded as she raised her eyebrow with a knowing smile. "Come, Plum, dear," she ordered. "We have been dismissed."

Merrily was grateful for the crackling fire that had been lit in the comfortable room. She enjoyed the cup of fragrant tea that a serving girl had left on a table near the fire to keep warm, and appreciated the soft cleanliness of the bed as she helped Plum lower her bulk onto it and slide over to her accustomed position closest to the wall. It was her concentration on getting Plum comfortably settled, bending as she was over the bed with her back to the door, that kept her from hearing the two men as they crept into the chamber. And because she was unaware, she did not see her attackers before they were upon her.

A large hand clamped over Merrily's mouth at the same time that a strong, male arm wrapped itself around her slender waist in a vicelike grip. Merrily struggled frantically, throwing her head back against the hooded face of her captor as she attempted to bump something sensitive and cause him enough pain to force him to release her. At the solid contact, the man yelped in surprise. And then Plum threw off the coverlet and began to scream.

"Silence her!" ground out Merrily's captor in a gravely voice.

Immediately the second man ran to the bed and, after a feeble struggle, wrestled Plum to the mattress. Then, casting about for something to use against the hysterical woman, he seized the pillow from under her head and stuffed one of the corners into her open mouth. Merrily's eyes widened with fear for her companion. She cried out against the muffle of the man's hand and renewed her struggles energetically.

"Quick, let us leave," hissed the man holding Merrily. "Those screams will have alerted the men below."

Before Merrily could counter his movements, he grabbed her two hands behind her back and forced her to lie down on the soiled carpet that lay near the bed. In an instant, he had subdued her squirming form and rolled her up into a tight coil of carpet, imprisoning her and effectively baffling her cries of outrage. The second man immediately left off his efforts to subdue Plum and ran to pick up one end of the rolled carpet. As soon as his companion had lifted the other end, they stumbled toward the door.

They ran into a solid wall. And the solid wall was Marc. The leader screeched with fright and dropped his end of the carpet. A muffled shriek from inside the carpet roll told the others that Merrily did not take such treatment kindly. It took only a split second for the other kidnapper to do the same, and even less time for them both to scramble across the bedchamber and throw themselves, in a shower of broken glass, out the window.

"Oh, do stop them!" cried Miss Plumley as she rose to her knees on the soft mattress and immediately toppled over.

"Go after them, Mack," commanded Marc in a calm voice as he looked toward the bed. The huge man was gone before the earl had finished speaking. It was immediately evident to the earl that Plum was disheveled and dazed, but essentially unharmed.

He entered the bedchamber, then, and stood for several seconds watching the wiggling, thumping, bulging carpet roll, trying to contain his seething anger. The bastards had tried to steal his lady! He would never let the woman out of his sight again. And what he would do to the two jackanapes who touched her when he caught them did not bear thinking about. At present, however, there was Merrily's welfare to consider. She was his most important concern now. He took a deep, cleansing breath and felt his anger fade somewhat. Poor darling! She must surely be frightened out of her wits. He would have to be gentle with her, solicitous. She would need his calm strength. With these thoughts at the forefront of his mind, he bent over and found the edge of the carpet. Then with infinite care, he gripped the tasseled edge with his strong fingers and yanked.

Merrily spilled out of the twirling carpet in a flurry of petticoats, muslin, and drifting lint. She hoisted herself to her elbow and reached up to steady her dizzily spinning head. She groaned, not as yet aware of her indelicate sprawl, and looked around a room that wavered in an unfocused blur.

"Are you all right, Plum?" she breathed unsteadily.

"Well, I . . . no, but . . . when they came in, you see . . . oh, I really do need my salts," she cried, and then reached like a woman possessed for her reticule.

"Hold on, Plum, dear," whispered Merrily. "I shall come to help you just as soon as I decide which end of the room is the top and which is the bottom."

Marc would have stooped to help her the moment she twirled out onto the floor. That had certainly been his intention. But he was halted in mid-crouch by the thoroughly enchanting display of Lady Mirthton's curvaceous legs. He was awestruck. Who could have known that such treasures would be hidden beneath her appalling skirts? They were perfectly proportioned, slim, and wonderfully dimpled at the knees. Perhaps they were not real. They could be merely the products of his wishful thinking. He owed it to himself to find out. He would only take one touch. Just one. And then he would set the wedding date.

"Lord Clairmont!" shrieked Miss Plumley as the earl bent to her charge and slid one large, warm hand up the length of her thigh.

The earl came slowly out of his daze. His eyes gleamed into Merrily's. She was real. Every beautiful inch of her. He smiled like a cat with a mouse in its claws. "Do not get in a pucker, Plum," he said smoothly, "I am merely checking Lady Mirthton for injuries."

Merrily lifted an eyebrow at that plumper. She swatted his hand away and, as quickly as she could, tucked her exposed limbs under her wrinkled skirts. She held out her hands, then, and the earl helped her to rise.

"Are you all right, my sweet?" Marc murmured as his arms closed around her.

"Yes, though I fear it will be awhile before my eyes stop playing cricket inside my head."

Marc smiled and picked a piece of lint out of Merrily's gloriously tousled hair. "If you keep looking at me so scandalously, my dear, I am going to climb right inside you to referee." He covered her gasp with another question. "Did you see the bounders?" he asked gently.

"No, I was in hopes that you had. They wore hoods, Marc."

"I know. Did they speak?"

"Just a few words," Merrily replied. "But nothing that would indicate who they were. Could they have been the same two who attacked you on Conduit Street?"

"From the shape of their physiques, I would doubt it. But I suppose it is a possibility."

A soft sound drew their attention toward the door in time to see Mack enter the room. Marc looked at him searchingly as Merrily crossed the chamber to help Plum rise. "Did you find them?" he asked quietly.

"Nay. The bloody bas—beggin' yer pardon, ladies . . . them two weasels was gone afore I could throw a saddle on Barbary. I looked, but 'thout knowin' the woods hereabouts, I couldn't find all the hidey-holes."

Marc nodded with a vexed twist to his lips. When he turned to Merrily, his jaw was rigid with displeasure. "We will be leaving for Rye momentarily, my dear. You and Plum must take a few moments to repair the damage done to yourselves during your ordeal. Mack and I will wait below. But I warn you, if you tarry longer than ten minutes, I shall come thundering up the stairs to rescue you."

"We shall be ready, Marc," said Merrily with a smile.

As Marc and Mack descended the stairs, Marc spoke softly. "What of our friends? Did they see the two assailants?"

"Saw 'em, but didn't know they was trouble. They didn't

know we was plannin' a trip, so they couldn't get agents here ahead o' us. They thought them two was just travelers leavin' th' inn.''

''There seem to be some definite holes in the protection they are able to give us, are there not?'' responded the earl. ''Well, at least they know now that we are headed for Rye.''

''Aye. They'll have men there ahead o' us this time.''

The earl nodded. ''Keep your eyes wide open, though, Mack,'' he ordered. ''There is something about all this that does not ring true.''

''What'd ye be meanin', yer nobleness?'' asked the giant man.

The earl thought for a moment, and then looked piercingly at his friend. ''Have you noticed, Mack, that on some occasions I am the one who is attacked, yet on others the target is Merrily?''

''Now that ye mention it, that be so,'' nodded Mack in response.

''I cannot be positive yet, Mack,'' said the earl as he whacked his crop against the side of his polished riding boot, ''but I think we have to be prepared for the possibility that a threat is coming at Merrily from not one source, but from two.''

Chapter 12

The cold drizzle that had plagued the travelers for the better part of the day finally drifted off to play havoc with the boats plying their trade in the Channel just before the earl's carriage passed through Land Gate into the ancient medieval town of Rye. Merrily drew back the drapery for a breath of refreshing, rain-washed air just as the massive stone towers passed by. She was entranced. The town had seen so much history. High up on the towers, holes could still be seen where long ago the town's defenders poured boiling oil down upon those who came against them. She studied the forty-foot towers with a shiver of respect.

The carriage continued on, rocking over the ancient cobblestones that paved the narrow, twisted, labyrinth of streets, while Merrily regarded in awe the odd jumble of buildings whose sagging roofs and crooked chimneys looked like a carpenter's concept of hell. In time the conveyance turned from busy Market Street into the quiet of East Street and came to a halt before the Durrant House Hotel. Marc helped the ladies alight from the carriage and watched while porters swept their bags inside and stable boys scurried to care for the cattle.

"Good evening, Lord Clairmont," cried the proprietor as the earl escorted the ladies inside.

"Good evening, Mr. Jenks," returned the earl jovially.

"You are known to him!" whispered Merrily in surprise.

"Yes, I have stayed here often. Many soldiers do. The hotel is a relay station for carrier pigeons, my dear. The government uses them to bring in dispatches from the war. And now if you will excuse me, I shall go make arrangements for our rooms."

"Of course," replied Merrily. "Plum and I shall warm ourselves by the fire while we wait. Oh but, Marc . . ."

"The gentleman always pays," asserted Lord Clairmont with a knowing grin, and he strolled away with the proprietor to the sound of Merrily's chuckles.

Marc was true to his word. He did not let Merrily out of his sight the entire night. After a delicious meal of turtle soup, salmon in a field of smelts, a joint of roast beef, stuffed grouse, sliced tongue, boiled potatoes, vegetables, and trifle, the earl made it very clear that he would be sleeping with Lady Mirthton. Plum hoisted herself into a ponderous pucker over the whole scandalous idea . . . until, that is, the earl explained that she would be there, too.

"Oh," said the very correct Miss Plumley.

"Yes," continued Marc convincingly. "Try to think of our situation as if we had been stranded in a stable on an isolated country lane during a blinding snow storm, Miss Plumley. We would all of us be sleeping together in that circumstance, would we not? And no one's honor would have been besmirched by morning because you would, of course, have kept careful watch over Merrily's virtue."

"Well . . ."

"You see the need, do you not, my dear Miss Plumley? Merrily was attacked only this afternoon."

"I suppose . . ."

"We were together once before, if you recall, and I was a pattern card of gentlemanly propriety," added Marc as he sensed the flustered woman's coming capitulation. He did not think that this was quite the best time to mention, though, that he had spent a good part of that night holding Merrily in his arms. The earl smiled to himself at the pleasant memory.

"Oh, very well," huffed Plum. "But I warn you, young man,

I shall be a veritable Amazon should you think to put something
by me."

"Never say so!" grinned Marc. "A regular out and outer
like you, Plum? What sort of cocklehead do you think me, my
dear?" he teased, and so the four of them had passed the night
together.

Early the following morning, Marc and Mack removed themselves to their own room to shave and dress for the day. Several
minutes later they met Merrily and Plum in front of the cozy
warmth of the arched brick fireplace in the common rooms.
While Plum was garbed in her usual somber black, Merrily
was wearing a chartreuse monstrosity with six pink flounces
and a nosegay of yellow and pink flowers dividing her breasts.
Marc moaned inwardly. Each day with Merrily was becoming
an adventure in forbearance. He could not wait to get his hands
on her in many more ways than the obvious. After breaking
their fast and gathering their cloaks, they set out at last for the
Church of St. Mary's.

Marc, mounted on Barbary, led the carriage down one tortu-
ous street after another toward the somber stone church, wondering how they were going to go about finding the list once
they got there. He let his eyes rise to the church's prominent
tower, whose heights were capped by a conical roof and a tall,
gleaming cross. A resonant bell began to chime and he glanced
immediately toward the carriage, smiling as Merrily's fair head
popped out of the window, anxious to watch the two gilded
cherubs, called the Quarter Boys, chime out the quarter hour
as they flanked one of the oldest clocks in all of England.

She takes such joy in everything, he thought as the carriage
pulled up in front of the ancient church steps. He loved that
about her. He needed it, too, he realized with a bit of a shock.
She wiped away the cynicism, the cold, aloof detachment, that
had gripped him since the war. She made him feel again, yet
softened that vulnerability with laughter. He thought, then, of
all the times he had arrogantly claimed that she belonged to
him and grinned. She did, of course. But suddenly he had come
to understand that that was not the half of it. Without even
being aware of it, she had woven bonds of joy around his heart,

capturing him as completely as a trap ensnares a hare. And he was well and truly caught. Now he belonged to her.

"Where shall we start?" asked Merrily as she took his proffered hand after he had dismounted and stepped from the carriage.

"I have been thinking about that," responded Marc, turning to help Plum descend. "Since your father used art as his clue, it would be logical to assume that he might have hidden the list among the works of art in the church."

"Simon was not a very logical man," interjected Plum as she stepped down to join them.

"Well, we shall just have to see, will we not?" said Merrily as she grinned at Marc.

"If we cannot find a clue among the art works," suggested Marc, "perhaps he gave a gift to the church at some time in the past and has hidden the list there."

"Yes," agreed Merrily, "but how will we know what it is?"

"There will be a record of it, my dear," said Marc. "I am persuaded your father would not have wanted to make your finding the list impossible."

"Just extremely difficult," laughed Merrily. "Well, we shall not find it standing here. Come along and let us get started."

A cursory search of the paintings and statuary that warmed the cold, stone walls of the ancient church proved fruitless. While Mack attended the horses and kept watch near the carriage, Merrily, Marc, and Miss Plumley resigned themselves to the necessity of a careful study of each art treasure, in the end even going so far as to lift the frames away from the wall in an effort to look behind them. Yet nothing even remotely resembling a wooden *sabot* was found. They did attract the attention of the vicar, though. Just as they had about given up hope of finding anything, the portly, balding man strolled to their side and offered his hand with a warm smile.

"I could not help noticing your . . . interest in our masterpieces, my lord," he commented after introductions had been made.

Marc laughed softly. "A rather uncommon interest, I wager you are thinking, sir," he replied.

"I own that it is not often a peer of the realm takes a greater interest in the back of our paintings than he does in the front, but to each his own, I always say."

"We are not quite as cork-brained as we seem, sir," said Merrily with a laugh. "We are looking for something, you see. We believe it to be in your church."

"Ah, a mystery!" cried the vicar.

"Just so," responded the earl. "However, our search of your paintings has turned up nothing, and it is rather important that we find it."

"Perhaps if you told me . . . .," hinted the vicar as his brows lifted expectantly.

"That we cannot do," said Marc with genuine regret. "But we would be grateful for a look at your parish records. Perhaps the item is listed among the gifts the church has received over the years."

"The records are available to anyone who wishes to see them, of course," responded the vicar, "but it is cold in the sanctuary this time of the morning. Would you not care to retire to my study to carry out your research? There is a nice warm fire going and I would be pleased if you would share a cup of hot tea with me."

"Delightful!" answered Plum before the rest could speak, and so, with a shrug of agreement, Marc followed the others down the aisle.

It was an hour and two pots of tea later before the vicar brought the record books to his study for the three to peruse. He excused himself, then, pleading parish business, but gave them permission to use his study and his teapot for as long as they needed that day. Marc divided the musty books between them and, with a fresh cup of steaming tea at their elbows, they turned the first pages and began.

Three hours later, Merrily was ready to rip up at the first person who walked through the door. She had never been so frustrated. She could not understand how Marc could sit so quietly, reading page after page, none of which told them anything, and not want to poke his fives into the nearest wall.

"It is no use!" she finally said testily.

"Have another cup of tea, dearest," said Plum absentmindedly.

Marc raised his head at her outburst and grinned at her.
"Finished your stack, have you?"

"Yes, and there is nothing. Oh, Marc, I am so vexed I could
stomp the Needles right into the sea."

The earl chuckled softly. "I think Plum has the right idea.
Have another cup of tea."

Merrily made a *moue* of distaste. "What are you looking at
with such concentration?" she asked him somewhat petulantly.
She circled the desk and came to sit beside him on the vicar's
well-worn leather sofa.

"The vicar gave us the parish birth and death records by
mistake. I was just following a hunch," the earl replied.

"Hmm, another one of those," responded Merrily as she
leaned closer.

"Yes, another one of those," he said as his eyes continued
to scan the pages and his arm reached around to pull her even
closer. And then he stiffened.

"What is it?" asked Merrily.

"Devil a bit!" he murmured.

"Marc, what is it?" insisted Merrily.

"It seems my hunch was correct, my dear," he said softly.
"What your father wanted you to find is here."

"The list?" cried Merrily as Plum hurried over to join them.

"No, sweet," answered Marc in a quiet voice. He placed his
finger on one of the records of birth then, and turned his eyes
to Merrily's. "Read this."

Merrily picked up the book from Marc's lap and read the
entry aloud. "Born to Sadie Dickerson, weaver, a boy, Boggs
Everett, 16 June, 1770. Father: Phineas Mirthton, Viscount
Collingwood."

"Pon my word!" breathed Plum. "Boggs was . . . a butter
stamp!"

"So it seems," said Marc softly.

Silence filled the small study for several long moments, while
each in his own way absorbed the shock of Marc's discovery.

Merrily leaned into the warmth of Marc's side, drawing on his strength and steady support.

"This means nothing now," she finally said. "Uncle Boggs is dead. And I do not understand why Father went to such lengths to lead me to this information."

"I think it was because it was the only way he could insure your inheritance, my dear," said the earl thoughtfully. "Acknowledged or not, Boggs Mirthton was the illegitimate issue of your grandfather. Because of that fact, his claim to the title and estate was shaky, if not nonexistent, as is Lucius's. No, my dear, it is my belief that Mirthton Manor rightfully belongs to you and that any court in the land will uphold your claim."

"'Pon my soul," muttered Plum.

"That would certainly explain Uncle Boggs's antagonism toward my father all those years," said Merrily, "but why would my father keep the information secret? Why would he feel the need to put clues to the truth in a painting?"

"Simon was not very logical," said Plum. "He was an odd duck. I always thought so."

Marc smiled. "I can only guess, of course," he replied, "but I think your father painted the picture as a sort of insurance policy for his father's legitimate heirs, my dear. You told me once that he was a wastrel. He must have regretted his weaknesses, knowing that his stronger, albeit illegitimate, brother would eventually outlast him. Perhaps Boggs held something over him that prevented him from exposing the truth. We will probably never know. But by providing a road map, so to speak, to the truth, he insured that at some time, among future generations, the true heirs would again take precedence."

"Oh, Marc," said Merrily as she rested her head against his welcoming shoulder. "So much was going on all around me, and I was so unaware."

"You were a child, my sweet," he soothed. "But you are a child no more. What will you do with this information?"

"I do not know," she replied. "I fear I am too stunned to do anything at the moment."

"There was no list," said Plum forcefully. "We have come all this way and there is nothing but a bit of ancient family history."

Marc caught Merrily's startled glance with his own. "Come now, Plum," he cajoled, "the information is rather important to Merrily's future, would you not admit?"

Plum stared at Marc for several seconds and then seemed to recover herself. "Of course, of course. Pray, pay no attention to me. I am an old woman, and have become overtired. Dearest, I have made a cake of myself, have I not?"

"Fustian," said Merrily with a smile. "We have now seen what we were meant to see, so I suggest that we go back to the Durrant House so that you can rest. Would you agree, my lord?" she asked.

"Indeed. We all need a chance to stretch our legs. I can tell you one thing I do not need, though," he said as he opened the study door.

"What is that, my lord?" asked Merrily gamely.

"Another cup of tea," he answered, and the ancient stone sanctuary rang with pleasant laughter.

Merrily snipped the last of the rose hips from the bushes behind Mirthton Manor the following afternoon and dropped them in the laden basket she carried at her side. She marveled at the tiny embryo of contentment that had been born inside her after the previous day's discovery, and nurtured it with an inward smile. She had a home! She did not see how her cousins could force her to leave it now. She did not want to force them to leave either, however. They were all the family she had left, after all, and were not responsible for the accident of their birth any more than she was.

But she knew their character, the toads! She would need to assert her rights as her father's heir because she expected that they would fight her every step of the way. There were so many things she wanted to do on the estate . . . things to make it more productive and self-sufficient . . . things she had wanted to do since before her father had died but could not for lack of money. But once she had turned the estate around financially, she could finally begin. The very thought filled her with excitement.

The carriage ride back to the Manor from Rye had proved, happily, to be uneventful and she had used the hours of quiet solitude while Plum napped to ponder her present state. It would be difficult for her as a woman to carry out her plans at first, she knew, but the tenants were good men and loyal. She would be able to count on their helpfulness. She was prepared for the fact that it would undoubtedly take years to reverse the Manor's financial picture, but she welcomed the consuming work, for the reality was that she would need toil for her mind and body if she were ever to be able to set aside her love for Marc. And set it aside she must. Whether they found the list or not, their time together was almost over and she needed to begin to deal with it.

Determined footsteps on the gravel nearby alerted her to his presence. She knew it was him even before she turned around. It was odd, she thought, how the heart could so easily sense the other part of itself. She turned, then, and let her bright smile reveal to Marc the fullness of her joy in seeing him.

"Had I known you earlier, my dear," he said with a disconcerting intensity in his gaze, "I would have used you in the war as a secret weapon." He gained her side, then slipped her basket onto his own arm while he raised the fingers of her hand to his warm lips. It was a very neat maneuver.

"Indeed," she laughed as his lips remained to nibble.

"Oh, yes," the earl finally said as he raised his head. "I would have simply turned you toward the enemy and asked you to smile, and the entire French army would have been stunned into immobility."

"What a hum," grinned the lady. "More than likely they would have been immobilized by fits of hysterics over the sight of my drunken teeth."

The earl shrugged. "Either way the result would have been the same," he said casually, and then he tucked her hand in the crook of his arm and grinned while Merrily's laughter fell like refreshing sunshine over the somber, sleeping garden.

"I have missed seeing my cousins yet again today, Marc," she said. "I believe that they must be avoiding us."

"Undoubtedly," he responded as he began to stroll with her down the barren path. "I wonder that we might not have made a very favorable impression on dear Lucius and Willard." Merrily's soft answering chuckles fell dully against the denuded trees.

Marc kept his comments light intentionally. He did not wish to reveal the fact that he had been anxious to see her cousins himself, but for a very different reason. If they had been, as he suspected, involved in the attack on Merrily in the inn at Hastings, then there was every chance that they had injured themselves in the fall from the window. It was true that there was a convenient stack of hay just below, but even if no bones had been broken, surely they would have received cuts from breaking through those panes of glass. Their continued absence suggested that he was right.

He had eagerly awaited their return the night before, even asking Mack and each of the footmen to watch for any sign of them, but he had been frustratingly disappointed. He had even sent Mack into the village to consult with Castlereagh's men, but they, too, had seen no sign of them. Finally, sensing that events were beginning to move more quickly, Marc had asked that the agents take up positions a discreet distance from the Manor house, and to keep themselves hidden and in readiness until their presence was needed. Marc ground his teeth and squeezed Merrily's hand as it rested trustingly in the crook of his elbow. As far as he was concerned, the bastards had as good as confessed their guilt. Now all he wanted to do was get them into custody.

"How am I to find the list, Marc?" asked Merrily softly as she walked beside him.

The plaintiveness in her voice tugged the earl back from his reverie and pierced his heart. "*We,* my dear. Will you never get it straight?"

She lifted her eyes to his and smiled gently. "Very well, my lord, '*we,*'" she answered. Slowly they left the main walk that passed through the rose garden and stepped onto a path that in early spring would be lined with the bright primary colors of tulips, crocus, and neat rows of daffodils.

"Your father may have had his vices, Merrily," offered the earl, "but he was not unintelligent. He did survive for a good part of his life as an active spy, after all."

"And he had the foresight to leave the clues his family would need in that picture," she added, "but what is all this praise of my scapegrace father leading to, my lord?"

"That he must have been able think clearly in tight situations, my dear," answered the earl, "and that he was in the habit of relaying information in other than the usual manner."

A bench was cradled near the ancient arms of a spreading yew, and Merrily drew Marc off the path to sit down upon it. "My father had no idea that I would be asked to recover his list, Marc," she stated.

"No," he agreed as he joined her on the cold stone bench, "but he was a man accustomed to dealing with dangerous spies. He was used to the keeping and revealing of secrets. A man who thought like a foreign agent would not have said anything about the list in the first place unless he wanted you to know about it, even if he were near death. He would have made his confession to you and let it go at that. No, my dear, I believe the information is there in something that he said. We have only to look closely and we will discover it."

"But I have told you already what he said, Marc," responded Merrily. "The only thing we have to go on is this 'sign of the *sabot.*'"

"That is what we have assumed, my dear. But what if the clue he gave you leads not to the list, but to the sign itself?"

"Then I would say that we are both bound for Bedlam, Marc. How can the words point to the sign itself?"

Marc shook his head, dislodging a golden curl. "I do not know . . . yet. But the answer is there. I know it." He sprang to his feet and began pacing back and forth before the bench, pinching his lower lip between his thumb and forefinger. Merrily watched him with growing amusement.

"You resemble one of my kneecaps, my lord," she giggled.

The earl halted his pacing and frowned at her. "It helps me

to think," he muttered, and then resumed his action. "Tell me the words again, exactly as you remember them."

"He said, 'Forgive me. I have spied against my country.' Then, 'There is a list,' and after that, 'the sign of the *sabot.*'"

"And a few mutterings after that?" queried the earl as he stopped to look at her.

"Yes," Merrily replied.

"Not much to go on, is it?" murmured the earl as he resumed his pacing.

Fifteen minutes later he again stopped. Shaking his head in frustration, he strode back to the bench and seated himself beside Merrily. "I cannot think of anything else the words could mean," he said with a sigh of resignation.

Merrily smiled and slipped her hand through Marc's arm. "Perhaps the clue is not in the words, my Friday-faced lord," she said.

"What do you mean?" insisted Marc with a piercing gaze.

"I am not quite sure," she responded with a shrug. "The thought just came to me while I was trying to think of something to say to cheer you up."

Marc's gaze softened and grew tender. "And what did you come up with, my sweet?" he whispered.

Suddenly Merrily was lost in the blue of Marc's eyes. She felt herself melting toward him, wanting to become a part of him. Her whole body thrummed with the desire to become one with his warmth.

"I-I could think of only one thing that might cheer you," she breathed as her hand drifted upward and, for the first time, touched a man's chest. The shock that swept over her was electric.

"Tell me," urged Marc, holding himself under tighter control than he ever knew he had the strength for. His eyes blazed at the passion he saw rising in the emerald depths of hers.

"I lo—t-trust you, Marc," she whispered.

He held the world in his hands. His body was a skyrocket leading the others at Vauxhall, bursting into the black vastness of the sky like an explosion of multi-colored happiness. He

was a cartwheel, spinning across England on winds of delight.
He was a shooting star, tearing a rent of joy across the night,
trailing sparkles of contentment in his wake. He was a prince
and a king, and the mightiest warrior that had ever lived. And
all because he now knew beyond all doubt that his lady loved
him.

"Ah, Merrily," he breathed as his hands molded themselves
to her flushed cheeks. He drew her lips nearer as he lowered his
to meet them . . . waiting, waiting for their first soft touch. . . .

"Oh, there you are," called Plum as Marc and Merrily sprang
apart. At the sight of them, she stopped short. "Why, never
say you were . . . embracing!" she gasped. One pudgy hand
flew to her bountiful breast.

"The lady had something in her eye," commented Marc
smoothly as he gave Merrily time to recover her composure.
Not that he was in much better condition, of course. Merrily
might be panting hard enough to blow his misplaced lock of
hair back where it belonged, but his arousal was hard enough
to drive spikes.

"Oh," replied the elderly lady, brightening considerably.
"Let me see, dearest," she added as she toddled near.

"It is not necessary, Plum," said Merrily somewhat breathlessly. She raised a hand to ward against her companion's
coming any closer and discovering the flush that radiated from
her cheeks. "Marc has removed it quite nicely."

Marc moved, then, to put himself between Plum and her
charge. He felt Merrily grasp his coattails with a shaky hand
and pull herself to her feet to stand behind him. He rigidly
controlled the impulse to smile when he felt her forehead sink
against the hollow between his shoulder blades. He could not
remember ever feeling so smugly arrogant. She not only loved
him . . . she wanted him!

"We were just discussing Lord Mirthton's last words to
Merrily," he told Plum, knowing that a change of subject was
high on the list of Merrily's priorities.

"Indeed?" responded Plum. "Such a pother. Such a pother."
She turned, then, to lower herself onto the bench while tugging

on the skirt of the gaudy chartreuse gown merrily had worn the day before. "Sit down, dearest," she said as she patted the warmed stone beside her.

Merrily shakily complied, not quite daring to look at the earl. He smiled at her reticence. "Yes," he continued, still keeping Plum's attention on him and not on her flustered charge. "Although we could make nothing out of the words that he spoke, Merrily had just suggested that the clue might have been given in something else that occurred that morning."

"Eating one's breakfast could hardly be considered a clue, my dear Lord Clairmont, and that is all that Simon did," uttered Miss Plumley with a sniff.

Marc smiled as Plum smoothed her skirts and then swung his gaze toward Merrily. She met his glance hesitantly, but returned his smile, letting him know that she was finally recovered. He caught a burgeoning flash of merriment in her green eyes and could not wait to get her alone again.

"I thought instead that his actions just before he died might be significant," corrected Marc more seriously. "Can you remember anything about them, Merrily?" he asked.

Merrily fisted her hands in her lap and dropped her gaze to her clenched fingers. "I remember being incredulous at the sight of him lying on the floor. I rushed to him . . . and then I-I pressed my fingers against one of his wounds. I remember reaching with my other hand to support his head, but I could not.

"Why?" interjected Marc as he came to stand before her.

"Because he was gripping my arms . . . yes, I remember that distinctly. He was holding on to me with a strength I could not believe a wounded man might possess."

"Keep the image in your mind, Merrily," urged the earl. "Did he hold you in that way while he made his confession?"

Merrily's eyes focused in the distance. "Yes. He did not release me until . . . until he had told me about the sign of the *sabot*."

"What did he do then?" inquired Marc in a tone of keen anticipation.

"He seized his own hand," she replied, somewhat mystified.

Plum stirred on the bench beside Merrily. "Must we dwell on this unpleasantness?" she asked softly. "Poor, dear Simon is gone from us now. Of what importance can the movement of his arms be to Merrily's cause?"

"Possibly a great deal, Plum," replied Marc earnestly. "It would all depend. . . . Tell me, my dear," he said as he again turned toward Merrily, "which hand did your father seize?"

Merrily looked at him questionably. "It was, let me think . . . the left one."

"You are sure?"

"Yes," she responded without hesitation.

"And did your father wear a wedding ring?" Marc continued.

"No, he never did. Only his ruby."

"Had he worn the ruby for many years?" the earl queried.

"Ever since I can remember," replied Merrily. "Marc, what are these questions leading to?"

"One more question and then I will tell you, my dear," said Marc. "Was your father wearing his ring when he died?"

"Yes, he was."

The intensity in Marc's gaze suddenly softened. "Then I am persuaded that we must take a very close look at your father's ring, Merrily. I believe that our answer lies there."

Merrily's eyes grew large. "You believe that in covering his ring my father was trying, with the last of his strength, to show me the clue, do you not?"

"Precisely," answered Marc.

"Then we shall go and get the ring immediately," she replied as she sprang to her feet. "Come, Plum, we must hurry."

In a short time the three of them were standing in a circle around the small desk in Simon Mirthton's bedroom. Merrily had retrieved the small lacquered box from the cabinet in her father's dressing room and had spilled its meager contents upon the desk top. She picked up the ring gingerly and turned it over in her palm.

"I can see nothing unusual about it, Marc," she said finally, "certainly nothing that resembles a wooden shoe."

"May I?" inquired the earl with a soft smile as he stretched out his hand. Merrily offered him the ring immediately.

The earl turned the ring in his fingers carefully, holding it closely both to his eyes and to the bright afternoon light streaming through the tall windows. He picked at the surface of the blood-red stone with his thumbnail, probing at intervals as if searching for the slightest irregularity. Suddenly his eyes flew to Merrily's. A triumphant grin spread across his face.

"Watch," he said as he moved the ring nearer to her. With both Merrily and Plum looking on in anticipation, Marc slid his thumbnail under a tiny ridge of gold and the ruby-studded lid of a tiny compartment sprang open.

" 'Pon my word," breathed Plum as she immediately began searching the depths of her abundant bosom for her salts.

"The *sabot!*" cried Merrily as her face lit with a grin so wide she could have tied it behind her neck.

"Just so," responded Marc smugly, and he looked again at the tiny golden seal that had been carefully shaped like a wooden shoe to be concealed beneath its guardian ruby. "Damme, but they did a clever job of hiding this!" exclaimed Marc suddenly. "If I had not seen similar rings when I was in Spain, I would never have known to look closely at this one."

"Then I must be even more grateful for the years you spent in that country, Marc," said Merrily happily, and then she frowned. "But do not expect my gratitude to extend to your time spent with Spanish dancers."

Marc laughed heartily. He placed the ruby ring in Merrily's hands and walked around the small desk to place a celebratory arm around each lady's shoulders. "Never say you are jealous, my sweet," he teased.

"Indeed not," Merrily huffed. "My eyes are naturally green."

Marc gave her shoulders a slight squeeze. "Have you any thoughts as to where we go from here?" he asked, dissipating a good measure of their elation.

"We still do not have the list," Plum pointed out unnecessarily.

"But we have made a start," encouraged Merrily. "We must not give up now."

"We *cannot* give up now, dearest," responded her companion bluntly, "else you shall be dead."

Marc's eyes found Merrily's just as bleakness was again gaining a foothold in her green gaze. He shook his head slightly, silently giving her support and courage through the warmth in his eyes. He saw that she was frightened, but hiding it well. He smiled at her, urging her without words to trust him. And when her answering smile displayed the fullness of her overlapping teeth, he once again rejoiced. She was his lady, and she loved him. He would move heaven and earth to keep her safe, and if that did not work, why then, he would unleash Mack.

So at last they have discovered the secret of the ring, came the thoughts of a nearby presence. *It cannot be long, then, before the list is revealed and I can move to tidy up all these loose ends. It is too bad of the earl that he did not take my warnings and cry off when he could. I have no wish to terminate him, after all. It is quite risky to harm a peer. But he knows too much now and, therefore, must be dealt with. Irritating, though, that he would continue to involve himself. It forces me to plan my moves carefully if I am to remain undetected. But, of course, I shall. Those stupid government agents will find nothing . . . no list, no ring, no French patriots, and certainly not I. All they will find are the bodies of two English fools who thought they could trust me. If I did not have to keep silent, I would throw back my head and laugh.*

Chapter 13

Marc poured himself an after-dinner brandy and crossed the drawing room to stand before the fire. His claret velvet dinner jacket hugged his muscular shoulders like a second skin as he lifted one wrist to rest it against the mantle. Happily, Charlotte had once again outdone herself. He absently rubbed a long-fingered hand across his abdomen, pulling his already clinging white inexpressibles even more tightly around his form. There was much to be said for a pleasantly full stomach. Mack had excused himself earlier and was even now in the kitchen expressing his own appreciation to the talented village woman. Marc smiled at the thought. He very much doubted that appreciation was what his large friend was engaged in expressing.

He turned then, to look at Merrily who was seated beside Plum on a threadbare sofa, idly flipping through the pages of a vintage copy of *La Belle Assemblie,* no doubt seeing a tasteful variation of her own ensemble reflected back from one of the fashion plates printed on its yellowed pages. Words could not describe the gown she had appeared in this evening. He hesitated to try, being quite happy to leave his dinner undisturbed exactly where it was. Sufficient to say, after tonight he would never look at the colors purple and peach in quite the same way again. The gown did have one advantage, though, he thought wryly. It tended to force him to keep his gaze securely planted above her neck, and that did wonders toward helping him control his growing ardor.

Yet her problem still remained. The two of them were no closer to discovering the whereabouts of the list than they had been when they had made their discovery of the *sabot* hidden inside her father's ring. All their hours of reasoning, of analyzing every bit of information they knew after finding the seal, had been for naught. Only one thing at this point was certain. They were sure that each of the spies must possess one of the *sabot*-shaped seals. Its mark on a sheet of paper or smear of sealing wax was obviously the way the authenticity of the communications passed back and forth between them was verified, and was in all likelihood the item Merrily's father looked for when trying to discover his compatriots' identities.

But where one has gone before, others can follow, Marc thought as he studied the fall of fire-kissed hair that spilled across Merrily's shoulder. Therefore, it was imperative that Marc show the ring to the agents surrounding the house as soon as possible. One of them would have to be dispatched immediately to carry a description back to Whitehall, for as soon as this information was in Peter's hands he could begin ferreting out the traitors as Merrily's father had done. Marc knew that, although it meant leaving Merrily without his presence in her room for a short time, he would have to try to contact them tonight.

Mack would be with her, of course, but it would not be quite the same. He would have to keep watch from the hall. Marc had vowed days ago that no matter how much he trusted his irreverent friend, no other man was ever going to enter Merrily's bedchamber again but him. Yet there was no hope for it. He would have to leave her. His mission was too important. He decided finally to wait until everyone had gone to bed, and then make his way secretly to Castlereagh's men.

"Do you suppose the fact that the *sabot* is a seal might be a clue?" asked Merrily suddenly. She rested her hand on an open page and looked toward Marc.

"At this point, anything is possible," he responded, drawing back somewhat from the consideration of his plans.

"Perhaps we should look for something sealed, then," she concluded.

Marc smiled slightly. "Have we not already opened everything in the house that has been in some way sealed? I cannot think of another nook or cranny that could possibly have remained unexplored."

"Hmm . . . you are right," she said, sweeping the cascade of curls back behind her shoulder. Marc gazed at the delicate, warm flesh she had uncovered and was astounded at how quickly he grew hot and hungry. It was difficult to keep from imagining his lips caressing her there. "A ring, then," she added brightly. "Could the list be in something shaped like a ring, or that had the word 'ring' in it?"

"I think we are beginning to grasp at straws, my dear," replied Marc as he shifted his elbow to the mantle and began to rub his upper lip to banish an insistent, yearning tingle.

"Well, what then?" she cried. "It is all well and good to have the ring, Marc, but it has given us no clue as to the whereabouts of the list. Whatever shall we do now?"

Marc glanced at her gently, understanding her frustration. It mirrored his own. They were close, he was sure of it, yet it seemed as if every path ended in a massive stone wall. And time would soon be running out. If they could not find the list before the deadline mentioned in Merrily's note, both their lives would be forfeit. Of course, under no circumstances would he allow that to happen. For their own good, he hoped that the bastards who had threatened his lady understood that.

"It has grown late, my sweet," he answered, suddenly anxious to meet with Castlereagh's men. "We will all of us be able to think more clearly in the morning. I suggest we retire and meet again after breaking our fast to discuss what our next step should be."

Merrily nodded with a sigh. "Yes. Things always look brighter by the light of day."

"That is a lovely ensemble, dearest," commented Plum as she pointed an embroidery needle toward the page Merrily held open on her lap. "I am persuaded that if I were to remove the flounces from the gown you are wearing and use them to decorate your bonnet, I could discover some most suitable cerise ostrich feathers among Beatrice's things with which to replace them. Would that not be perfect? You would be dressed to the nines then, my dear."

Merrily heard Marc groan and saw his head fall heavily into his tapered hand. She hid a grin before she commented, "I am quite fond of this gown just as it is, Plum. Besides, I have far greater need for a new shawl and I would be happy if you made it for me. Do you think I might trade a few bushels of our peaches for some of Thomas and Betsey's wool?" Marc's eyebrows rose to skim his hairline.

"An excellent idea," exclaimed Plum as she patted Merrily's hand.

"A maggoty notion," vowed Marc when he could stand no more. Something inside him rebelled at the idea of his future wife bartering for goods as if she were punting on tick. Of course, from what he could see, she most certainly was, and that made him all the more anxious to get this business of the list taken care of so he could finally start providing for her. "You shall not be trading peaches for Thomas's wool, you impossible woman!" he stated more boldly. "If you get wool from anyone, it shall be from me!"

"You have need of peaches, Marc?" asked Merrily in astonishment.

"Certainly not. I have greenhouses full of them," he replied with heat.

"Then what will you take in trade?"

"Trade?" echoed Marc as his vexation coalesced.

"Yes," Merrily laughed with a hint of exasperation, "what will you take in trade for your wool?"

Marc's eyes suddenly lit with an unholy gleam. So she wanted to trade, did she? His mind spun with the possibilities. A slow grin began to curl his lips, but then halted. Plum was still present. His eyes swung to the elderly woman, narrowing slightly. *Damme!* He would have to be circumspect; certainly more cognizant of the proprieties. He would have to thwart his masculine impulses and ask for something simple, something impersonal, something with which she could readily agree.

"Well?" reminded Merrily. "What will you take, Marc?"

"Every single one of your dresses."

A heavy snow had begun to fall by the time Marc was able to slip out through the back of the house and begin to make his way toward the place where he knew the head of the agents was hiding. His boots crunched noisily over the moisture-laden crystals and he cursed his luck that he could not move more silently, but lifted his collar against the stinging snow and kept on going. He clutched Simon Mirthton's ring in one hand while the other slipped to the closures on his greatcoat, sealing it close to his body against the piercing bite of the storm-driven wind.

He had informed Mack of his plans as soon as the ladies had sought their beds earlier. Merrily had made no comment on the fact that he was not following her up the stairs to his own room. She was not aware, of course, that he had instead been sleeping with her. It was one thing to share a room for her protection when they stayed at an inn, but this was her home. He had no wish to compromise her in front of her servants. And so he had made it his practice to creep into her room as soon as he knew she was asleep and curl up at the foot of her bed. He made sure he was gone before the first rays of dawn ever warmed her cheeks, too, though it was becoming increasingly difficult to do so. She looked like a kitten curled into a somnolent, warm ball when she slept, and Marc would have given his head of hair to be lying smack in the middle of that soft, enticing curl.

A footstep sounded softly behind him. Marc whirled around, ready to do battle.

"Hold, my lord," laughed a deep, male voice softly. A diminutive figure separated himself from the moon shadows and strode forward.

"Pettigrew," mouthed Marc as his muscles, one by one, relaxed. "You almost got yourself killed."

"Been tried b'fore, my lord," the wiry man said with a grin as he reached Marc's side. "This ain't fit weather for man nor beast. You must have trouble if you're out in it."

"We've made a breakthrough," said Marc intensely. "I have something to show you, and then word of what we've discovered has to be relayed to Eversley as quickly as possible."

"By all means," replied Pettigrew with sudden seriousness. "We've fashioned a screened fire to ward off the cold over past that line of trees. It'll give us light enough to see what ye've brought." As the smaller man swung away he commanded, "Follow me."

Marc approached the small fire to see man after man approach the warmth of the flames from one direction, huddle near the light with outstretched hands for several minutes, and then move off into the darkness again, but in the opposite direction. He raised an eyebrow questioningly and his companion gave him a half-grin.

"The men are moving in a slow circle around the Manor," he explained. "That way they have a chance to keep their blood warmed by their movement, and periodically can spend some time thawing out their fingers over the fire."

Marc nodded and took the last steps into the circle of dim light. Immediately he squatted down next to the fire and opened his hand. The ruby captured the glow of the meager flames and shone blood red.

"This is Simon Mirthton's ring," he began. "Lady Mirthton told me that he wore it all of her life. Now watch." With a swift flick of his thumb, Marc revealed the seal of the *sabot*.

Pettigrew whistled softly. "So that's what ye've been looking for. Ingenious!"

"Yes," responded Marc, "though we're no closer to finding the list than before. However," he continued soberly, "a description of this ring has to be taken to Whitehall immediately. It is my belief that each of the spies in the ring carries something similar to this. Eversley needs to know about it right away so that he can set his men working on finding the rest of them."

"Aye," Pettigrew replied, and then he turned toward the government agent who was just appearing to take his turn before the fire. "McPhee," he called softly, "over here if you please."

As Pettigrew explained the situation to the second man, Marc stretched his hands toward the fire. It looked to be a long night. He knew that McPhee would ride through the rest of the evening and on into the next day, not stopping until he reached London, but anything could happen between now and then. His horse could pull up lame, or the storm might make the roads impassable further north. There were any number of things. If only he could shorten the distance back to the capital. And then he snorted. Might as well wish the man could fly.

Marc's head popped up. *Fly!* He twisted toward the two men who were examining the ring. "You must ride instead to Rye, Mr. McPhee," he commanded.

"Aye," replied Pettigrew after a moment. "The carrier pigeons!"

"Just so," responded Marc with a nod of excitement. "If you leave immediately, McPhee, a bird can be at Whitehall before morning."

The taciturn man's eyes narrowed as he nodded his assent. He took one more look at the ring, memorizing it so that he could recall it in detail to the message scribe in Rye, then turned on his heels and was gone into the snow-swirled night.

Mack watched the butler, Grimes, walk stiffly down the corridor toward him, carrying a small silver tray upon which a china cup was balanced. He stopped before the giant man and looked up at him warily.

"Howd' do," Mack murmured assessingly.

"Very well, sir," the butler replied, "though I confess to being weary. The days are quite taxing with so many in residence."

"You bin makin' more trips up and down this hallway than a donkey 'round a corn grinder," Mack commented amiably.

"Yes, well," Grimes hedged, "you have perhaps noticed that the nobility can be rather demanding."

Mack grinned. "Where I come from, ain't no nobility," he said.

"Ah, yes, America," sighed the butler as he shifted to his other foot. "I should perhaps like to go there some day."

A heavy silence fell between the two men. Mack kept still, waiting for the somewhat discomfited man to reveal his reason for being there. He was not unduly concerned that the man seemed a trifle nervous. Most men were around him. Still he held himself ready, watchful.

"I could not help but notice your presence before Lady Mirthton's door, sir," Grimes finally began.

"I'm powerful hard to miss," replied Mack.

"Yes, well, I just wanted you to know that I think it is timely that someone is watching out for her."

"Is that so?" commented Mack as he crossed his thick arms before his immense chest.

"Indeed," responded Grimes. "I do not think the lady safe here."

"Why is that, do y' s'pose?" Mack's eyes narrowed imperceptibly, but otherwise he did not move.

"It is the two lords, sir," replied the man as his eyes flicked from one end of the corridor to the other. "They do not care for her presence here," he added in a whisper.

"You heerd somethin' I oughta know about, fella?" asked Mack as his hands fell in hamlike fists to his sides and he straightened to his full, towering height.

"Gracious n-no," stammered the smaller man. "It is merely a feeling, that is all. One can sense the enmity coming from the two lords, sir. I merely wish to do what I can to assure Lady Mirthton's continued good health."

Mack relaxed back against the wall outside Merrily's room. "You wanna help?" he questioned.

"Yes, indeed," Grimes replied hastily. "Anything. Anything at all that I can do."

"Then keep yer eyes open," Mack ordered. "Find out if ye can whar them two bastards is went to, an' fer sure let me know if'n they come back."

"I-I shall certainly do so, sir," Grimes agreed; "and first

thing in the morning, I shall begin to interrogate anyone on the estate who might know of the two lords' whereabouts." He hesitated long enough to receive Mack's nod of approval and then turned away. When he had gone only a few steps, he again turned back toward Mack. "Oh, I quite forgot," he smiled. "I brought this cup of mulled wine for you before I retire. I thought perhaps you might like it. A man needs something to chase the chill away in this cold corridor."

"Obliged to ye," answered Mack as he took the offered cup and downed its contents in one swallow. He wiped the residue from his lips with the back of his hand, then watched as the butler stepped back from him across the corridor to lean against the opposite wall. The smile on the servant's face never faltered. Oddly, it distorted instead, pulling on the diagonal into a leering, snarling, sneering grin that shifted wildly before Mack's eyes. He shook his head to clear his vision as the butler's body rippled like the image on a wind-touched pond. He heard the smaller man's chuckle echoing inside his head with the sound of a thousand mocking voices. It was the last thing he remembered before nothingness crowded in.

Moonlight played over the aging rosewood furnishings in Merrily's bedchamber, yet was repeatedly shunted aside by the dipping shadows of the bare-branched trees that resisted the persistent winter wind. The cold light flowing through the parted curtains bleached the pale yellow damask wall hangings into near translucence. A pool of still-malleable wax supported a blackened nub of wick in a dish on the table beside her bed, bearing silent testimony to Merrily's restlessness.

She had fallen asleep only a short time before, worried to the point of anxious wakefulness because Marc had not come to her. Something was wrong, she knew. If it were not, he would have come sneaking into her chamber like he had before, settling himself with all the stealth of a warthog at the foot of her bed so that she might relax into deep sleep by the comfort of his presence. But he had not come. Merrily had stayed awake

s long as she could waiting for him, but exhaustion after the
xcitement of the day had finally overcome her resistance, and
he had drifted into sleep. She did not hear the metallic snick
s a key turned in her lock, nor was she aware of the soft sigh
f her door as it swung open to admit two hooded figures who
tepped gingerly over the mound of Mack's body and crept
ilently toward her. The gloved hand that clamped across her
nouth muffled her scream.

Merrily's body arched against the restraining hands that
eized her arms and dragged her out of bed. She twisted franti-
ally, jerking her arms as she struggled to free them until the
arger of her captors shoved one of them behind her back at a
>ainful angle and of its own accord, her body nearly doubled
>ver. She felt her bare feet snag against the ragged carpet and
ried to use them to trip or kick her assailants, but the smaller
f the two dove at them and forced them into stillness.

"You should have left when you had the chance," hissed
he male voice behind her as he tugged her fisted hand even
iigher between her shoulder blades.

Merrily renewed her struggles, trying to free her mouth to
cream or at least find out who the bounders were, but the
gloved hand remained pressed like an iron band across her
ender lips.

"Hold still!" commanded the harsh whisper behind her. The
viry arm fastened around her waist tightened, forcing a gust
)f air from her flared nostrils as her breasts heaved from her
utile exertion. With her body held immobile, Merrily's brain
inally began to function, overriding the stark terror that had
:laimed her faculties thus far. She realized immediately that
here were two of them, and that she was not dealing with riff-
·aff from the London stews. The voice behind her was cultured,
:ducated. She was being held captive by a gentleman.

"You thought you could get away with it, did you not?" the
voice continued. "You should have known that we would be
ible to see through your petty schemes. But you shall not be
illowed to get away with it, do you hear? You shall be made
:o suffer for what you tried to do!" As soon as his words were

finished, the two assailants began to drag her toward the snow draped window nearest her bed.

Merrily used a moment of inattention to jerk her mouth free of her captor's hand. "Who are you?" she gasped as a flow of cold air raced into her lungs. Instantly the hand clamped back over her bloodless lips. She felt her legs drop heavily to the floor and watched as the second man moved to twist the latch and throw open the window, raising his arms to ward off an icy blast of wind-driven snow that stole the remaining warmth from the room. In her thin wool nightgown, Merrily began to shiver, feeling the frigid currents swirl around her feet and legs. At last she understood what they meant to do. She was going to be thrown to her death from the second-story window. Panic knifed through her. She pushed back against her captor, trying to brace her feet against the floor, but the snow-covered surface was wet and slick, and gave her no purchase. Slowly, steadily she was forced toward the gaping opening, then lifted once again in the two men's straining arms.

"You should have left when you had the chance," repeated the harsh whisper against her ear.

Before she could even begin to grasp her assailant's meaning her legs were tossed out the window to dangle in the icy bluster of the elements. Even more quickly, her arms were released and forced to clamp onto the snowy ledge. The two men stood back then, and stared at her silently through the ragged eye holes that were cut haphazardly in their hoods. Merrily's fingers scrabbled for purchase on the icy ledge. She felt her limbs tremble violently and grow unfeeling in the numbing cold. Wet snow blew against her, clinging in a heavy coating to her thin gown, and time slowed to a crawl as her captors continued their vigil, unmoving. Merrily's strength was slipping away. She rested her head against the ledge and then slowly lifted it, drawing on the last of her reserves to once again face her assailants. It would solve nothing. It would not save her. But she had to ask anyway. Her eyes sought out her captor's. Her lips, almost too cold to move, formed the silent whisper. *If I am going to die, I must know.*

"Why?"

*   *   *

Things are finally drawing to a conclusion, thought Marc
with satisfaction as he made his way up the wide drive toward
the Manor, *and it cannot come too soon. The bastards are close
now, but we will be ready for them. I can almost feel my fingers
around their necks.*

Marc hunched his own neck deeper into the collar of his
greatcoat and raised a gloved hand to his beaver, holding it
firmly on his head against the increasing wind. The storm had
almost become a blizzard in the short time he had been out in
it. His eyes scanned the park with steady precision, constantly
searching, seeking any aberration that might signal danger. *I
must get Merrily out of here and back to London as soon as
his case breaks. The hoyden gets into too much trouble by
half. I shall get a special license. It does not signify what she
might feel about it, she will marry me, and that is that! It is
the only way I can protect her. The only way to keep her safe
from the bounders who seem to be drawn to her like bees to
honey.* And then he grinned. *But who will keep her safe from
me?*

The wind whipped one of the capes of his greatcoat against
his face, forcing him to look up suddenly. His glance took in
the facade of the Manor before he once again turned his face
away from the force of the wind. And then the sight he had
seen so fleetingly registered in his cold brain. Someone was
hanging out of the upstairs window! His eyes flew to the Manor
again and locked on the slight, still form hanging on so precariously to the snow-laden ledge. *My God, Merrily!*

In an instant, he was plowing through the accumulating drifts,
and in moments had gained the steps leading up to the Manor.
He did not hesitate. Throwing his shoulder against the stout
door, he broke through the lock as if it did not exist and hurled
himself up the stairs. He vaguely heard someone roar an ancient
battle cry filled with rage and anguish, but did not concern
himself with it. Instead, he thundered down the corridor toward
Merrily's room, stopping only to feel for a pulse in Mack's

neck before kicking down the bedroom door and crashing int
Merrily's chamber.

The sight before him turned him cold, calm, contained. H
was a pistol primed to explode. Two hooded figures were des
perately attempting to pull the cold-stiffened body of his lad
back into the negligible warmth of her room. He did not sto
to analyze what they thought they were doing, he merely bor
down on them, letting the rage inside him boil out through hi
gaze. They dropped Merrily, then, as soon as he launche
himself through the door, leaving her to hang half-in, half-ou
of the window while they squeaked with fright and cowere
against the damask draperies on either side of the opening a
Marc came inexorably on. He reached them quickly, sayin,
nothing as he filled his fists with their clothing and jerke
them, whimpering with terror, to their feet. Disgusted with thei
cowardice, he cracked their heads together with a loud cruncl
and let them fall into insensibility upon the floor.

His heart began to beat again then . . . a pounding rhythn
of anxious fear that spurred him into a flurry of action. Instantl·
he was at Merrily's side, lifting her gently into his arms as h·
closed the window, and carrying her with infinite tendernes
to her bed. He moved quickly to her wardrobe and rifled througl
it until he found a clean nightgown, then, without allowin;
himself to think about what he was doing, he ripped off he·
sodden gown and gently dressed her in the dry one. Quickl)
he tucked her insensible form under the heavy quilts, and
after smoothing her hair back from her icy brow, strode to th·
fireplace, where he knelt down and in minutes had a roarin;
fire going. He stepped, then, into the hallway and dragge·
Mack's limp form toward the warmth of the fire. Running hi:
hands over his friend's body, he quickly ascertained that Macl
was uninjured, but more than likely drugged. He left him t·
warm and wake naturally, while he returned to deal with th·
two assailants.

He knew who they were, of course, but pulled off their hood:
none too gently just the same. Lucius and Willard were reveale·
to him just as he had known they would be, and were sprawle·
on top of one another in their unconsciousness like a basket o·

eels, eliciting from Marc a grunt of distaste. He reached, then, for the cords which bound the draperies and used them to secure their feet and wrists, then fashioned stout gags with torn strips of sheeting and tied them securely in place. There would be plenty of time to deal with them later, once he was sure Merrily would be all right. He propped them up uncomfortably in a nearby corner and returned to Merrily's side.

The slight blue tinge to her translucent skin frightened him. His brow creased with worry. She looked so small and frail to him. He knew she was not warming fast enough. He sat on the bed and put his fingers to her neck. Her pulse was not strong. He knew of only one thing to do. As quickly as he could he slipped out of his clothes and slid into the bed, then took her limp form into his arms. The shock of her cold body as he drew her flush against his was enough to cool the odd and assorted sensual notions that persistently flitted through his head at finding himself in the place he had craved to be for so long, yet, as his hands worked to warm her contours, he did not chide himself unnecessarily for his thoughts. He knew that he would have to be dead to keep from reacting to Merrily's body. He knew, too, that the time would come, and soon, when he would lie with her like this and make her his own. He could be patient, he decided with a grin. The prize was so worth the waiting.

He turned, then, and curled himself around her, giving her his total warmth. He tucked the quilts close around her neck and raised himself just enough to kiss the tender spot right behind her ear. It had been a long day. A productive one, but still, a very long day. He smiled in satisfaction just before he drifted off into a deep, untroubled sleep.

Merrily's eyes opened slowly, lazily, contentedly. She had never been so warm and comfortable in her life. A bright stream of sunshine blazed a path across her bed, warping across the contours of one . . . dear heavens! . . . *two* sets of legs! She sat up like a sprung catapult.

"Merrily, for heaven's sake!" grumbled Marc's voice from

beside her. "Your elbow struck me right in the eye." She
whirled around in time to see the earl grind the heels of his
hands into his eyelids and sleepily sit up beside her. The quilts
slowly pooled around his waist.

"My lord!" she gasped as her eyes fastened on the soft curls
covering his chest, "remove yourself from his bed at once!"

"No," the earl responded in a voice made husky from sleep.
He grinned roguishly then and let his appreciative gaze slowly
sweep over her. "You are lovely in the morning, my dear," he
murmured.

Merrily's eyes grew as wide as clay pigeons. She swallowed
slowly, feeling like her whole torso had just caught fire. "Why
will you not get out of the bed?" she whispered, unable to
break away from his compelling gaze.

"Because I am naked, my sweet," he answered. "You would
be even more embarrassed than you already are if I should do
so."

"True," she breathed, noting the fine dusting of whiskers
on his cheeks that snagged the morning sunlight. "Am I?"

Marc chuckled and stroked her warm, flushed cheek with
his finger. "Would that you were, my dear," he said with
amusement, "but, alas, you are covered neck to toes in wool."
Marc had never felt so relieved. She was warm again. Actually,
he considered with a wry grin, judging by the arousal he saw
melting her green eyes, she was hot. He mentally cursed the
circumstances that kept him from doing something about it.

"Would you consider telling me why you are in my bed,
my lord?" Merrily asked softly. Personally, the lady thought
with a silent sigh, she really did not care, since having the earl
in bed with her was all that is wonderful, but still she felt she
deserved some explanation for propriety's sake.

Marc smiled and then settled himself back against their hastily propped up pillows. Without warning, he pulled Merrily
back against him and wrapped his arms around her. "I am
keeping you warm, love," he whispered against her ear.

Hot waves of tingles washed over her. Merrily gasped at the
sensation. She felt incredibly foolish. She had not been able to

take her eyes off Marc's naked chest since she had awakened. For all she knew, the bed could be floating in the middle of the sea. What was this devilish power he had over her? And worse. How did she always manage to get herself into these situations with him?

"This is most improper, Marc," she managed to say at last as she pushed away from him. "If anyone should see us I shall *really* be compromised."

"Oh, but they have," he said matter-of-factly as he pulled her back close to him and tucked her head against his neck. "Look around you, my dear," he suggested.

Merrily bolted rigidly upright . . . and came face to face with her cousins, still bound, gagged, and sagging together against the wall. Muffled noises began to issue forth from them as their eyes pleaded with her for release. She could do nothing but stare. And then she blinked.

"I remember now," she breathed, and then her eyes flew to Marc's. "What has happened to Mack?" she cried as her hands rested upon his chest.

"He is behind you," Marc soothed. "He was drugged, though I have not spoken to him yet to find out how."

They both turned, then, to see Mack leaning groggily against the wall nearest the fireplace. The fire had burned down into embers, and so he rolled unsteadily toward the wood pile and put on another log.

"It were Grimes," he said in a voice that sounded like fog. He pulled a chair close to the newly aroused flames, then held his hands toward its warmth.

"So he was in league with these two after all," murmured Marc thoughtfully. "Well, man, are you all right?"

"Feels like m' head's bin run thew a cider press," Mack responded, "but I'm comin' 'round."

Merrily sank back against Marc's body. "What has been going on in here, my lord? Why are my cousins bound?" she asked.

Marc tucked her head back where it belonged. "They were the two hooded men who tried to kill you," he answered as his eyes pierced the two mewling men with his anger. He felt Merrily stiffen slightly, and winced as her fingers gripped a goodly portion of his chest hair.

Out of the corner of his eye, he saw the two cousins squirm in denial. Their actions sickened him. He felt his anger build to the boiling point. Surely the bounders did not think to try lying their way out of what Marc had seen with his own eyes? Was there no end to their spineless perfidy? Merrily had almost died because of them. He would have no more. They may be Merrily's last remaining family, but, by God, they would meet their fate bravely or he would throw *them* out the window! Without thinking, he threw aside the concealing covers and leaped from the bed to stand before the wiggling shapes in all his naked magnificence.

"Silence, you craven bastards!" he shouted as Merrily shrieked in shocked delight. From the chair by the fire, Mack burst into deep, rumbling laughter, slapping his huge hands on his thighs like beaters against a dusty carpet.

Marc spun around, it having finally occurred to him what he had done, and grabbed for one of the quilts to hastily wrap around his waist. He was too late. From the doorway, rolling over the room like the voice of the Archangel, came Plum's stentorious censure, "Merrily Mirthon," she boomed, "you have been compromised!"

Chapter 14

"Come in, Plum," invited Marc pleasantly. "Mack, give our noble chaperone your chair, if you please. We may as well all discuss this together." He deftly flipped aside the concealing quilt and, in less than the tic of an eye, rejoined Merrily in the bed.

Merrily groaned at his never-ending audacity and fell back against the curve of his arm. "Plum, dearest, I am persuaded that there is a perfectly logical explanation for why Lord Clairmont was . . . er, *is* in my bed."

"Continue. I am most anxious to hear it," replied Plum past her scowl.

"I am rather anxious to hear it myself," murmured the earl as his breath tickled Merrily's ear.

"Behave, you bounder!" hissed Merrily. "I am in a deuced coil here!"

"Tut, tut, such language, my sweet," whispered the earl with a grin.

"I am waiting," reminded Plum.

"Well, as to the explanation, dear, I have not heard it yet myself . . . but I am most sure that it will uncompromise me in a moment." She glanced at Marc with a hopeful grin that begged confirmation, but she was to be disappointed. He kept silent. Her look of hope slid into a glare.

"I wish to know what has transpired here, sir," Plum demanded. "Why are you in obvious . . . oh, dear! . . . *déshabillé*, in my charge's bed, I might add, and why are dear Lucius and Willard bound and gagged? This is a havey-cavey business all around, and I will have an explanation."

"Of course," replied Marc smoothly. "Mack, go and fetch two more chairs for Merrily's illustrious cousins, will you?" And then his voice turned to ice. "Condemned men have a right to face their accusers, do they not?"

When Mack had returned with the chairs, Marc directed him to tie the cousins into them, but to leave their gags in place. There was a great deal of scuffling and muffled cursing that followed Marc's order, but soon the two men were once again securely bound.

"Lord Clairmont, you are still . . . mercy! . . . unclothed. I must insist that you take yourself away from Merrily and clothe yourself!" demanded Plum. "Please remember our maidenly sensibilities."

"I suppose that is not too much to ask," he replied, "but I shall have to rise from the bed unclothed before I can become clothed again in my clothing," he reasoned quite seriously. Merrily rolled her eyes.

"Then we shall cover our eyes while you fetch your clothing and clothe yourself, my lord," asserted Plum in all maidenly earnestness.

"To clothe or not to clothe, that is the question," recited Marc with a finger in the air. "Hide your eyes, my dear," he said to Merrily as he threw back the covers, "I feel a soliloquy coming upon me."

Merrily clamped her hands over her eyes and moaned. "Marc, in the space of a few hours I have been frozen, thawed, seen my cousins bound and gagged, and been well and truly compromised," she said between the edges of her little fingers. "How is it that you can not only joke at a time like this, but wax poetic?"

Marc stuffed his shirttail into his newly donned pantaloons

and grinned. "You may open your eyes now, love," he said, "and as to the other, it is merely my way of holding my anger in check . . . anger, by the way," he said as his gaze slid toward the cousins, "which I am about to unleash."

"Oh, dear," sighed Miss Plumley. "Your tone does not bode well for dear Lucius and Willard, I vow. Yet I suppose we must get to the bottom of all this. But I cannot approve of our holding this meeting in Merrily's bedchamber . . . and her still abed!"

"It is a bit late to worry about that now, dear," said Merrily. "Everyone has already seen what there is to see."

Plum sighed heavily. "Very well. Then I will have an explanation first, my lord," she said primly. "What were you doing . . . oh, goodness! . . . unclothed! . . . in Merrily's bed?"

"I was warming her, Plum," the earl offered sincerely. "I found these two jackanapes hanging her out the window in the middle of the storm, and she was near to being frozen solid. It was the only way I could think of to bring her temperature back up to normal."

"'Pon my word!" exclaimed Plum as her eyes sought out Lucius and Willard. "Why ever would you do such a dastardly thing, my dears!"

"Obviously they wanted her dead," said Marc flatly. He did not allow the violent twists of the two cousins' heads and their muffled sounds of agitation to sway him as he turned to face them fully. His eyes blazed with anger. "It is my belief that they are behind everything. These two are not only murders, but traitorous spies." Again the two cousins shook their heads, struggling violently against the gags which kept them from speaking. "Just look at their faces," accused Marc. "They are covered with cuts. Proof enough that they were the ones who tried to kidnap you from the inn at Hastings, Merrily. I, myself, saw them attack you on the road to Brighton. And now, this attempt. It is a cruel death, freezing. These scum do not even deserve the quickness of hanging."

Merrily's eyes filled with unwanted tears. She had no liking for her cousins, but they were still her family. More than anything she wanted to believe that they were innocent of her father's murder. And there were still pieces to the puzzle of their involvement that did not fit. She was determined to find out the truth. Angrily she dashed the tears from her eyes with the backs of her hands and spoke.

"I wish you to remove their gags, Marc," she said softly.

He whirled around to face her. "To what end? The truth is gouged into their faces from that leap from the window!"

"There are some holes in your assumptions," she said reasonably.

Marc stilled. Then the rigid contours of his face softened. "All right," he began on a soft sigh, "explain them."

"In order for them to be the spies, they would have had to kill their own parents, Marc. They are mean, and sometimes vicious, but they were mirror images of their father. They got along with one another like three boils on the devil's rump. There would be no need for them to exclude him from knowledge of what they were doing. They would be able to count on his support for their activities no matter what they were." The cousins nodded a frantic agreement.

"I concede that you might have a point," Marc agreed grudgingly.

"And then there is their age, Marc," she continued. "They are still in school . . . still foolish boys. I am persuaded that they do not have the brains or experience to be deep cover spies."

Marc remained silent and thoughtful for several moments, then walked toward the two men and removed the gags from their reddened mouths.

"We are not spies!" cried Lucius. "Not murderers!"

"We do not know what you are talking about!" whimpered Willard. He writhed against his bonds as tears threatened.

"Then give us the truth!" commanded Marc harshly.

Willard's eyes flew to Lucius's. "L-Lucius?" he questioned hesitantly.

"Pull yourself together, you sniveling brat!" spat Lucius.

"B-but we have to tell," whimpered Willard. "W-we will be hanged as spies, else!"

"Oh, I doubt it will get that far," interjected Marc casually as he buffed his nails on his shirt. "We would want for Merrily's

sake to avoid a messy, scandalous trial, would we not? No, I
am persuaded that the best solution for everyone all around
would be to turn you over to Mack."

Even Lucius gasped. "You cannot! There are laws in England . . ."

"Which you have broken!" shouted Marc.

"Tell them, Lucius!" wailed Willard.

"Oh, all right, all right!" his brother cried in disgust. "But
you have just made everything impossible, you craven worm!"

"What has he made impossible?" asked Merrily calmly.

"The enclosures!" spat out Lucius with a snarl. Merrily
gasped. "Father and I had planned from the time he assumed
the title to enclose the land, but we could do nothing with you
still in the way."

"Then you did plan to kill me?" concluded Merrily as her
face whitened.

"No, of course not!" cried Lucius. "We are not murderers!
We only meant to frighten you away, since you did not seem
to be falling in with Father's original plan of banishing you to
London to find yourself a husband. If you had only done what
you were ordered to, none of this needed to have happened. A
husband would have kept you with him ever after and away
from the Manor."

Merrily sank back against the pillows at this revelation.

"Why did Merrily have to be gotten out of the way?" asked
Marc angrily. "You had the title and the power to do anything
you wanted with the estate."

"It was a financial decision," responded Lucius with an
uncaring shrug. "Father wanted to restore the Manor to the
condition it was before my scapegrace uncle inherited it." Merrily winced visibly. "In order to do that, he had to come up
with a way to squeeze every drop of profit from the estate that
he could."

"But to enclose the land, Lucius," breathed Merrily. "How
could you do that? Our tenants would lose their homes."

"And that is exactly why you had to be removed from the
Manor, dear cousin." His eyes slewed toward Marc then. "You
may have noticed, my lord, that the tenants on Mirthton land

are rather loyal to Merrily. If she were here to give them a reason to fight against the inevitable, the cost of removing them and maintaining a watch against their retaliation would eat up any profits we might realize from the plan. It was imperative, therefore, that my dear cousin be kept out of the way. We did not count, however, on our little Merrily's own offering of revenge."

"What are you speaking of?" questioned Merrily. "What revenge?"

"Do not play the innocent with me, cousin," snarled Lucius. "Willard and I were perfectly content to allow you to remain unmolested in London until this business was completed, but you could not let it go at that, could you?"

"Watch your tone with the lady," snapped Marc, "and explain yourself. Just what is it that Merrily supposedly did?"

"Of that you are well aware, my lord," replied Lucius with venom, "since you aided her yourself. Oh, do not think that we were ignorant of your part in it, Clairmont. We knew . . . and we warned our cousin at the Bear that no matter who she got to help her, it would do no good. It seems we were wrong, however. You and that scheming bitch are standing there, while Willard and I are tied to these chairs!"

Marc backhanded him across the face.

"Marc, please!" cried Merrily as she forgot propriety and jumped from the bed to seize his arm.

Marc's breathing slowed. By force of will he allowed the tension to leach out of him. He turned, then, and took Merrily into his arms. "Very well," he said with even control, "explain what it is you think the two of us have done."

"You hired men to ransack the Manor and steal from us," he accused. Beside him Willard nodded his agreement. "You were so jealous of my father, and then I, coming into the title that you thought to ruin us, to strip away even what little wealth remained at the Manor. You connived your way into Clairmont's protection and then, while Willard and I were away from the Manor discussing the enclosures with our overseer, you set a pack of thugs on our home to strip it bare."

"I did not!" cried Merrily.

"You lie!" retorted her cousin. "It could only have been you! We could not prove it, of course. You were too clever for that. But we vowed to get the proof we needed."

"So you left the remainder of your term at Oxford and followed her to London," concluded Marc quietly.

"Yes," affirmed Lucius angrily, "and we watched every move she made, knowing that at some time or other she would make contact with those she hired. But the only one she made contact with was you, Clairmont. We knew then that she had somehow managed to make you her partner in crime. Somehow? Huh!" he grunted. "After this morning, her method seems more than obvious."

Marc grabbed Lucius's shirt front in both fists and lifted him, chair and all, to within inches of his outraged countenance. "You will apologize to your cousin," he said between gritted teeth, "and you will never malign her in such a way again."

Lucius thought he had been terrified by the threat of Mack earlier. He now knew what real terror was. His eyes bulged and sweat peppered his face as he tried to swallow his fear long enough to speak.

"I-I d-do beg your p-pardon, cousin," he stammered.

Marc slammed his chair back down on the floor. "Continue," he commanded.

"W-well, uh, I, that is, we, could get no proof of what we suspected, so when we saw that Merrily was taking the stage to Brighton and knew that she was returning to the Manor, we decided that our only recourse was to try to frighten her away until the enclosures could take place."

"We only meant to frighten her," added Willard in a whine.

"We thought that threats might do it," explained Lucius, "so we told her we knew what she was up to and that it would never succeed. But then you came to her rescue and put a period to that."

"Why did you try to kidnap her in the inn at Hastings?" demanded the angry earl.

"It was another attempt to get her out of the way. We thought that we could bring her back to the Manor and lock her in one of the attic rooms until the enclosures were over. No one would have heard her if she cried out, and we have so few servants, they would never think to go near that area to service it.''

''And last night?'' growled Marc with lowered brows. ''I suppose you will call that 'frightening' her, too. Well, let me assure you, gentlemen, I call hanging a woman out of a window in a blizzard until she is blue with cold attempted murder, and that is what I will see you charged with before this day is through!''

''No, my lord, you cannot!'' cried Willard. ''Oh, please,sir, we did only mean to scare her. Did you not see us trying to pull her back in when you entered the room? We never realized how quickly she would get so cold. Please, sir, please!''

Marc's eyes narrowed into slits as he glared at the two craven bastards. He felt Merrily shudder in his arms and tightened his hold comfortingly. ''Tell me something,'' he began softly, ''did you two enjoy setting fire to the tails of cats when you were boys? Did you make necklaces out of living tadpoles? Did you pull the wings off harmless butterflies?''

Lucius's face grew dusky with rage. He twisted his hands against his bonds and lifted his lips in a sneer. ''Make your point, Clairmont,'' he uttered.

''The point is,'' answered Marc in a deadly voice, ''that I have never met two more despicable, unnatural men in my life. When I think of the hurt, the fright, that you have put Merrily through, I can assure you, you are fortunate to be alive.''

''You have no right to judge us!'' cried Lucius. ''We may do whatever we want. This is my estate!''

''Unfortunately, that is not true,'' said Marc evenly.

''What do you mean?'' said Lucius, totally taken aback by the earl's calm statement.

''There was a purpose in our recent trip to Rye,'' Marc stated. ''We had need to search the church records there and quite by accident discovered the record of your father's birth.''

''But Father was born here,'' said Willard.

''Alas, no,'' replied Marc. ''He was born to a commoner, and, as I am sure you must be comprehending by now, she was not your grandfather's legal wife.''

''Then . . .,'' began Willard.

"He was a bastard," finished Lucius as the color drained from his face. Suddenly his eyes flicked to Marc's. "You could be making this up," he accused.

"I could, but, on my honor as a gentleman, I must again state that it is true," Marc vowed. "If you need further proof, the records are still there in the Church of St. Mary's. Oh, and I left a message for the vicar there . . . a very nice man, by the way . . . that there might possibly be a dispute regarding an inheritance because of the information we uncovered there, and that the record might need to be protected. I am sure he has the book under lock and key by this time should you take it into your heads to try and destroy the evidence."

Lucius began to fume. "It seems you have us at your mercy, my lord," he sneered.

"I do, do I not?" he grinned.

"Perhaps you would be so kind as to tell us of your intentions," the vexed young man ground out.

"I would be delighted. Merrily, you are shivering. Get back into bed, love," ordered the earl. "Mack, another log or two for the fire, please." When each had complied, Marc began to pace before the two bound men. "As I see it," he began thoughtfully, "you are guilty at the least of malicious mischief, and at the most of attempted murder. Either charge can be easily proven. You have broken the law and are now without a home, income, or prospects."

"Oh, Marc . . .," began Merrily from the coziness of her bed.

Marc held up an arresting hand. "Allow me to continue, my dear," he said as he smiled at her. "Now I know that you are bounders of the worst kind, but you have insisted that you meant no permanent harm to Merrily, and, oddly enough, I believe you." He heard Merrily sigh with relief. "Therefore, I am persuaded that the next step is to examine your options. I could, of course, have you arrested on any number of charges, but a trial would put a period to Merrily's already somewhat unorthodox reputation. On the other hand, I might force you to emigrate. This option particularly appeals to me, as I never wish to see either of you again in my life." Marc regarded the cousins as a wave of panic marred their already bruised features. "However, there is a third option, gentlemen." Marc watched as the brothers' eyes grew round. "You could return to Oxford, finish your schooling, and I will give to each of you a sum of money at the completion of your studies upon which to build your future wealth. Well, gentlemen, which shall it be?"

Merrily was upon him in seconds. "Oh, Marc," she cried as she flew into his arms, "it is too much, but you have made me the happiest of women!"

"Now why did I not think to give the rascals money sooner?" murmured the earl as he reveled in her soft body pressed so tightly into his.

"Behave!" Merrily chided as she pushed back from him. Then her face grew serious. "Why are you doing it Marc?" she asked. "They are nothing to you. They are barely anything to me."

"They are the last of your family, love," he replied gently. "I would not have you worried about them for a moment." He lifted his head, then, and sought out his friend. "Mack, I am persuaded that we no longer need fear for Merrily's safety. Release her cousins, please."

When Mack had completed that task, Lucius and Willard slowly approached the earl. They rubbed their wrists as much out of nervousness as the need to restore their impeded circulation. "My brother and I would like to return to school," stated Lucius in a voice that told of his shattered pride.

"Very well," replied Marc. "That is a wise choice. I will see to it that you have an allowance as well as paying your tuition, but there are two conditions."

The cousins raised their eyes to Marc's. "What are they?" asked Lucius finally.

Marc took a deep breath and let it out slowly. "I have done what I could for you because you are Merrily's family, but I cannot excuse what you tried to do to her. From this day forth, you are never to attempt to see her or contact her in any way again. Do you agree?"

The two young men stiffened. Marc saw the second blow to their pride strike home like an arrow to the heart, but he would not waver. He waited, silent, until at last they both nodded.

"We agree," Lucius affirmed. "And the second condition?"

"You have heard us speak this morning of spies. I will not speak of the matter to you in any more detail than to say that it was they who broke into your home and killed both Merrily's father and your parents, and ransacked the Manor later. Needless to say, if any of this becomes known and is bruited about, Merrily's reputation will be irreparably ruined. Therefore, my second condition is that you are never to speak of this matter in any way to anyone. If I ever hear word of it, gentlemen, I will know from whom the information came and I will come after you." The menace in Marc's calm voice was palpable. "Do you agree to this condition?"

Lucius's eyes moved to Merrily. He regarded her for long moments, and then smiled softly. "I give you my word of honor," he vowed. As soon as Willard, too, had agreed, they turned and left the room. They were gone from the Manor, and Merrily's life, in less than an hour.

"The spies ransacked the Manor again, did they not?" concluded Merrily softly as her arms tightened around Marc's waist.

"I would wager my life on it, my sweet," agreed the earl.

Merrily nodded sadly, and then let the warmth of Marc's surrounding arms chase away her threatening fears.

Later that afternoon, as the sun blazed forth from behind the retreat of the low, scudding storm clouds, the steady drip of fresh snowmelt joined with the songs of newly twittering birds to form a pleasant symphony of early winter. Marc took the opportunity to saddle Barbary and ride toward the base camp of the government agents, looking for all the world as if the only thing he had in mind for the afternoon was a pleasant solitary outing.

He reached the camp quickly and held a short conversation with Pettigrew in which he was informed that McPhee was resting now, but had returned to camp only moments earlier, reporting that everything had gone well during his dash to Rye. The information about the rings was now in government hands, and Marc was sure, knowing Eversley as he did, that the intrepid man was already hot on the foreign agents' trails.

He spurred his mount forward down one of the paths bisecting the park. He thought he may as well make his ruse into a reality. The day was warming nicely and the paths had cleared somewhat. He felt the need for a hard gallop, but knew that that would be foolish on ground soggy with snowmelt.

His thoughts drifted back to Merrily, as they always seemed to do these days. It was a relief to know that her cousins would no longer be a concern for her. But perhaps even more of a relief for him. He had always known that they presented a threat to her, but he was chagrined to find that he had given them too much credit. Merrily had been right. They could no more have carried off the role of foreign agents than she could. Marc remembered his feeling from days ago that there were two separate threats against Merrily. He now knew that to be true. He had eliminated one, but the other still hovered just out of reach like a malignant cloud, worrying his lady and making the evil deeds of her two contemptible cousins seem not so bad after all.

The time for the confrontation was near, he knew. He could sense it with every instinct of his soldier's mind. Would he be ready? He very much hoped so, for death would be the punishment for his error. His tightened lips relaxed into a slight smile. *Ah, Merrily, love,* he thought as he began to grin, *when I think of the way you feel in my arms, I become rather fond of the idea of staying alive.*

Chapter 15

Merrily's half-boots squeezed a print of moisture from the damp soil as she and Marc walked in the rose garden the following morning. It was really not a suitable day for a leisurely stroll, the day having arrived blustery and cold, but Marc had seen immediately that his lady had needed a diversion and so had bundled her up after breaking their fast in an appalling collection of antiquated outerwear and hastily squired her outside. His gloved hand rode her elbow as a precaution against slipping, and, of course, just because he liked it there.

"Do you regret not being able to apprehend Grimes, Marc?" Merrily questioned to the accompaniment of steady sucking sounds beneath their boots.

"Not really, my dear," he replied. "He probably absconded from the Manor the instant I broke your door down, and even if I had not been otherwise occupied, I would have been hard-pressed to follow him in the storm. However, you must not be concerned about him. Scum always rises to the top, love. He will turn up again to receive his just compensation."

"Yes, I suppose," she allowed flatly.

They walked along in silence until Marc squeezed her arm lightly and she smiled up at him. "Are you still worried about your cousins?" he queried.

"Oh, no," she answered readily. "If Grimes is the scum, they are the bilge water he is floating upon, Marc. I have only an overwhelming sense of relief and gratitude that they are no longer a part of my life."

"What then?" probed the earl as he worried over the lack of sparkle in Merrily's viridescent eyes. "Plum?"

The lady chuckled softly. "Ah, yes . . . dear Plum. I did not tell you before, Marc, but I caught her attempting to send Lucy out into the storm after you had taken Mack down to Charlotte for one of her tonics to help clear his head of the aftereffects of the drug."

"Indeed! Merrily, dear, I am aware that Plum is sometimes . . . shall we say, fluttery in her thinking, but why ever would she do something as foolish as that?" asked Marc with an unbelieving smile. He steered Merrily down a fork in the path that led to the dormant tulip garden.

Merrily broke out in giggles. "S-she took a notion to send the p-poor girl to Thomas and Betsey's cottage with a demand that he come at once with his stoutest pitch fork to p-prick your conscience, as it were, into making an honest woman of me."

"Never say so!" exclaimed the earl on a huff of laughter. "Am I to assume, then, since the nether regions of my anatomy are still unbroached, you were able to change her mind?"

"Oh, yes, indeed," laughed Merrily. "Once I had succeeded in convincing her that the walk would not do poor Lucy the least bit of good, it was only a matter of time before I had her talked down into a weapon she was more suited to wield."

"Explain 'talked down,'" requested Marc with a wide grin. He felt himself relaxing. The sparkle had returned to Merrily's eyes. He thought that he could continue watching her and listening to her charming narrations forever.

"Well," gurgled Merrily as she gently cupped his biceps with her other hand, "at first Plum wanted to hie into the rear courtyard for one of the meat cleavers in the butcher shed, but I was able to persuade her that no lady of breeding would allow herself to handle what was so obviously a man's implement."

"A close shave," commented Marc mildly. "Then what?"

"Then she insisted upon one of Charlotte's kitchen knives."

"Such a sharp intellect," said Marc as he led Merrily along the tulip path. "Obviously you were able to dissuade her."

"Obviously," responded Merrily smugly as she came to a halt near the bench she and Marc had rested upon some days earlier. "I merely reminded her that in order to wield a weapon effectively, one must also be prepared to use it."

"I get the point," uttered Marc with an amused tilt to the corner of his mouth. "What, then, did the dear lady finally settle upon?" he asked as he noted the dampness of the stone seat and prevented Merrily from lowering herself upon it. "A knitting needle?"

"Oh, no, my lord," chided Merrily, "much harder to drive the point home, would you not agree?"

"Absolutely. An embroidery needle then?"

"How you puncture my schemes with the sharpness of your wit, my lord!" remarked Merrily. "But, alas, no. One cannot get a good grip on the skinny little things, don't you know. And just the tiniest bit of blood left on the needle could ruin a fine piece of embroidery in a trice."

"Such penetrating logic, Lady Mirthton," complimented the earl. "But, much to my regret, I am out of guesses. What weapon did you finally convince your companion to use against me?" he asked with mischievous anticipation.

"One that a lady could use with the utmost propriety, my lord," began Merrily, biting her lower lip against laughter.

"Do continue," urged the earl as he struggled to maintain a straight face.

"One that is both easy to wield and t-tidy," she added mirthfully.

"I am panting with anticipation," chuckled the earl as his grin spread wide. "What is this marvelous weapon?"

"T-tweezers," blurted Merrily and her voice dissolved into gales of laughter. "I c-convinced her that if she c-caught the s-septum of your n-nose between her tweezers, s-she could force you into anything."

Marc's answering shouts of laughter rolled throughout the garden. Tears streamed from his eyes as he swung Merrily into his arms and hugged her tightly to his body, rocking her back and forth in the blustery winter wind. She snuffled into his neckcloth, clutching at the lapels of his coat weakly. How he loved her! She had given him more happiness in the last few days than he had experienced in his entire life. His heart swelled with the struggle to contain his emotions, but slowly, and with great difficulty, he put her from him.

"Well," he began, taking out a clean handkerchief to wipe his eyes, "I shall probably be the first cad in the history of England to be tweezed into marriage."

"Fustian," countered Merrily with renewed laughter. "You and I both know that I am still . . . well . . ."

"Er . . . yes, we do," agreed the earl.

"And no one who was present will say anything," she added, "so there is really no reason for you to feel honor bound to offer for me at all."

"No, there is not," confirmed Marc, "except . . ."

"Except what, my lord?" questioned Merrily in surprise.

"Except that you, my dear, at least had a nightgown on. I should think you would be honor bound to offer for me," he stated as his nose rose haughtily into the cold, winter air.

Merrily's silvery laughter once again brought warmth and life to the drab grayness of the winter-bound garden.

A few hours later, as they were leaving the garden, Merrily stopped along the path to touch the brittle remains of what was once a vibrant tulip. She knelt down beside it and stroked one of its crisp, fragile leaves, watching as it crumbled back into the earth from which it had come.

"It is most odd, Marc," she commented, "but the Manor seems much different to me since we have been here."

Marc stepped closer and knelt beside her. "How is it different?" he asked.

She looked at him with a soft smile and then answered. "It is as if, even though everything is familiar, nothing is the same." She removed her glove and poked her finger into the soft soil, then gave a mirthless laugh. "Oh, I suppose I am making no sense at all," she said, looking up at him again, "but perhaps what I am trying to say is that Mirthton Manor no longer seems like home."

"I think I understand," nodded Marc. "All the people who made this your home are gone now."

"Yes, that is it exactly. Now it is a place that I think of fondly, but it is only a place." She dug more of her fingers into the moist earth, dislodging as she did the end of a short, perfectly straight stick.

"You need to fill it with children, Merrily," Marc said softly, "with love. Then it will become a home again." As their eyes locked, Marc allowed all the love he felt for her to show in his tender gaze. He reached for her, sliding his warm hand down her slender arm until he captured a glove full of stained fingers, dirt, and a short, but very sharp stick. "Damme!" he muttered as the stick scored his exposed wrist.

"Oh, dear," breathed Merrily, mortified that such a tender moment had been so painfully interrupted. Her eyes found the dirt-incrusted stick at the same time as Marc's did.

"What the deuce . . .?" grumbled the earl as he took the stick from Merrily's hand. He scanned it quickly and handed it back to the lady. "It seems you have found an old garden stake, my dear. Either that, or you are experimenting with alternate weapons for Plum."

"Oh, I remember these!" exclaimed Merrily with a sweet smile. "Our old gardener, back in pre-history when we still had one, of course, used these to mark the different varieties of tulips he had planted. There were scores of them in the tulip bed as I recall." She began to rub her thumb vigorously over the enlarged head of the stake, softly scrubbing away the years of accumulated dirt.

"Booby-trapping them, more likely," Marc grumbled, rubbing the red streak on his wrist.

"Don't be such a baby," grinned Merrily as she began to see the color of a painted design beneath the dirt.

"I have been out of short pants for years," countered the earl with mild huffiness, totally unaware that Merrily had suddenly stilled. "I am wounded," he continued as she finally looked

up at him, open-mouthed, and held the grubby stake before his
eyes. "I am cut to the quick," he groused as his gaze at last
focused on the stake. "I am . . ." Merrily watched as his voice
tapered to silence and his eyes grew wide.

". . . looking at a picture of a wooden shoe," she finished
for him breathlessly, and then, with the most blatant impropriety,
she stabbed the stake back into the soil with a shriek and threw
herself across the short distance into the earl's arms, where she
tumbled him backward into a sprawling heap, the momentum
of which sent them both, shrieking with laughter, on a wild
roll down the soggy garden path.

The tulip bed had been destroyed by nightfall.

As soon as Merrily and the earl had been able to untangle
their limbs and stagger to their feet on the muddy garden path,
they had raced for the Manor, determined to enlist every able
body in the house to help in digging for the list. They had
banged into the kitchen, flushed and breathless, only to surprise
Mack and Charlotte as they had been engaging in some rather
private amusements.

"Having a cooking lesson, are we?" the earl had needled
after Mack had practically dumped Charlotte off the table top
and onto the floor in their haste to spring apart.

"Aye," the earl's recalcitrant man had grinned. "Charlotte's
learnin' me all about gettin' steamed."

Marc had noted Merrily's puzzled expression and stifled a
threatening smile. "Yes, well . . .", he had begun as his lips
twitched suspiciously, "school is over for the day. Merrily and
I have made a discovery and we want both you and Charlotte
to bundle up and come out to the garden to help us. Merrily,"
he had said as he turned toward her, "ask Plum to join us too.
We shall need every hand that is available to us."

"I shall go right away," Merrily had agreed, then she had
turned and had quickly left the kitchen.

In only a short time, the old gardener's shed had been rifled
for digging and sifting implements and the five of them had
begun the seemingly monumental task of locating each of the

old garden stakes, then digging beneath them for some sign of the list. Plum took it upon herself to slowly rake her fingers through the soil until she located one stake after another, while Marc and Mack performed the heavy work of digging deep holes in the still-sodden soil. It remained for Charlotte and Merrily, therefore, to sift through the large piles of damp, black earth for anything that might relate to the list. As darkness approached frustration descended, for the only things that the two of them had discovered were hundreds of tulip and daffodil bulbs and a fisherman's feast of earthworms. The men had not fared better. In the time that they had been working, they had managed to transfer the entire contents of the tulip bed down to a depth of three feet onto the gravel path that marked its border. As they stood surveying their handiwork, they realized that not only had the list not been discovered, but that there was no more soil left to dig.

"It is time to call a halt, I think," said Marc wearily. He had long ago removed his coat, though the wind was still biting, and now ran a soiled sleeve across his brow, dampening it with earth and perspiration. "The list is obviously elsewhere."

"But it must be here!" insisted Merrily as she struggled to rise from her cramped stoop beside the piles of dirt. Marc hurried to her and seized her elbow as she cried out when her spine refused to straighten. "Marc," she said, looking at him dolefully, "there is nowhere else to look."

"Yet I am persuaded that the list is not here, my dear," he replied in a voice that was gentle, yet firm. "Only consider it, Merrily. Your father wanted you to find the list. Would he have made it so difficult for you by hiding it under three feet of dirt in a large tulip bed? I think not. If we have not located it in the soil we have thus far uncovered, I cannot believe that it is here at all."

"Oh, Marc," sighed Merrily, "what you say does seem likely, but . . ."

"I know, my sweet," he said tenderly. "What is there left for us if this is not where your father hid his list?"

"Exactly," she breathed despondently.

Marc slid his arm around her shoulders. "We are all

exhausted, my dear," he said reasonably. "It is impossible to think clearly now. I suggest that we go inside and each of us take a relaxing, hot bath. Then perhaps Charlotte can lay out a light collation for us since she has had no time to cook this afternoon. Once we are warm and fed, we shall be in much better spirits and shall adjourn to the drawing room to think this whole situation through."

Merrily's shoulders lifted in another sigh, but she nodded. "Very well," she said with a soft smile. "It is not hopeless yet, is it, my lord?"

Marc adored his lady's unflagging spirit. His answering smile told her just how much he did. "No, love, it is not hopeless yet."

Mack walked Charlotte and Plum back to the Manor to begin heating water for their baths, while Marc and Merrily together collected the digging tools and returned them to the shed, stopping for a moment beside the rusted blade of a hand-held plow to scrap the thick layer of mud from their boots. Marc brushed scattered clots of dirt from his greatcoat before slipping back into it, and then, looking down at himself, he laughed ruefully.

"I doubt I would be able to set one foot in St. James's Street in these without being stoned," he remarked as he regarded his torn, filthy clothing.

Merrily's eyes sparked with emerald as she grinned up at him. "Have no fear, my lord," she vowed, "I shall undertake to correct the sad state of your clothing this very evening."

"You shall not," the earl countered. "You are tired. Besides, you shall be too busy talking with me."

"You mistake my meaning, my lord," she said with a mischievous smile. "I shall not actually deal with your clothing."

"Oh?" responded Marc, wary of what was coming.

"Oh, no," the lady replied. "I shall do what I always do."

"And what is that?" queried Marc, knowing he should never have asked.

"I shall turn the whole problem over to Plum. You know what wonders she works for me." Merrily skittered aside as the earl took a healthy swipe in the direction of her *derrière* and giggled happily.

"Just try, my dear," laughed Marc as he pointed toward the Manor and gave the vixen a gentle shove. "Just you try."

Bowls of hot mulligatawny soup awaited them when they had finished bathing. It was a pleasant and much appreciated surprise. Charlotte had kept the leftover course from the previous night's meal chilled in the icy pantry, and, when warmed and complemented with rounds of fresh bread and preserved fruit, sliced beef and assorted cheeses, the five weary residents of the Manor soon found themselves well rested and satisfied. While Mack remained behind to help Charlotte in cleaning up the kitchen, as soon as the meal was over Marc escorted both Merrily and a yawning Plum into the drawing room to discuss a solution to the puzzle of the elusive list.

Marc crossed immediately to the brandy decanter which had been left to warm on a small table near the fire and poured himself a generous measure. "Ladies?" he inquired, raising his glass in question.

"Oh, dear, dear, no!" gasped Plum. "Why, I should never . . . why, a lady would not . . . dear, me . . . but, perhaps if it was just a little taste . . ."

Merrily laid a warm hand on her companion's arm. "I should like a glass, too, Marc," she stated as she shared a smile with him.

Mark nodded and, after pouring their drinks, carried them toward the sofa the two women shared and then took a chair across from them. He relaxed against the worn cushions and crossed an ankle over his knee. The light from the nearby fire seemed to set the brandy in his glass aflame as he stared for a time into its depths. "Well," he said after long moments of contemplation, "where do we begin?"

"Where I left off, of course," answered Plum. Both other sets of eyes swung toward her in surprise. "One cannot do embroidery all higgledy-piggledy, don't you know."

Merrily grinned at Marc. "Lord Clairmont was speaking of finding the list, dear," she corrected softly.

"What? Oh, the list. Yes, of course," murmured the elderly lady. "Well, I do not have it anyway."

"The list?" questioned Marc.

"No, no, dear boy," scowled Plum with a shake of her head, "my embroidery. Please try to pay attention." With a quick flip of her glass, she downed her brandy in one swallow, then dabbed at her upper lip with the lace edge of a handkerchief she had withdrawn from her sleeve like a skilled magician. "I neglected to bring it into the drawing room before supper and now I must go and fetch it." With surprisingly agile movements, Plum heaved her bulk into a standing position and toddled from the room.

"Yes, of course," responded the somewhat dazed earl as he stood politely, but belatedly. He looked at Merrily, then, with an eyebrow artfully raised in question, shrugged, and finally settled himself on the sofa beside her.

Merrily merely smiled. "It is no use trying to figure her out, Marc," she advised. "You shall be a candidate for Bedlam if you do."

"Perhaps that is what happened to your father," he said without thinking.

Merrily's face fell. "Perhaps," she replied quietly.

"Ah, Merrily, forgive me," he said as he moved closer and pulled her into his arms. "That was a stupid thing to say. I am a cork-brained idiot."

"I have noticed that," she said, her words muffled against the intricate folds of his neckcloth.

The earl began to chuckle. "Imp," he murmured as his hand slid caressingly up and down her velvet covered arm. "But you must say the words, Merrily. I must hear them. Do you forgive me?"

"Yes, of course," she replied as her head rolled to his shoulder and she absentmindedly tucked her body beneath his arm. "But neither your words nor my forgiveness excuses what my father was, Marc. When I think of how his life was wasted, I am unbearably sad."

Marc's heart swelled with tenderness. He turned his body toward her and cupped the smoothness of her cheek, letting his long fingers bury themselves in the soft fragrant wisps of hair that trailed from her temples. His eyes blazed into hers, laving her with all the power of the love he felt for her, assaulting her with wave after wave of tingling emotion that left her weak and trembling against the strength of his side.

"His life was not wasted, love," he whispered, bare inches from her sweet mouth. And then he smiled. "He made you."

Slowly, with imperceptible movement, Marc lowered his lips to hers. He brushed them tentatively, gently, against hers, acquainting her with the feel of him. Merrily shuddered and her hand rose to rest lightly on his chest. Marc touched his lips to hers again, more firmly this time, letting her know in the age-old way that there was more, much more. Her breathing quickened; her fingers curled into the green satin of his waistcoat. He pressed harder, pulling her against him more firmly, and felt her arch into the curve of his body. Gently, with infinite care, he let his tongue ride the seam of her lips, back and forth, back and forth, slowly dissolving the bond that held them closed against him, tantalizing her with what awaited her next. She moaned softly and responded, relaxing in his arms and opening to him like a flower to the sun.

"I have never been kissed before, my lord," she confessed when at last, and very reluctantly, Marc lifted his mouth from hers.

"I know," he replied as he tucked a strand of her hair that had caught on the point of his collar back into place.

"I did not know that one used one's tongue," she said somewhat nervously.

"I know that, too," murmured the well-satisfied earl in reply.

"I did wonder, though," she began hesitantly, "if it might not be better if you did not play with a lady's teeth quite so much."

Marc controlled his laughter. "Did my actions distress you, my sweet?" he asked as he toyed with a wayward curl.

"Oh, no," she responded uncomfortably. "I was merely concerned that you might have gotten stuck."

"Stuck?" repeated the earl on a swallowed chuckle.

"In my overlap," Merrily said seriously.

"I adore your overlap," growled the earl, and, with his intentions written plainly on his face, he proceeded to show her exactly how much.

"Really, my lord," said Lady Mirthton some time later, "you must stop doing that. I cannot even remember my own name when you are kissing me."

"Which is my intention, of course," grinned the earl smugly.

"But we have work to do," she reminded him.

"Tyrant," he muttered, and then he sighed. "Very, well. Let us consider once again what we know." He rose to his feet and brought the brandy decanter over to refill their glasses. Then, setting the bottle on a table near his elbow, he settled himself again at Merrily's side and fitted her against him.

"We know where the sign of the *sabot* is," began the lady, taking a small sip of the aromatic liquid.

"We do indeed," agreed the earl, "and your father's ring is the only tangible evidence we have that we are certain relates directly to your father's role as a spy. Everything else, the picture, the records in Rye, the garden stakes, the attacks by your cousins, all those have been nothing more than blind alleys."

"And we are once again back at the beginning," continued Merrily quietly. "We wasted so many days thinking that the sign of the *sabot* was the focus of our search, but it seems to have no importance at all."

"I would not say that, love," encouraged Marc as he lifted his glass to his lips. "Certainly it is a link to the other members of the spy ring, and was important enough for your father to mention it specifically, but I do agree that there must be something else . . . something that we have overlooked so far that will make sense out of all of this."

Merrily unconsciously snuggled deeper against Marc's side. "But all we have are his words before he died, Marc, and you know those as well as I."

Suddenly Marc straightened slightly. "I know the words you understood, Merrily," he began with intensity, "but what about the ones you did not understand."

"What do you mean?" she said as her eyes widened.

"What if your father gave you the solution, but in his weakness or because of your sobbing you missed it?"

"Then it would be lost to us, Marc," she said as her eyes filled with tears. "I can remember no more than what I told you."

"Try, my dear," he urged. "Close your eyes and try to remember exactly what happened that morning."

As Marc applied gentle pressure to Merrily's shoulder, she sank back against the curve of his arm, closing her eyes as she struggled to recall the events of that tragic day. Marc watched as her eyes flitted anxiously underneath her pale lids, wishing that he could make her memories easier.

After long moments, her moss-colored eyes popped open and she sat up abruptly. "Nothing. I can remember nothing," she stated with obvious disappointment.

"You are wound tight as a clock spring," observed Marc. "I am aware of how difficult it is for you to recall that day, Merrily, but you must try to relax and let the memories come."

"I cannot relax, Marc," she cried. "All I can remember is Father telling me about the sign, and then . . . blood. There was so much blood."

"All right, my dear, all right," soothed Marc as he again pulled her into his arms. "I would not overset you for the world. Think no more about it."

"But you think that the answer is there, Marc, do you not?" persisted Merrily as her head bobbed up from his shoulder.

"I believe that it must be, love," he answered, tucking her soft curls back under his chin.

"Then I must continue to try and remember," Merrily vowed, popping back up again.

"It is too painful," countered Marc, anchoring her pesky head against him again.

"Nevertheless . . .," began Merrily, and Marc caught her curls in mid-bob.

"Merrily, for heaven's sake!" he grumped loudly. "Deuced woman," he added in a grousing mutter. "One tries to be a gentleman . . ."

Merrily bit back a grin. "Thank you, Marc," she said sincerely. "Now, let me see. How is the best way to go about recalling a misunderstood word?"

"There is one way, perhaps," he offered in rather suspicious tones.

"What way is that?" asked Merrily as she relaxed back against him.

"Well," began the earl, "the idea is to relax one's body to the point where one's mind can float freely from thought to random thought, quite like a daydream. Only in this, of course the one doing the thinking has to endeavor to keep his idle thoughts from wandering too far from the subject at hand."

"How can this help?" asked Merrily curiously.

"Quite often, my dear, things that one has hidden in his subconscious come forth in this way."

"I see," pondered the lady. "But I cannot seem to relax when I think of that morning, Marc," she added.

The earl smiled broadly. "As to that, I have another solution." His eyebrow rose like the Matterhorn and his gaze dropped to her lips.

"I am afraid to ask," murmured Merrily as she became aware of the direction of Marc's regard.

"I am going to give your body something to do other than tense," whispered the earl as his mouth brushed hers. "It is a sacrifice for me, of course," he continued as he nibbled on her lower lip, "but I am willing if it will help our cause." He raised slightly to give the same tantalizing treatment to her upper lip, then stroked her delicate inner tissues with his tongue.

"I cannot think at all," breathed Merrily after several moments of this delicious torture.

"Yes, you can," whispered the earl. "Just relax and let your mind go free."

His fingers traced curls up and down her ribs and Merrily floated on the delicate sensations. She turned her thoughts toward the image of her father as she had seen him that last day. Marc's tongue touched warm and damp behind her ear. She shivered. Her father's mouth was moving, goosebumps skittered across her skin. She heard his rattling cough, saw the blood gush from his mouth, felt Marc's lips draw upon her earlobe with gentle sucking tugs . . . she floated . . . soared. His mouth rode her jaw, leaving a wet, shivery trail. *The sign of the* sabot . . . the words echoed inside her mind. His hand rose higher, higher . . . *the sign of the sabot* . . . his fingers found her breast . . . exquisite, it was exquisite. She could bear no more. *The sign of the* sabot . . . *under* . . .

Merrily sat bolt upright, spilling Marc onto the threadbare carpet like a bucket of slops. " 'Under!' " she cried joyously. Marc looked up at her uncomprehendingly. "Father said 'under,' Marc," she shouted.

Marc dug the heels of his hands into his eyes as he forced his body under control. He shook his head, feeling like its contents were half a step behind his skull during the motion. At last he dared to look again at the lady who had nearly brought him to the brink, dumped him into a vat of ice water, and had no idea she had done either. It was going to be a long night.

" 'Under?' " he murmured dazedly.

"Yes, 'under!' " she exclaimed as she dropped down on the floor beside him. "Will you please stop shaking your head like a wet dog and listen? Your idea worked! I remembered that after Father said 'the sign of the *sabot*,' he said 'under.' "

" 'Under!' " breathed Marc as his eyes finally widened in comprehension.

"Yes!" cried Merrily as she threw herself into his arms.

"Merrily, go and get your father's ring," commanded Marc as he batted down his lady's petticoats and untangled his appendages from hers.

"What are you thinking?" she asked breathlessly, accepting his hand as he hauled her to her feet.

"I am thinking that you have just located the list, love," he said with a rakish grin. "Now go and get your father's ring."

Merrily hesitated only a moment before turning on her heels and flying out the drawing room door. Her excited voice soon rang out as she sprinted up the stairs. "Plum! Oh, Plum, you will never guess what has happened . . ."

Marc smiled even as his mind grew wary. The end might be in sight, but the danger had just increased a hundredfold. He gritted his teeth against the helplessness he felt. He had no clue as to the identity of the enemy. He knew only one thing, that it was time for Castlereagh's men to be brought into play. The situation was too fraught with peril, else. He slammed his fist into the curve of his hand and strode quickly toward the door. It was time to bring things to a close. Before Merrily returned to the drawing room with her father's ring, he would have Mack riding with a summons to Pettigrew.

Chapter 16

Marc had already returned to the drawing room by the time Merrily burst in carrying her father's ring before her like a link boy's torch in a thick London fog. As soon as she had given it to him, he flipped the tiny latch on the side with his thumbnail and the ruby-studded lid sprang open.

"What are you going to do?" asked Merrily as her gaze, bright with excitement, left his to rest upon the image of the *sabot*.

"If you will remove your beautiful curls from in front of my nose, I shall show you," responded the earl.

Merrily gave him a ruefully lopsided grin. "I still do not understand how one simple word can give you the solution to the whereabouts of the list," she commented when she had pulled back enough for the earl to once again see the ring.

"Simple, my dear," said the earl airily. "You collect that I have always operated on the assumption that your father meant for you to be able to find the list."

"Yes, I know," agreed Merrily encouragingly.

"Therefore, it follows that, knowing that he was alone with you and mortally wounded, he would not feel the need to speak in riddles."

Merrily thought for a few moments as Marc dug into the

inner pocket of his evening coat and brought out a small knife. "You are saying that my father's words should be taken at face value, are you not, my lord?" she said finally.

"Just so," he responded with a quick grin. "And that is precisely what we are going to do. Your father told you about the sign of the *sabot*," he continued as he opened the knife to expose its sharp, pointed blade, "and then he said 'under,' and that, my sweet, is exactly where we are going to look." With a deft movement, he jimmied the point of his knife between the edge of the seal and the base of the ring and gave it a quick twist. Instantly the small metal disk popped free of the ring and dropped to the floor, where it rolled into anonymity among the tribe of dust bunnies residing beneath the overstuffed sofa. "Unless I miss my guess, my dear," said the earl with a triumphant smile, "we have just come to the end of our search."

Merrily's gaze was fastened on the ring. Just under the place where the disk had rested was a small circular compartment, and within this tiny space lay a carefully folded piece of paper, so small and thin in form as to be almost transparent. With a sudden release of an anxiously caged breath, Merrily slipped it from its place of concealment and carefully unfolded it, staring in amazement at the miniscule words written thereon.

"We'll need a magnifying glass," murmured the earl. "Is there one in the desk?"

"Yes, in the center drawer," responded Merrily, never once taking her eyes from the precious paper. She closed the distance to the nearest candelabra and seated herself nearby.

When Marc returned with the magnifying glass, he took a seat beside her and gingerly seized the list in his long fingers. Holding it close to the light, he began to read.

"Good God, Merrily, the first name on the list is a man I know!" exclaimed Marc as his brows shot up in surprise.

"Who, Marc?" she questioned with shock.

"Peter Finchley," the earl responded with a snarl. "He is an officer on Castlereagh's own staff. Comes from a fine family. Merrily," said the earl with eyes filled with anguish, "he is a lifelong friend of Eversley's father. Peter is named for him, for God's sake!"

"Oh, Marc," she whispered, "what kind of people are we dealing with here?"

"Devious bastards," spat Marc, "with cover so deep I would never have believed their guilt in a hundred years if I did not have the evidence of their perfidy right here in my own hands. Just look at the next name on the list."

"Whose is it?" asked Merrily quietly as she slipped a comforting arm around Marc's shoulders.

"Frederick Warner's," replied the earl grimly. "Probably the best placed man of them all."

"I do not recognize his name," Merrily said softly.

"I daresay you would not, my dear. He is one of the oldest and most trusted of the waiters at White's. Oh, damme, Merrily," cried the earl as he jumped to his feet and began to pace, "what ingenious placement! Who else has carte blanche to slip unobtrusively near to one private conversation after another . . . never regarded, never even noticed. Just continually, silently present, like a piece of familiar furniture, soaking up tidbits of information from drink-loosened tongues like ink drawn into a blotting paper. Every member of the club might have given away secrets. My God, Merrily! What might I have revealed?"

"Stop it, Marc," said Merrily quietly. "This serves no purpose."

Her calm logic stilled him. His eyes met hers and he drew strength from her, finally nodding his agreement as his shoulders slowly sagged. "No, it does not," he said as he smiled faintly. He crossed the room, then, and once again sat down beside her.

"Are there other names on the list?" she inquired.

"One other, though, happily, I do not know him."

"What is the name?"

"Bevis Martin," replied Marc. "Beside his name is the word 'Eastbourne.'"

"The town is only a short distance away from here, Marc, but it is not much more than a small resort and fishing village."

"Which is also only a short distance across the Channel from France, if you are possessed of a sturdy boat," remarked the earl.

"So you think our Mr. Martin might be a fisherman?" she asked.

"By day, perhaps," commented Marc as his jaw clenched. "By night, I suspect he is the courier who transports the information into France."

"Do you think that Father was the one who supplied his information?" asked Merrily as she began to draw sobering conclusions.

"That would be my guess," replied Marc gently, "because he lived so close to the village and could come and go unremarked. He would not have had direct contact with Mr. Martin, though."

"No," Merrily agreed. "We know that none of them were aware of each other's identity. There must have been drop-off points," she concluded.

"And pick-up points as well," he added as he slipped the ring and the tiny list into his pocket. "I vow, I would give much to know where those points are."

"Then I shall tell you, dear boy," came an amused voice from the doorway, "and then you shall give your very life for what you know."

Startled by the menace so evident in the voice of the new presence in the room, Marc and Merrily spun around to face the intruder, both recognizing the familiar voice, yet not able to reconcile the person's identity with the threat so implicit in the speaker's tone. As soon as their eyes locked on the doorway, they were stunned into near paralysis, their minds refusing to accept the truth. It had to be a mistake; and yet it was not. The proof was right before their eyes. Anguish unlike any Merrily had ever known rivered through her as she was forced to believe what could no longer be denied. Her heart crumbled, for, standing at the threshold of the drawing room, two pistols wavering in her soft, pudgy hands, stood the last person either of them would ever have suspected: Plum.

"Of course," said Marc as understanding finally dawned and he willed his muscles to relax. "It all makes perfect sense now."

"None of this makes sense!" cried Merrily as she started forward. "Plum . . ."

"No, Merrily," commanded Marc, seizing her wrist and pulling her back to his side.

"Plum?" she questioned plaintively. "Please, dear, I cannot understand . . ."

"Be silent!" ordered Plum viciously.

Merrily shrank back against Marc, stalwartly suppressing the tears that threatened to inundate her. "It was you? All this time, it was you, Plum?"

"Of course it was I, you silly chit!" snarled the elderly woman as she brandished one of the pistols in Merrily's direction. Marc immediately shoved her behind him.

"But . . . but, why?" pleaded Merrily as images of her life with this woman she had come to think of as a mother flashed through her bruised mind.

Miss Plumley sniffed and then let an evil smile flit across her features. "I suppose it does no harm to tell you. You will not be able to make use of the information, after all."

"As you say," remarked the earl as he immediately comprehended the need to keep the woman talking while Mack made his way back through the deep snowdrifts to the Manor with help. "How . . . when did it all begin, Miss Plumley?" he asked evenly.

"In glorious France, of course," she replied as her eyes glowed with patriotic fire. "I was born there, you know, in the beautiful Loire valley. My father was an important man in the Revolution."

"Indeed," commented the earl.

"But you came to England to escape the purges," argued Merrily, still too shaken to speak steadily.

Miss Plumley only smiled. "That is what I told your family, of course. I needed to gain their sympathy so that I could ingratiate myself into their midst, you see. And I did have a claim, my dear. I am distantly related to you through my mother."

"Who sent you?" asked the earl.

"The Revolutionary council. Because of my distant family here, I was given orders to establish myself and recruit agents who would work with me to spread our glorious Revolution abroad to England." Miss Plumley laughed then. "It was no problem to find Englishmen who were sympathetic to our cause," she continued scornfully. "Your radical societies founded to promote our revolutionary ideals were full of them. No . . . the difficulty came when your country foolishly went to war with Napoleon. Some of my recruits grew reluctant then, having suddenly developed a rather tardy vein of patriotic fervor. They insisted that there was a distinction between the revolutionary idealist and the traitorous spy, so it seemed. It was a most annoying time for me, I assure you, but between blackmail and political sanctions, my agents soon became firm once again in their loyalty to me."

"Sanctions?" questioned Merrily.

"She means murder, my dear," responded Marc quietly. "How did you recruit Simon Mirthton?" he asked, turning his attention back to the elderly woman. "Was he sympathetic to your ideals?"

"Goodness, no," laughed Miss Plumley. "He was only interested in money. It was easy to recruit him. When one is deep in dun territory one has little trouble justifying questionable behavior, especially if the behavior is lucrative enough."

Merrily winced, then rested her head against Marc's back. Immediately, his fingers reached to entwine with hers and squeeze them gently. "What did my father do for you?" she finally asked.

"Actually, he was my most important agent," Plum replied. "He was not aware of this, of course, but it was quite true. He was perfectly placed, you see. He was a gentleman, assumed to have a gentleman's honor, a member of White's, a man possessed of a Manor near Eastbourne, and a man who had been a friend since Eton of a certain Sir Philip Ardmore, who happens to work at the Foreign Ministry. Ah, I see by the fire in your eyes that you understand his value to me, my lord," she commented. "He was the tie that bound all my agents together. No one would remark a man going often to visit his

old friend. It was a simple thing for Peter Finchley to slip a
packet of information into a secret place in Sir Philip's office
where your father could retrieve it when his friend was not
aware. After all these years, poor Sir Philip still has no idea
how he is being used.

"It was even easier, of course, for him to pick up an envelope
that had been fastened to the underside of a certain table in the
gaming room at White's. Who would think it odd that one of
the Town's most renown wastrels was again gambling away
his blunt? And again, no one would remark if Viscount Collingwood appeared in Eastbourne. He had grown up in the vicinity.
The town folk had been used to his presence on their streets
since he was a child. It was all so very natural . . . so perfect.
Do you not agree?"

"Ideal," commented Marc, "yet Simon Mirthton did not
have your name on his list. How did you recruit him without
his knowing your identity?"

"Oh, do use some intelligence!" snapped Plum. "I contacted
him through several of my henchmen, of course. They were
the ones who approached him . . . and they were hooded, so
he could not identify them, either. They followed him one
night, waited until he was thoroughly cup-shot, and made the
proposition to pay him for carrying messages from Sir Philip's
office to a location in Eastbourne."

"Then he did not know what he was doing," cried Merrily
at once.

"Not at first, dear," responded Plum. "But he knew later.
Of course, by that time, it was too late. He was in far too deeply
to ever get out." Plum stepped farther inside the room then,
and, reaching behind her without removing her gaze from her
captives, she quietly closed the door.

"Yet he did try, did he not?" questioned Marc.

Plum shrugged her fleshy shoulders and the corners of her
mouth sagged distastefully. "Oh, yes, he tried," she said with
disgust. "The fool's conscience began to bother him. I could
see it happening. He began to stay at the Manor for long periods
of time, ignoring my directives that he had messages to relay
to Eastbourne. He spent more and more time with Merrily,

filling the stupid twit's head with all the things he was going to do for her. He was even planning a Season for her! It was the outside of enough! I knew then that he was up to something and I began having him watched."

"And you discovered that he was trying to learn the identities of the other agents," added Marc, prodding her to continue talking.

"Oh, yes," Plum replied casually, "and once I learned that, of course, I knew that he would not be trying to gather such information unless he intended to use it against me."

"Blackmail?" questioned Merrily.

"Just so," answered Plum. "I do not blame him, of course. I was, after all, blackmailing him. Why should he not try to do the same to me? I could not allow it, however," she mused as she scratched her temple with the barrel of a pistol. "It was unfortunate, but he had to be stopped."

"And so you had him killed," concluded Marc through clenched teeth.

"Goodness, no!" gasped Plum. "I did the job myself, dear boy." Merrily gasped, and had it not been for Marc's tight grip on her arm, very likely would have collapsed. Plum, though, remained unaware of her charge's state. Caught up in the telling of her story, she smiled widely and continued. "I confronted him when I knew Merrily was out on her morning ride. It was most amusing, my dear. You should have seen the look on your father's face when he found out I was the head of the spy ring. It was simply priceless!" she chuckled. "I shall never forget it."

"You are a monster!" Merrily whispered, but Plum was oblivious to her pain.

"Tell us what happened that day," said Marc with a softly spoken command.

"I called his bluff," answered the elderly woman flatly. "I told him that I did not believe in the existence of his so-called list. I knew that I had hidden the identities of my agents well, and truly did not believe that he could have uncovered them. I told him so in no uncertain terms."

"Then what?" urged Marc.

"He panicked, I suppose," replied Plum with a shrug. "He must have come to believe that I was not going to agree to his terms, and he simply panicked. The foolish man actually attacked me," she commented with a wondering shake of her gray head. "I was armed, of course. I would have preferred to leave his sanction to one of my minions, but as I was the only one about, the untidy business had to be done by me."

"You had a dagger?" asked the earl.

"Yes, dear boy. I always carry one. One never knows in this business when it might be necessary to use it."

Merrily was horrified. Her fingers dug into Marc's and she gripped his hand as if it were a lifeline to sanity. "You are mad," she breathed, more loudly this time.

"Mad? Never say so, my dear," replied Plum with a gay laugh. "I am a patriot. Nothing more, nothing less. Your father tried to use his knowledge of our organization to blackmail me for enough money to see you and him safely out of the country. He threatened me with exposure, dear. His action was nothing less than an act of war against me and my country. Consider that the muttonhead died in battle, if it makes you feel any better."

A shiver of revulsion raced through Merrily's system. Marc felt it, and stroked her hand with his thumb reassuringly. "I assume, then, that you are the one who sent Merrily the threatening note," he said, seeking once again to stall for time.

"Ah, yes, the note," smiled Plum in reply. "Rather a desperate move, was it not? But, unfortunately, necessary. I rather lost control of events for a period of time after Simon's death, you see. Almost immediately after Boggs became the next Viscount Collingwood, he began to press for Merrily's removal to London in order to find herself a husband. I had no more knowledge of his plan to get her out of the way so that he could begin the enclosures than she did, of course, but I had noted that Merrily had become uncharacteristically subdued after her father's death, as if something more than grief was blue-deviling her. I began to wonder if Simon had told me the truth. Perhaps there was indeed a list of my agents, and perhaps he had somehow conveyed that list to Merrily. I knew that I must discover the way of it. That meant, of course, that I would have to place myself in Merrily's company, and her trust, at all times until whatever she might have learned from her father might be revealed."

"So that is why you pressed to accompany me to London as my companion," breathed Merrily from behind Marc's broad shoulder. "I told no one that my father had even spoken to me before his death because I knew that the knowledge of my father's activities would shame Uncle Boggs to the point where he would never be able to forgive him, yet you knew."

"I just said that I did not!" snapped Plum. "I merely suspected." And then Plum smiled. "I must say, though, my dear, that you cooperated with my plan beautifully. We had not been in London but a few days before you confessed all to your dear, sweet, trustworthy companion."

"I did trust you!" cried Merrily as she stepped out from behind Marc. He reached for her, but she would not be denied. "I trusted you as I would have trusted my own mother."

"Hmm, well, that proved to be a stupid mistake, did it not, dearest?" remarked Plum. "For I then knew that the list did indeed exist, and it became a matter of great importance to get it back."

"So you sent men to search the Manor," concluded Marc.

"Yes, the cork-brained loobies!" exclaimed Plum vehemently. "They thoroughly botched everything. They were only to make the search look like a robbery, but the idiots chose one of the few nights when Boggs and Beatrice were not off visiting the local gentry, trying to impress them with their new roles as lord and lady of the Manor. My men were caught in the act and had no choice but to kill them."

"And when we traveled back to the Manor to attend their funerals and I wanted to remain, you sided with Lucius and Willard to force me back to Town because you had not yet found the list and wanted your henchmen to search again, is that not correct?" concluded Merrily, trying to control her mounting anger.

"Yes, my dear," responded Plum with a slight nod. "Lucius and Willard had their own reasons for wanting you away from the Manor, of course. I did not know them at the time, but it suited my purposes to fall in with their desires in the matter. I had only to recall to your mind that your father wished with all his heart that his beloved daughter might have a Season, and your tender filial sentiments played perfectly into my hands. I confess that I did make a mistake, though. I incorrectly assumed that the dear boys would return immediately to Oxford.''

''But they did not,'' added Marc grimly, ''so when your men broke into the Manor the second time, Merrily's cousins were still living there, only they were away at the time talking over the enclosures with their overseer.''

''And I was blamed,'' said Merrily flatly.

''I take no responsibility for that,'' pouted the heavy-set woman.

''Then tell us please why you found it necessary, after once getting Merrily away from the Manor, to send her a note that would immediately send her back,'' commanded the earl.

''It was expedient to do so,'' responded Plum with a negligent wave of her hand. ''My dunderheaded men had failed twice to find the list at the Manor. I knew that if it were ever to be found, it would have to be done so by Merrily or me. I could not let her out of my sight, however, so I had to devise a way that would force her to accompany me. I also knew that Merrily's knowledge of her father's mind would be necessary if I were to be successful. Thus, I sent the note.''

Marc's mouth eased into a tight smile. ''Your plan was rather nicely ruined, was it not?'' he commented evenly.

''If you are referring to her cork-brained idea to involve you, Lord Clairmont,'' sniffed Plum, ''it was irritating . . . but hardly insurmountable. In the beginning it merely meant that I was forced to devise certain strategies to discourage you.''

''Such as having me attacked in front of Weston's,'' concluded Marc quickly.

Merrily gasped. ''And that is why you held me back when I tried to run to Marc's aid!'' she cried.

''Yes, my dear,'' confessed Plum. ''It would not have done for you to interrupt my men before they accomplished their task. That is exactly what you ended up doing, of course, but that is water under the bridge," she sighed.

"When you got in the way of the men who tried to go after them," continued Merrily, "that was done on purpose, too, was it not?"

"Again, yes," said Plum agreeably. "It would have been a very serious matter if the authorities had gotten hold of my men. And quite an annoying complication for me," she added almost as an afterthought. "It would have been a great deal of trouble for me to plant someone in the gaol with them to make sure they did not talk. And most untidy. I do dislike untidy things."

A moment of appalled silence descended upon the room. "And the second note?" queried Marc when at last he could speak.

"Merely another effort to discourage you, dear boy," said Plum with a negligent wave of one of the pistols. "You ignored it, of course, as I was certain you would do, but still it was most foolish of you."

"Because by that time I knew too much to be allowed to live whether I paid the note heed or not," concluded the earl.

"Exactly so," agreed Miss Plumley with a sweet smile.

"You then began your attempt to eliminate me in earnest, did you not?" continued the earl. "I must say, the poison in my food was a nice touch. And you did throw me quite off the scent by being the first to scream at the sight of the lifeless kitten who had eaten from my plate. Tell me, Miss Plumley, did you arrange for the brawl as well?"

Plum laughed gaily. "No, indeed. A happy coincidence, that. But it served my purposes quite nicely, do you not agree?"

"Yet there were no more attempts after that," continued the earl. "Why?"

"I began to think it foolish on my part not to make use of you," Plum confessed with a shrug. "You would have to die anyway, of course. You knew far too much to allow you to live. But it seemed only sensible to delay the inevitable until your usefulness was over. And now, it seems, it indeed is.

Merrily, dearest, please come out from behind the earl. I am most sorry, but it is time for you both to die.''

Merrily watched in horror as Plum's jaw clenched with resolution. Out of the corner of her eye, she saw Marc's hands form into fists as Plum raised both pistols and leveled them at his chest. She knew in that moment that as surely as there was no way for him to avoid being shot, he would also not hesitate to do so in order to give her a chance to flee. She could not . . . no, she would not let that happen. Before her terror at what she was contemplating consumed her and held her rigidly to her fate, Merrily grasped the sides of her head and moaned loudly, striding across the room, and away from the stunned earl, as if she had been suddenly rendered mad with grief.

''Ohhhh,'' she wailed as she stumbled farther away from Marc. ''Ohhh, dear God in heaven! I can take no more,'' she cried as she pulled at her hair and surreptitiously stole glances at Plum. ''So much blood,'' she moaned, weaving farther away from Marc. ''Oh, dear God, I do not wish to die!''

''Come back here,'' demanded Plum as her eyes followed Merrily's progress. ''What is the matter with you?''

Marc watched as one of the pistols shifted its aim away from him and wavered somewhere in between the two of them. His eyes gleamed as he quickly understood what Merrily was attempting. Confound the impertinent baggage! The further apart the two of them were, the less likely that Plum could shoot them both with accuracy. She would have to take time to aim her second shot, and in that time, one of them would have a chance to escape. Marc gritted his teeth in exasperation. He was well aware that by her actions his lady was choosing to draw Plum's first fire. A wave of love flowed through him so powerfully that it almost brought him to his knees, and almost, *almost,* overcame his burgeoning urge to throttle her.

''I simply cannot believe it, Plum,'' cried Merrily as she continued to ignore Miss Plumley's commands. Great tears streamed down her flushed cheeks as she dipped and wove her way dramatically toward the opposite wall. Suddenly she stopped. Her hands dropped to her sides and she stared piteously at her companion. Plum's gaze became riveted on her. The second pistol slowly swept in her direction. "Oh, Plum," Merrily gasped dramatically, "you . . . you killed my f-father!" As soon as the words left her lips, Merrily threaded her fingers through her hair and released an ear-splitting scream.

It was all the diversion Marc needed. Instantly, he dove for the elderly woman, rolling his big body across the floor until he crashed against her fleshy legs. The loud report of a pistol sounded almost simultaneously with Plum's screech of outrage as her feet were swept out from under her and she fell heavily to the floor. Marc scrambled to his feet, ready to block the next shot with his body, but there was no need. Plum lay unmoving, her head resting aside the clawed foot of an ancient table. Quickly Marc knelt beside her, placing his fingers against her throat. Her pulse was shallow, but steady. Finally he rose to his feet and gathered both pistols into his arms, carrying them to rest safely on the mantle far away from Plum. At last he turned toward Merrily.

"Come here, love," he said huskily as he opened his arms to her.

Merrily needed no second invitation. She flew into his embrace and buried her face in the disheveled folds of his Mathematical, sobbing against him until her sorrowing heart ran out of tears and finally grew numb.

"Oh, Marc," she confessed, hiccoughing softly against his now sodden cravat, "I have never been so afraid in my life."

"Nor have I, you little scapegrace hoyden," he murmured against the soft curve of her neck. "What could you have been thinking? If you had only stayed behind me I would have protected you from harm." Just the thought of what might have happened sent a shudder coursing through Marc's body and he crushed Merrily tighter against him in reaction.

"But then I could not have protected you," she said with the first stirrings of a smile.

Marc leaned away. from her and slowly shook his head, watching in fascination as Merrily's eyes changed from moss to the viridescence of the sea. His heart swelled, and he marveled at this evidence of the resilience of her spirit. He would treasure it for the rest of his life. His laugh came hesitantly at first, and softly, as if he could not quite accept that the nightmare of the last few minutes was over and she was finally safe, but her answering smile and the sparkle of relief that shone brightly in her eyes melted the last of the tension that rode his muscles. He threw back his head and shouted in sheer joy. Lifting Merrily up by her slender waist, he hoisted her high in the air and spun her around and around while she squealed with happiness, then lowered her into his exuberant embrace.

It was just as Merrily's feet again gained the floor that Plum shook off her muddled wits, staggered to her feet, and started toward them. Gales of delighted laughter masked the slow scrape of her footsteps as she closed the distance between them. Stealthily, with the cunning of a zealot, she drew her concealed dagger from the folds of her gown and lifted it high. She knew that she would have to be quick. She could not afford to give them time to mount a defense against her. She must strike while the earl's back was toward her and Merrily's view was blocked. She set aside the throbbing pain that weakened her. Nothing must be allowed to keep her from her goal. Before they knew what was happening, she must be upon them. The decision had been made long ago. They both had to die. She took each step carefully, drawing nearer, nearer. Then, with an agility that belied her bulk, she gathered her remaining strength and ran straight for the earl's broad back.

She was only a few feet from her goal when the drawing room door burst open, allowing Mack and Castlereagh's men entrance. Marc spun around instantly, shoving Merrily behind him as he realized their peril. Quickly he threw up his arm, his hand snagging Plum's arm just as her dagger plunged toward his heart. He stopped the blade's descent with inches to spare. As Plum screamed in frustrated rage, Marc squeezed her wrist, forcing her weapon out of her benumbed hand to drop harmlessly to the floor. Pettigrew was on her in moments, binding her heavy arms quickly behind her and handing her over none too gently to one of his agents with orders to secure her in one of the carriages and then leave immediately for London.

"Sorry we couldn't arrive sooner, my lord," said Pettigrew

as he collected the dagger and guns. "Can't say as I ever remember the snow drifting so high this time of year. 'Twas devilish hard to wade through."

"I can hardly complain," responded Marc with a slight grin. "You timed your arrival perfectly."

"A little too perfectly," said Merrily as she stepped shakily out from behind the earl. "Marc, who are these men?"

"Ah, yes," replied the earl with a slight flush, "I do owe you a bit of an explanation, do I not? These men work for Castlereagh. I have been in league with him since shortly after you came to me."

"Even though I told you that you must not involve him?" cried Merrily as her eyes flashed green fire.

"Yes, my dear. In my judgment, it was the only thing to be done. Now, are you going to spend the rest of the evening ripping up at me?" Marc grinned at her then, a winning one that had her legs turning to aspic before his teeth even showed.

"No," she replied softly, "I am not so rag-mannered as that. I will thank you instead, my lord, for your good judgment saved your life."

She heard sounds from outside, then, and turned to stand near the window overlooking the drive. Plum was being helped down the snow-covered steps by Pettigrew's men. Merrily watched as her companion's familiar form struggled defiantly against her bonds while she was being escorted to the awaiting carriage. Just before her head was forced through the narrow doorway, she shouted in a voice that rasped with fury, *"Liberté! Egalité! Fraternité!"*. Her screams of rabid patriotism continued until the horses were finally whipped into motion and the carriage jolted down the drive and out of sight.

"She is mad, Merrily," said Marc softly as he joined her by the window.

"I know that now," she replied soberly, "and I know what she has done, but how will I ever reconcile it to what she has been to me all my life?"

"I cannot answer that, my dear," responded the earl thoughtfully, "but I do believe that you must give it some time. You have had a tremendous shock, Merrily. Why not seek your bed now? Mack and Charlotte will straighten up here. Tomorrow you will feel more the thing."

Merrily lifted her gaze to the earl and studied him for a long moment before nodding. Slowly she turned toward the door and made her way from the room. He was right, of course. It would not be long before her brightness of spirit would overcome the hurt Plum had caused her and she would begin to go on with her life again. But how could she tell him that he was also very wrong? How could he know that an even greater pain was the knowledge that their time together was over? Her love for him was already a constant ache. How could he understand that it would never go away? Yet she knew that she would let him leave on the morrow and not try to stop him. It was only a matter of hours before all London would know what her father did. Once that happened; all of the *haute monde* would shun her. Even if by some miracle he wanted to, the Earl of Clairmont would never be allowed by society to join himself with the daughter of a spy and still be accepted by his peers. And she could never let that happen. No, come tomorrow she would smile and thank him and let him go. And she would spend the rest of the coming night wondering how the deuce she was going to accomplish it.

Merrily hesitated outside the door of the breakfast room the next morning, pasting a bright smile on her sleep-deprived countenance and screwing her courage firmly in place. She knew that Marc was already inside. She had seen him go down the stairs earlier to talk to Pettigrew and supervise the packing of his things into his carriage. She took a deep breath and released it slowly, then before she could think of better of it, pushed open the door and strode into the room.

"Good morning, my lord," she said perkily as she swept toward the sideboard.

Marc looked up from the pages of his newspaper and followed her progress with discerning eyes. "Good morning," he replied evenly.

"Well, you must be most anxious to be off, my lord," said

Merrily brightly as she filled a plate with eggs, kippers, deviled kidneys, and sliced fruit.

Marc folded the paper and laid it on the table beside him, watching his lady carefully. "Not particularly," he commented in response.

"Fustian," remarked Merrily. "You must be in alt to be free of the bumblebroth I dragged you into." As Merrily placed her plate upon the table, Marc rose to seat her. "And I have not even thanked you, have I? How remiss of me! I do, you know," she chattered on. "I thank you most kindly for everything you have done for me, and ask your forgiveness for all the pother you have had on account of it. *And . . . "* she added on a cheerful giggle, "I promise never to interrupt your conversation at a ball again." With a flourish of white linen, Merrily settled her serviette upon her lap and stabbed at a soft fold of egg.

Marc was not even the tiniest bit fooled. He knew exactly what his little baggage was up to and he would have no more of it. He reached for Merrily, seizing her by her shoulders and hauling her to her feet, overturning her chair as he did so and sending it to the floor with a loud crash. He pulled her tightly against him and slipped his hands up to bracket her radiant cheeks as he devoured her with his intense blue gaze.

"Oh, I do not think so," he murmured softly. "I expect that you will be interrupting most of my conversations for the rest of our lives, my dear. But that is quite all right with me. As long as you love me to distraction the way I love you, you may stomp all over my melodious phrases. I shall not mind in the least."

"Love?" breathed Merrily as the dull ache in her breast miraculously vanished. "You love me?"

"Incredibly. Overwhelmingly. Incapacitatingly," answered the earl as his mouth descended.

"But you cannot!" gasped Merrily as she drew back slightly. "The news about my father must even now be making the London tabbies purr. You must not associate yourself with me."

"One of the advantages of being at war, love," answered the earl as he dropped a tender kiss on her trembling lips, "is that government activities can be kept secret and all records of them sealed. No one will ever know of your father's involvement, Merrily. Your father's reputation is safe."

"But what of the others in the ring?" she asked, clutching at his pristine lapels. "Will they not tell someone?"

Marc's eyes hardened. "I received a message from Eversley early this morning," he began. "Thanks to your father's list and agent McPhee's forethought in bringing a few carrier pigeons back with him from Rye, we were able to get the names to Peter so quickly that the men were all captured before they were even aware of their danger." He inhaled deeply and sighed then, clutching Merrily to him more tightly. "This is war, Merrily," he said without emotion. "The agents have already been dispatched."

Merrily stared ahead in silence until finally her forehead dropped to his neckcloth. "Then it is over," she breathed unsteadily. "Really over."

"All but the ceremony," replied Marc softly.

"Ceremony?" questioned Merrily as her head bobbed up.

"Mm-hmm. Our wedding ceremony," responded Marc as he kissed the tiny ball on the end of her nose. "I had Peter procure a special license for me. It arrived with his message this morning. And, unless I miss my guess, that door opening in the hall is Mack arriving with the nearest clergyman he could find. So, what say you, my dearest love? Shall we go get leg-shackled for life?"

Merrily marveled at how her eyes could fill with tears at the same time that a broad smile stretched across her face. She shook her head and forced back a sob of joy. "Yes," she said tightly, as her emotions threatened to overflow. "Yes, my darling Marc, we shall."

"So this is what it is all about," murmured Merrily sometime later. Marc was buried to the hilt inside her and was playing with her overlap with his tongue.

"Hardly," groaned the earl as he lifted his head to grin at her. "I have only just begun, my love," he whispered as he withdrew slightly and returned with an even deeper stroke.

Merrily gasped and sighed, discovering to her delight another
set of opposites her body could do at the same time. "This is
most enjoyable, Marc," she whispered as her hands learned the
planes of his back, "but I have a question."

"Now?" queried Marc with more than a tinge of exasperation.

"Yes. What will happen to the Manor?"

Marc responded to the worry in his wife's voice with love
and an inordinate amount of patience. He lifted himself to his
elbows and filled his hands with her luminous hair. "We will
live a part of each year here, my sweet, and part in my other
estates, but the Manor will always belong to you. Whatever
renovations you wish to make, or new farming techniques you
wish to try, you may do. I will make sure you will have all the
money you need to do it."

"Oh, Marc," Merrily cried, "my tenants will be safe. Oh,
darling, do you know how very much I love you?"

"I was rather hoping you would end this conversation and
show me, love," growled the earl as he ground his hips against
her and pushed deeper.

"Ohh," gasped Merrily, "what a very good idea, my lord.
What shall I do first?"

"I shall do the doing, my love," replied the earl on a groan,
feeling his control slipping away. "Draw your legs up around
my waist. Yes, that's right. Now squeeze . . . oh, Merrily!"

The earl became overwhelmed in sensation. He felt surrounded in sweet warmth, felt his lovely wife stroking his
shoulders, his hair, beating against him . . . *beating against
him?* Slowly, painfully, Marc pulled back from the sensual haze
that buoyed him, fighting for threads of control while he stared
questioningly at Merrily's face. Her eyes were dark with desire.

"Merrily . . . love . . . do you wish for me to stop?" he
rasped. It was the hardest question he had ever had to ask.

Merrily stared at him blankly. She blinked. "No," she finally
whispered huskily.

"Then why are you beating against my ribs?" asked Marc,
amused that in her passion she had not even realized what she
was doing.

Merrily blinked again. "Marc, darling, how can I be beating against your ribs when all my fingers are tangled in your hair?" By way of demonstration, she clenched her fingers and waggled his puzzled head.

"Then what . . .?" wondered the earl as he raised himself on his wrists and pivoted his torso slightly to see.

Lady Clairmont finally understood. She gasped with embarrassment and pulled her husband back down to her. Her fingers wrapped themselves more tightly in his thick blond hair and she braced his face securely before her.

"Kneecaps," she whispered sheepishly.

"Good Lord," uttered the earl.

He lowered his forehead to hers on a disbelieving huff of air, but did not laugh. He could not. For Merrily suddenly wriggled enticingly beneath him and, as an indrawn breath shuddered back into his lungs, the Earl of Clairmont once again became lost in the continuation of his task.

Note from the Author

You might have noticed a rather clumsy use of the very formal title, Lady Mirthton, throughout the first part of *A Merry Escapade*. By now, of course, you have discovered the reason for it, but just to set the record straight, in actual Regency times hardly anyone went around "my Lording" or "my Ladying" the nobility except the servants. In fact, according to Daniel Poole's book, *What Jane Austen Ate and Charles Dickens Knew*, even the queen allowed "Ma'am" on occasion, and the Prince of Wales would accept "Sir."

So why did I repeatedly "Lady Mirthton" my poor, loveable character? Because as the daughter of a viscount, in reality she would probably have been addressed as the Lady Merrily. Ah, now you can see the problem. If I had addressed her less clumsily, it would have been much more difficult to include what I think became a very special part of the story.

I hope that I might be forgiven the bit of license I took at Merrily's expense, but you should know I have no remorse. I am afraid that when given the choice between absolute correctness and a good laugh, I take the laugh every time.

ZEBRA REGENCIES
ARE
THE TALK OF THE TON!

A REFORMED RAKE (4499, $3.99)
by Jeanne Savery
After governess Harriet Cole helped her young charge flee to France — and the designs of a despicable suitor, more trouble soon arrived in the person of a London rake. Sir Frederick Carrington insisted on providing safe escort back to England. Harriet deemed Carrington more dangerous than any band of brigands, but secretly relished matching wits with him. But after being taken in his arms for a tender kiss, she found herself wondering — *could* a lady find love with an irresistible rogue?

A SCANDALOUS PROPOSAL (4504, $4.99)
by Teresa DesJardien
After only two weeks into the London season, Lady Pamela Premington has already received her first offer of marriage. If only it hadn't come from the *ton's* most notorious rake, Lord Marchmont. Pamela had already set her sights on the distinguished Lieutenant Penford, who had the heroism and honor that made him the ideal match. Now she had to keep from falling under the spell of the seductive Lord so she could pursue the man more worthy of her love. Or was he?

A LADY'S CHAMPION (4535, $3.99)
by Janice Bennett
Miss Daphne, art mistress of the Selwood Academy for Young Ladies, greeted the notion of ghosts haunting the academy with skepticism. However, to avoid rumors frightening off students, she found herself turning to Mr. Adrian Carstairs, sent by her uncle to be her "protector" against the "ghosts." Although, Daphne would accept no interference in her life, she *would* accept aid in exposing any spectral spirits. What she never expected was for Adrian to expose the secret wishes of her hidden heart . . .

CHARITY'S GAMBIT (4537, $3.99)
by Marcy Stewart
Charity Abercrombie reluctantly embarks on a London season in hopes of making a suitable match. However she cannot forget the mysterious Dominic Castille — and the kiss they shared — when he fell from a tree as she strolled through the woods. Charity does not know that the dark and dashing captain harbors a dangerous secret that will ensnare them both in its web — leaving Charity to risk certain ruin and losing the man she so passionately loves . . .